THE BRIDE
WORE SCANDAL

First published in Great Britain 2010
Paperback edition 2011
Harlequin Mills & Boon Limited,
Eton House, 18-24 Paradise Road, Richmond, Surrey TW9 1SR

© Helen Dickson 2010

ISBN: 978 0 263 87851 6

Harlequin Mills & Boon policy is to use papers that are natural, renewable and recyclable products and made from wood grown in sustainable forests. The logging and manufacturing processes conform to the legal environmental regulations of the country of origin.

Printed and bound in Spain
by Litografia Rosés, S.A., Barcelona

THE BRIDE
WORE SCANDAL

Prologue

On reaching the bank of the wide river, the lone rider dismounted. After doing a quick scan of the surrounding area, with no one else in sight, he removed his frock-coat. The day was hot, the water too tempting to resist. Unbuckling his belt, he sat down on a tree stump and removed his boots. This done, he removed his breeches and shirt, laying them out on the ground. Moving to the water's edge, he stretched his arms high above his head, the muscles rippling beneath the firm flesh of his magnificent body showing a ready, capable strength, gleaming golden brown under the hot rays of the sun.

Moments later there was a splash, followed by the lesser sound of a body, like a dark, sleek blade, cutting its way just below the surface of the water with slow, controlled strokes.

Meanwhile, just half a mile away, a young woman trotted along on a grey mare, following a narrow and twisted path, the tall trees—mainly beach and oak—through which she rode dappling her glorious mane of fair hair and body with shades and light. In the pungent smelling undergrowth, small animals foraged, and above her head squirrels darted along the branches of trees, birds fluttered and sang and starlings flew frenziedly in the blue sky. Ahead of her, in a meadow bordered by a wide meandering brook, a spread of deep pink-and-white campions, ox-eyed moon-daisies and golden buttercups brightened the gloominess.

The dark-haired man emerged naked from the river, droplets of water clinging to his bronzed skin and tinier beads sparkling in the dark furring on his broad chest, while, following a narrow, well-worn path, Christina Atherton rode in the shadow of the sturdy stone walls that surrounded Oakbridge, her home. Having ridden her horse hard for the past hour, she now rode at a more leisurely pace, breathing in the humid, sweet scented air. She was hot and tendrils of damp, ash-blond curls clung to her cheeks.

The brook offered the only relief in sight and the temptation to dip her bare feet in the cool, flowing water was almost overwhelming. She guided her mare across the meadow, and on reaching the brook she dismounted, patting the sleek chestnut neck before turning her attention to the stream. She took a moment to turn and gaze back at the house, beautiful in its ancient splendour, with appreciative, loving eyes, refusing for now to allow herself to dwell on the tension that existed within its walls and the worries that awaited her there. Turning her head in another direction, she gazed at the slope of land, to the gentle fold of hills that went on into the hazy distance. She was quiet, deep in her own thoughts, distracted by the splendour of what lay about her.

As she approached the brook, her walk was graceful, the gentle sway of her hips seductive, causing her mane of softly curling hair to lift and bounce about her shoulders. Sitting on the grassy bank, she removed her shoes, casting her eyes about her to make sure she was quite alone, before raising her skirts and peeling down her stockings. The look on her face was one of pure rapture as she dangled her feet in the ice-cold water, raising them now and then before dunking them back in, disturbing the tiny minnows darting about beneath the surface.

So absorbed was she in her pleasure that she was unaware of the lone horseman watching her from the shelter of the trees a short distance away, or the smile that curved his lips when she hitched up her skirts and stretched her long and slender legs out in front of her to dry.

Christina lay down on the dry grass, letting the fronds touch her face. The ground was vibrant with life. Through half-closed lids she saw a shiny black beetle scurrying away, and here and there tiny blue-and-white flowers. After a while, on a sigh she sat up and reluctantly donned her stockings and shoes.

The watcher sat on his horse without moving. The beauty of the young woman was such that he could not tear his eyes away. It brought home to him the starvation of his long celibacy. Her light blond hair tumbling over her shoulders was rich and luxuriant. Golden strands lightened by the sun shimmered among the carefree curls. He felt a great temptation to cross the meadow and run his fingers through the soft tresses. It was with a will of iron that he kept a grip on himself and did no more than watch.

Mounting her horse, about to ride towards the house, Christina heard a loud yelp followed by a whimper coming from the trees. Without a thought, she rode towards the sound, entering the dark coolness of the woods once more. She was surprised to see a small white dog of indeterminate breed caught up in some bramble bushes.

The distressed dog was familiar to Christina and, dismounting quickly, she went to try to set it free. Cleary frightened, it growled and bared its fangs, trying to back off.

'Toby—good dog. Dear me, what a pickle you've got yourself into.' She bent her head to smile at him. 'Don't struggle so. You know who I am,' she murmured, holding out her hand in an effort to calm him down, relieved when he recognised her voice. Knowing he could trust her, he reduced his growl to a whimper; crawling forward on his belly as far as the clinging barbs would allow, he licked the end of her bare fingers with his sloppy wet tongue. 'Hold still now and you'll be out of there in a trice. Don't wriggle so. You'll make it difficult for yourself as well as for me.'

Falling to her knees, she carefully began prising away the brambles curling round his lacerated body, wishing she had worn her riding gloves when she felt the sharp prick of the barbs. They drew blood and spattered her gown. Hearing the heavy tread of someone coming up behind her, although her heart jumped, with a force of will she managed to ignore him, for she believed it to be the dog's owner. But she could not quell the tremor of fear that gripped her on knowing she was alone with him in the woods.

'I've told you before about letting your dog run wherever it pleases,' she reproached crossly, her own pain from her hands and the suffering dog sharpening her tone. 'There are sheep in the next field and Farmer Leigh is likely to take a gun to him if he worries them, so if you care for him you'll see he's fastened up in future.' Unable to set the dog free, she sighed with frustration; sitting back on her heels, she wiped her damp forehead with the back of her hand, smearing it with blood. 'I'm afraid you'll have to do it. I can't release the brambles.'

Someone squatted beside her, the lean, hard muscles of his thighs flexing beneath the tight-fitting breeches, and it wasn't until he spoke that she realised he wasn't the dog's owner.

'Here, let me,' the stranger said, producing a knife. Methodically and deftly his long brown fingers cut away the offending brambles. Not until the dog was free and wagging his short, stubby tail and licking his hand as he ruffled his ears, checking that the animal was unharmed apart from a few surface lacerations, did he turn and look at the young woman beside him. She did not smile, nor speak, but her startling eyes, a dark and mysterious blue, tilted to look up at him.

'There, it is done. The owner, whoever he is, will be

grateful to us for having freed it. It would never have freed itself. No doubt it was after rabbits.'

Three things hit Christina at once: his eyes were deep and piercing—a strange colour of silver grey—while his voice was richly textured, cultured and deep, and the hands that had released Toby from the briars had the strength in them of a man who was not afraid to dirty them in his chosen profession, yet giving the impression of a creative man of some refinement. The combination sent a peculiar warmth up her spine, and nothing had prepared her for the thrill of quivering excitement that gripped her now, beginning in her chest where her heart lay, and radiating to every part of her body. He looked steadily at her. Then he moved his head closer to hers.

Hypnotised by those passionate silver eyes, which were coming nearer and nearer to her own, Christina found she couldn't move—she had neither the desire nor the strength to do so. Her heart thumped so wildly in her breast that she could hardly breathe. Cupping her chin in his hand, he placed his mouth on hers. Without ever being aware of it, she yielded her lips to his. His kiss was both gentle and compelling. The world around her seemed to vanish away, leaving only this stranger and herself locked together in a charmed circle against which dull reality crumbled away.

She was aware that this was a moment of great importance, that she stood on the threshold of a great revelation, but could not yet understand the substance of it. Her heart swelled with an emotion of such pro-portions she was overwhelmed. It was as if she were being sucked down into a pool of deep, dark, swirling water, a turbulence of longing—a longing for something she had never known before, but which this man could provide.

Releasing her chin he pulled away. 'Well, well,' he murmured. 'I can see I shall have to come this way more often.'

'I should not have let you kiss me.'

He smiled. 'No, you shouldn't—any more than I should have attempted to. Do you mind?'

She shook her head. 'No, no, I don't.'

'Then there's no harm done.'

They continued to look at each other. Christina saw that his thick, dark brown hair was curiously wet and drawn back, accentuating high cheekbones, a heavy lock falling carelessly over his wide brow. A firm, clean-shaven chin, well-formed nose and strongly sensual mouth added to the enigmatic character of his bronzed face. His eyebrows were inclined to dip in a frown of perplexity over eyes that were ever watchful. He was very handsome, but there was an aggressive virility in his bold gaze that made her uneasy. They looked at each other with startled eyes, a look that lasted no more than a moment and yet seemed to last an eternity before she lowered her eyes.

When he straightened and she stood before him, the dog content to sit at her feet, she was conscious of the hard lines of his body beneath his clothes, of how tall he was, how lean and superbly fit, how proudly he carried himself. His eyes observed her with frank interest. She felt she should be nervous, in the woods all alone with a perfect stranger, but she wasn't and she couldn't

have said why. He appeared to offer no threat to her, tall
and arrogant-looking as he was, a complex man who
would be as elusive as smoke, a man who would break
the heart of the woman who loved him.

'I—I'm sure you're right about Toby,' she murmured,
giving him a wobbly smile. 'He's badly scratched, poor
thing, but had he become caught in a poacher's snare, he
would not have fared so well. Thank you for what you
did. I'm sorry I spoke sharply. I—I thought you were
Toby's owner.'

'You will have a few choice words to say to him when
next you meet, I am sure. You are well acquainted with
him—the dog's owner?'

'I—I—no,' she stammered, cursing herself for being
flustered. 'Not very.'

'Then if you tell me where he lives, I would be happy
to return the dog.' He saw something flare in her eyes,
something akin to fear. It vanished as quickly as it had
appeared. His curiosity was roused. 'I promise you it
would be no trouble.'

'No,' she said—too quickly, the stranger thought,
noticing how her glance flitted hesitantly away from
him. 'I'll take care of it myself.'

'As you wish.' He looked down at her face upturned
to his, tempted to caress the delicate, unblemished
cheeks blooming with colour. Her features seemed perfect. Her soft pink lips were slightly parted, tantalising
and gracefully curving. Her brows were gently arched
above eyes that were clear and blue, brilliant against
the thick fringe of jet black lashes. They stared back

at him open, yet as unfathomable as any sea he had gazed into.

As he looked at her he felt burned—scorched—by her beauty. He was quite bewildered by the emotion he felt in the part of his body where he supposed his heart lay. He couldn't describe what he felt because he didn't have any words. It was then that he saw the colour that stained her cheeks darken, sensed her breath catch in her throat and felt momentary wonder. Could she, too, be feeling the lure of deep attraction awoken by the kiss?

'Are you far from home?' he asked, amazed at his concern, for what did he care about a woman riding in the woods alone? Perhaps it was because of her vulnerable femininity, or was it her total lack of concern over her own safety? Whatever it was, it annoyed him slightly, since he didn't really have the time or patience to be fretting himself over a woman he did not know, but something about this young woman intrigued him, made him want to get to know her better.

'Oh, no, I live quite close,' she replied, regarding him steadily, not the slightest bit alarmed at his large, male presence.

'And where's home?'

He was smiling, and his smile was luminous, joyous, heart-stopping. 'As I said, not far.'

Unexpectedly, he reached out and took her blood-smeared hands, bending his head and frowning at the scratches. 'I see you have not fared so well yourself. You'd best get along home and have them tended—although I suppose you could clean them in the brook.'

Something in his tone alarmed Christina. Her eyes snapped to his and she gasped, slowly pulling her hands from his gentle grasp. 'It's nothing. They'll soon heal—but… Oh! You were watching me, weren't you—when I…?' His smiling eyes captured hers and held them prisoner until she felt a warmth suffuse her cheeks.

'I saw you dunking your feet in the brook, if that's what you mean.' His white teeth gleamed and his bold eyes laughed at her as his leisurely perusal swept her face, delighting in her confusion. 'And what pretty feet you have, as perfect as any I have ever seen.'

At this questionable familiarity, mortified, Christina suffered through a scorching blush. His having taken the time to watch her—no, spy on her would be a more appropriate word—as she removed her stockings, told her his manners were somewhat lacking. 'And how long were you standing there ogling me?'

Having leisurely observed the beauty to his heart's content while she indulged herself in the brook, he made no effort to curb an amused, all-too-confident grin. 'Long enough to know I won't forget what I saw in a hurry. It would be impossible. You have pretty legs, too, by the way.'

'Oh!' She jumped as if she'd been stung and her mouth flew open to speak her outrage. 'You should not have looked—or you should have made your presence known so I could have covered myself.'

'I did not want to intrude on what was, to me, a very gratifying moment—although on second thought,' he murmured, smiling lazily and his eyes narrowing to gleaming slits, 'had I thought you would welcome my presence and allow me to share your...paddle, then I might very well have shown myself.'

'And got yourself dunked in the water for your cheek,' Christina retorted, meeting his predatory stare, feeling much like a hen before a wily fox and expecting to be devoured at any moment. She was unable to believe the man's audacity. The moment of enchantment—the kiss and the care and kindness he had shown Toby a moment before—was forgotten.

'I'd have been more than willing to risk it, to verify with more credible evidence that what I was seeing was actually mortal and not some wondrous vision I'd conjured up.'

Christina's ire flared. 'A kick on the shin would have supplied that evidence just as well.'

He chuckled softly. 'Had I but known such beauty was so close at hand—a beauty who shares the same enthusiasm for water as myself—I would have invited you to share my dip in the river just now, which I found most gratifying and refreshing on such a hot afternoon as this.'

Christina's slightly sunburned nose snubbed him. 'You are shameless. You, a stranger, can hardly expect me to welcome your advances,' she retorted angrily.

His grin was wicked. 'You had no objections a moment ago.'

'You may be accustomed to easy conquests, but being a lady, I find the thought of sharing anything else with you utterly distasteful. Who are you, anyway?'

'My name is Simon. Until recently I was a soldier.'

'And now?'

He shrugged nonchalantly. 'I haven't decided—besides, you do not want to hear about what I do.'

Christina lifted a sleek brow. 'Why would I not want to hear? I am curious about all manner of creatures, including soldiers and men who haven't decided what they want to be,' she said coolly, hoping to sting him into a retort.

The stranger's eyes narrowed, but he was only considering whether or not to answer her question. She could see the moment when he decided not to. She found she was disappointed, which was foolish. Why should he tell her anything about himself, and why should she care?

'What I do—or what I might do—cannot possibly be of interest to such a gracious young woman as yourself.' Suddenly the stranger's eyes gleamed with devilish humour, and his lips drew slowly into a gentle smile. 'I ask you to forgive my boldness. You are a delight to my eye. Have mercy on me.'

His eyes slid over her like a touch, making Christina shiver despite the heat of the day. She lifted her chin with a show of bravado. There was arrogance in the tilt of his head and a single-minded determination in the set of his firm jaw that was not to her liking. She had an uncomfortable feeling that her angry words, far from discouraging him, had acted as bait to this handsome stranger called Simon. 'It passes through my mind that you are too much of a rake for me to do that.'

'There are many who would agree with you—but

believe me when I say that never have I met so lovely or charming a woman as you.'

Confused by the gentle warmth of his gaze and the directness of his words, Christina could find no words to reply. In her innocence, it was impossible for her to determine whether he mocked her or told the truth. He was not like any man she had ever met. Suddenly aware of the confines of the trees, which seemed to be closing in on them, the closeness of this stranger and the danger he might pose—why, he might be a thief, a molester of women or even a murderer for all she knew—sanity heavily mixed with panic had her turning from him and striding to her horse.

In amused silence the stranger watched her, admiration in his eyes as he watched the sway of her hips and the arrogant toss of her head. So, the young woman was a lady—or at least she thought she was. She was also a lady who needed a lesson in manners. And the stranger knew he was just the man to give it to her.

With a quick movement he was behind her. Clamping his hands tightly about her narrow waist, she was seized and lifted and settled into the saddle as if she weighed nothing at all. A gasp caught in her throat when he very boldly led her knee around the horn.

Snatching the reins and controlling her restless horse, after calling to Toby she looked down at the man with cool disdain. 'May I ask what you are doing here? The woods are out of bounds.'

He grinned, a wicked pirate's grin. 'I'm a stranger to these parts. I am merely finding my way about.'

'Then might I suggest that you find your way about

somewhere else. You are not welcome here.' With that and setting her heel to the mare's side, she rode off, Toby following dutifully in her wake.

'Considering the pleasant interlude we have shared,' the stranger called after her, admiration and merriment lighting his eyes, 'I think I should at least know the name of such a captivating companion.'

Christina ignored him, riding on, his mocking laughter still ringing in her ears long after she reached the house.

Tom Bradshaw rushed to assist her when she rode into the stable yard, casting a disapproving glance at the dog close on her heels.

Tom was a middle-aged groom who had worked for the Atherton family since he was a lad. He was a man of few words, a decent, discreet man, whom Christina could rely on. He also had a remarkable way with the horses and had taught both Christina and her older brother William to ride as soon as they could sit a horse. He was also the only person at Oakbridge who knew what went on and that the young master had got himself into something that wouldn't be easy to get out of.

'See to the dog, please, Tom,' Christina instructed as she slid from the saddle and handed him the reins. 'I found him in the woods caught in brambles. He isn't badly hurt, but perhaps you could clean him up a bit before you return him to his owner.' She gave him a meaningful look, sarcasm curling her lip. 'I'm sure you know where he can be found—although at this hour it's highly likely he'll still be abed.'

With that she strode into the house, determined to forget her meeting with the stranger, a thoroughly obnoxious man she hoped never to have the misfortune of setting eyes on again. And yet, she thought on a softer note when she remembered the tenderness of his kiss and the gentleness that had warmed his eyes to soft grey velvet, this was not exactly true. Her meeting with the stranger had been her first encounter with the intimacy and power of strong attraction between a man and a woman, of desire that melted the bones and inflamed the flesh and caused all coherent thoughts to flee.

Chapter One

It was 1708 in the reign of Queen Anne. Plots and rumours kept up the intensity of political strife. There was activity in all the underworld of Jacobite agents, who were working against the vested interests of the nation to remove the Queen and place the Catholic King James III on the throne. An association was formed. They collected arms and enrolled troops, and money had to be raised to pay for it. Some Catholics in England were generous and sent money to France, to the young James Edward Stuart; others, the not-so-principled and scrupulous Catholics, used more devious and often murderous means, and thought nothing of turning to crime to fund the Jacobite cause.

To Christina Atherton, who had planned the evening's gathering and entertainment with cards, supper and dancing and a stand of fireworks in the extensive grounds of Oakbridge Hall, thoughts of Jacobites and rebellion could not be further from her mind. The guests were due to arrive in half an hour, and she was checking the preparations when a man's voice echoed round the hall. She turned from the huge urn of fresh flowers she had been rearranging to face her brother.

'Christina! Where the devil are you?'

'I am here, William, ready to receive our guests.'

The young man looked and saw her standing before the urn of flowers. Her heart-shaped face surrounded by a halo of golden curls seemed to have a delicate, ethereal quality, and her light blue gown gave her a look of fragility.

'Dear Lord, Christina, you are never there when I want you,' he complained irritably, fumbling with his cravat.

'I am never far away, as well you know. Is there something wrong?'

He stared at her, as if her words surprised him, then he answered crossly. 'Of course there is. Everything is wrong.'

Christina knew by the tone of his voice that something was amiss. The deep frown that creased his brow attested to this. She sighed, walking towards him, then calmly straightened his cravat for him. 'What can be wrong? Everything is prepared. The musicians have arrived, the food tables set up, the fireworks—'

'Damn the fireworks!' he exclaimed fiercely. 'That wasn't what I meant.'

'Then what has happened?' she asked, alarmed, for she realised by the very intensity of his tone that he was upset.

Ashamed of his irritation, he said, 'Forgive me, Christina. I'm in one hell of a tangle and I'm damned if I know what to do about it.'

'You haven't been gambling again, have you—and lost? Oh, William, I hope not.'

'No, of course I haven't. It's worse than that.'

'Tell me.'

'We have an extra guest tonight—Lord Rockley. What is more, he is to stay the night.'

'Lord Rockley? I don't believe I've heard of him. Who is he?'

'Trouble, Christina. The worst. Hell and damnation!' William exclaimed angrily, pushing his fair hair from his forehead in frustration. 'Why does he have to come tonight—just when things are going well?'

'Then why did you invite him?'

William looked at her as if she'd taken leave of her senses. 'Invite him?' he burst out. 'I didn't invite him. Rockley invited himself. I was at Middleton Lodge to take a look at Sir Gilbert Rosing's recently acquired stallion when he just turned up. When Gilbert mentioned that he was coming here tonight, in a calm and disarming way Rockley told me he was new to the district, and that because of the increasing assaults on travellers, which is causing the Lord Lieutenant a great deal of concern, he has been appointed to the area to curb the illegal activities of the highway robbers who persist in evading the law. What better place to start, he said, than by getting to know the local gentry at a gathering here at Oakbridge—if I didn't mind him trespassing on my hospitality.'

Christina was shocked. 'Oh! What did you say?'

'What could I say other than that I would be hon-oured to have him as a guest and to stay the night, since he is residing with his brother five miles away—too far from him to travel back late at night.'

Despite the fear beginning to quake through her, Christina managed to sound calm. 'But—this is terrible news. Do you think he suspects what goes on here at Oakbridge?'

'I don't think so—at least, I hope not. I have no idea what is in his head—what he expects to find.' He shook his head in exasperation. 'I'm no good at all this sub-terfuge, Christina, no good at all.'

'I'm glad you're not.'

'I'm sure I must have guilt written all over me.'

'No, you have not and you must try to stay calm,' Christina said soothingly. 'What is he like—this Lord Rockley?'

'A cool one, I can tell you—a retired military man—with a reputation to instil fear into the stoutest heart.'

'Even Mark Bucklow's?' she asked quietly, hoping and wishing this would be so.

'As to that, we shall have to wait and see. To his enemies, Rockley is the most hated and feared of all Marlborough's commanders. They believe he is a mon-ster, a barbarian, more evil than the Devil himself—and more dangerous, for whereas the Devil is a spirit, Rockley is flesh and blood.'

Suddenly the atmosphere was filled with gruesome predictions of violence and death; Christina stared at her brother in mute horror, for surely no man could be as bad as that, and hoped that what William said was pure hysteria passed on by word of mouth from Lord Rockley's enemies. But despite her doubts, at that moment a bank of cloud passed over the house and darkened the room. A cold shiver ran down her spine, as if nature herself brooded at the mention of such evil.

'Dear me, this Lord Rockley sounds quite fearsome. And this is the man who is to stay at Oakbridge?'

William nodded. 'He looked me straight in the eye as he spoke—it was a challenge almost, as if testing my reaction. Such men are better dealt with in calm deliberation, not youthful bravado, so naturally I had to agree that it was high time someone brought these fellows preying on innocent travellers to justice and left it at that.'

'But—tonight of all nights. What shall we do? Mark has it all planned. Lord Rockley could ruin everything.'

'No, he won't,' William countered fiercely, pacing the small area of floor between the flower-filled urn and Christina. 'We must see to it that he doesn't suspect a thing.'

'Oh, how I wish we could cancel the party—to send word to everyone not to come.'

'It's too late for that. Besides, Mark wouldn't allow it. You know the rules,' William uttered with bitter irony, having come to rue the day he'd met Mark Bucklow and fallen into his clutches. 'Tonight the gentry are coming to Oakbridge to make merry. The windows will be blazing with light and the drink flowing—enough to sodden their wits for their journey home. Do as he says, keep him happy and we'll be all right. But, by God, if you open your mouth and squeal, Christina, he'll break us both.'

Christina faced her brother, holding her hands in front of her so they wouldn't tremble. 'I understand, William, and I've never gossiped in my life. It doesn't matter to me what Mark Bucklow does or what company he keeps, I'll do what he asks and he'll have no cause to grumble. But if he hurts you in any way, I'll go and find a magistrate and bring him here. I'll have the law on him. Then let him try and break me.'

Her show of spirit brought a grim smile to William's lips. 'That's a pretty speech, Christina. Scratch you and you show your claws, but Mark has more sense and cunning than the law and we both know it. The constables are too scared to shove their noses into what he does.'

What he said was true. All her life Christina had felt content in the quiet, comfortable, well-to-do existence into which she had been born. And yet, it had only taken William's meeting with Mark Bucklow to set the wheels of fate in motion, precipitating her from the tranquil monotony of her familiar world into the future, whose far-reaching horizons were hazy and unknowable and often frightening.

Mark Bucklow was one of the most dangerous and feared men Christina had ever met or heard about. There were many in the fraternity who were in awe of him and feared him. Mark's rule over his gang of thieves was supreme. The fraternity's meetings took place at Oakbridge, in a labyrinth of ancient tunnels running beneath the house. The chamber he used was at the exit of the tunnels, the perfect hideaway, so well situated for his organisation that he and his associates could come and go as they pleased with comparative ease.

Oakbridge was in the heart of Mark's domain, where constables were reluctant to venture. Mark knew every highway and byway, every house and hiding place and escape route, every type of thief and scoundrel who worked for him and owed him a cut of their earnings, and if any dared take their plunder elsewhere, he'd be floating in the river before the day's end. Only the most hard-bitten thieves and cut-throats defied Mark Bucklow, and brave though he tried be, William wasn't one of them. Mark had threatened to kill him if he didn't comply with his wishes. It was no idle threat. William knew this and he was right to be afraid—not only for his own life, but for Christina's also.

Christina had no illusions about her brother and she had to stop herself from conjuring up all the gruesome outcomes of his involvement with Mark Bucklow of which her imagination was capable, lest she frighten herself into an early grave. She loved William dearly, but she could not ignore the fact that he was inclined to laziness.

Their father had dispatched him to Balliol College at Oxford University to read law. Their father had died while William was at university, leaving him a wealthy young man. Elevated to a position of importance, he had left his studies for the seedy delights on offer in London. Here he had taken up with a wild, rakish set of young men. Awestruck, his new cronies introduced him to the private clubs of the elite and to the high-stake games of chance that flourished within these establishments. It had been a heady temptation that he could not resist. Lacking any kind of guidance, he had recklessly gone his own way, and within two years his wealth was exhausted.

It was at this desperate time that William became associated with Mark Bucklow. Seduced by Bucklow's talk of riches beyond belief, William had taken the money Mark offered to pay off some of his most pressing creditors, with the promise of paying it back when his circumstances improved. Truly believing he was on his way to Eldorado, he had fallen for every word that dripped from the villain's silken tongue. It certainly meant a new and profitable beginning for him, and further confirmed the steadfast belief that he was in full control of his own destiny and would now have whatever he desired. How wrong he had been.

'Mark cannot go on doing what he does for ever,' Christina said. 'He likes the idea of easy money and associating with wealthy people. Little good it will do him when he is caught.'

'I don't think it's like that. In fact, it's rather difficult to decide what he does with the money he gets from the robberies—none of it has come my way, that's for sure,' William complained bitterly. 'In fact, Christina, I don't know anything about Mark at all. When he's not in London, his business dealing seems to radiate from a room in an inn somewhere.'

'How do you know this?'

'I keep my ears open. He meets with other men there—at the Black Swan Inn over at Wakeham. It's all very secretive. The lot of them usually scatter after the meetings, going in different directions.'

Christina frowned, curious as to what else other than highway robbery Mark was mixed up in. 'Whatever else he's involved in, I hope you keep out of it. You're in deep enough as it is. How I wish you'd never met him, but we both know why he approached you. Mark is clever, scheming and cunning—and he has murdered more people than I care to know about. He had his eyes set on Oakbridge—a house in a splendid isolated location and full of secret places. What better place for him to operate his network from—and you, with your pocket to let, provided him with the perfect opportunity.'

Embarrassment tinted William's handsome face with a ruddy hue. 'I know and I'm fed up with saying I'm sorry.'

'And I'm sorry. So very sorry.' Christina's heart went out to him. He was not bad, she thought, merely weak. 'But it is better to live in poverty than this.'

'What can I do? I am involved up to my neck—even though I haven't received a penny piece from him in all these months.'

'I'm glad, because that would make you as big a criminal as he is. It has all worked out to his advantage—just as he planned it. It pains me to think I have to take part in it. I hate it, William. I hate what we do—the anxieties and the misery of it all. And tonight, being forced to hold this party, I shall die a thousand deaths should the crimes he and his cohorts carry out on the guests returning to their homes be traced back here.'

'As long as we keep our mouths shut we'll be all

right. At Oakbridge we have comfort. Would you prefer the squalor of prison while you await the hangman's pleasure or transportation?'

The cruelty of his words lashed into her, and with tears burning the backs of her eyes, she turned her head away. 'Please don't say that. I am frightened. I hate the hold Mark has over us and I fear greatly what will become of us. If you should put one foot wrong, William—or me—he will not hesitate to kill us.'

Aware of the intensity of her feelings and her fear, William softened. 'I know, which is why we must do as he says. Here you are safe, Christina.'

'What I want is peace of mind and security, and a life without Mark Bucklow. When you took up with him, I recall warning you to be careful what you wished for— that you may get it, but at a cost. And your association with him may cost us dear.' She gave him a meaningful look. 'I don't think Squire Kershaw would be quite so eager to allow your marriage to Miranda to go ahead should he find out about your association with Mark.'

William blanched visibly. Becoming betrothed to Miranda was the one good thing that had happened to him in recent months, and he dearly wanted to make her his wife. She was sweet and gentle and he loved her dearly. Her father was in favour of a match between them, but William knew Squire Kershaw would pull back if it became known that thieves were using Oakbridge as their base with his permission. He had taken Miranda to London to visit relatives. They were expected to leave for their home in Cirencester very soon, and were to call at Oakbridge on the way.

'I know the situation, Christina,' William replied crossly, her persistence to continue harping on about it hardening his mood. 'Must you turn everything into a high tragedy? I can only hope to God Squire Kershaw doesn't find out about what goes on here.'

'For your sake, so do I. If Mark chooses to make his living from outwitting the gullible, then that is his affair. But if things go wrong, then it will be you who will pay the price, not Mark. They say the devil looks after his own, and they don't come much uglier than Mark Bucklow. I know him well enough to despise him—as much as I do this Lord Rockley for inviting himself to Oakbridge and making me afraid and uncertain,' she uttered crossly and meant every word.

She imagined him to have an ugly face with a bent nose, close-set eyes and yellow teeth, a man who would hardly care about the havoc he had brought upon his enemies and her nerves. How dare he have the effrontery to invite himself to Oakbridge? She would dearly like to shatter his composure to her satisfaction and give him a tongue-lashing that would lay him low for a week and make him think twice before coming again.

'Whatever happens, we must be clever and see that he has not the least suspicion about what goes on here at Oakbridge. I doubt Mark will forgo the opportunity of obtaining thousands of pounds' worth of goods, but we must make him aware of the danger. When the guests have arrived, you must slip away and warn him. You'll find him in the usual place, organising the night's work. After that it's up to him.'

Christina paled. 'But—you know how much I hate that tunnel, William. I cannot...'

'Yes, you can,' William said roughly. 'You must. If you leave during the firework display, your absence will be least noticed.'

Christina hesitated for a moment, then, determination in the set of her small jaw, the expression in her eyes almost truculent, she said, 'Very well, but you know how I feel about facing Mark and his band of ruffians.'

'You'd best have a room made ready for our unwelcome guest—and his valet, I suppose—the blue room in the West Wing, which is far enough away from the entrance Mark will use, should he have need to come back here later. With any luck, Rockley will leave after breakfast without suspecting a thing. If he is suspicious, we must make sure he knows nothing definite. Hopefully he will go away and we'll see neither hide nor hair of him again.'

When William had left her, Christina thought of the evening that stretched before her, shrouded with gloom and foreboding. She tried to prepare herself for her meeting with Lord Rockley, her stomach twisting into sick knots of fear. William had told her he was clever. *How clever?* she wondered. Under close inspection she studied her image in her dressing-table mirror, considering her features only for what hazard they might pose. Was there something in her eyes and her expression that might prove to be a liability, something that would betray them all?

The face that stared back at her was an attractive

face, the features soft, the eyes appealing. She quickly pulled herself up sharp. This was a time for survival, not for girlish fancies and longings. With a hardness of purpose born of necessity, Christina gave her mind over to how best she might carry out her deception, entertaining no concept of a day when these self-same features might cause a man to forget what other goals he had in mind.

One after another, the carriages came slowly up the short avenue of poplars leading to the entrance to Oakbridge, lit up from the basement to the roof for the occasion by lights flaring cheerfully in the darkness. Built in Tudor times of warm red brick, it was large and rambling. Sadly, its tasteful furnishings and exquisite decorations were showing signs of neglect. Fabrics had become faded and frayed, carpets worn, and there were pale rectangles on the walls where paintings used to hang; although it was months since they had been taken down and sold, their absence never failed to remind Christina of William's debt to Mark Bucklow, or the vicious threat he posed to their lives.

Only the most eminent of the local gentry had been invited to tonight's party, so that the guests felt themselves highly privileged persons. It was clear, early as it was, that the event would be a success. In the days of Christina's grandfather, whose wealth had surpassed most of his contemporaries and the estate had exuded good, well-funded stewardship, from its carefully landscaped grounds to the house itself, grand, memorable events had been held at Oakbridge, balls and parties that were still talked about today. Her father had carried on the tradition and it had been expected that William, now Lord Atherton, would do the same. The tradition was about to be continued, but sadly, it was not William who called the tune or funded the entertainment, but Mark Bucklow.

Christina was breathtakingly beautiful, standing beside William to receive their guests in the doorway of the large drawing-room on the first floor, from which one of several doors led into the long gallery where the dancing was to be held. The ice blue of her dress blended perfectly with her eyes of a slightly darker shade, as did the setting of the diamonds and sapphires that adorned her throat. They had belonged to Christina's mother, and Christina had steadfastly refused to part with them to pay off William's debts. The diamonds flashed in the bright light, rousing an answering flash of envy in the eyes of every woman present, and of their male escorts, although their desires were attracted more to the wearer than the jewels.

Christina could see and feel the admiration directed at her, but how they would sneer, she thought bitterly, if they knew how miserable she was, how heavy her heart, which lay in her breast like a stone. She could not understand how she managed to function at these events. She hated them, but she managed to collect her thoughts sufficiently to respond with grace to the comments of their guests. Her smile was charming, but like the sun, it was more brilliant than warm.

A man, a stranger to those present, entered and detached himself from the receiving line. His figure was distinctive, his shoulders broad and his walk combined gracefulness with strength. He coolly and carefully examined the faces that made up the assembly, of ladies in ball gowns and men in elaborate wigs and evening dress moving about to the strains of violins.

Then he turned his eyes on his host. The same procedure was repeated. William Atherton was a slender, fair-haired young man with an open, boyish face. His gaze moved on to the lady by his side. From his enquiries he knew Atherton to be unwed, so he surmised the lady to be his sister Christina. Much had been talked about her beauty, but, not given to listening to idle gossip, he had thought little of it. Now, as he inspected her with the interested look of an entomologist discovering some rare insect, he was all attention.

Tall and lithe and looking like some fantastic Grecian statue, Christina Atherton was exquisitely lovely, ruling her domain like a young queen. She wore her golden tresses piled and curled in glorious chaos atop her head, with tendrils wafting against the curve of her neck. But he could be forgiven for thinking that he preferred her as he had last seen her the day before, with her hair in a delightful disarray of golden lights, her feet bare and splashing in the brook.

There was a fragile, waif-like quality about her that appealed to him, a naïve freshness in her eyes that stemmed from innocence. It was a trait absent in the women of his acquaintance, but beneath it all, Christina Atherton reminded him of a fine silver rapier blade, made of steel. He could not keep his eyes off her as she spoke to the guests, her gloved hand resting lightly on her brother's arm. Her gems caught his eye. They were beautiful and fine cut and matched the deep, uncommon colouring of her eyes, eyes lit by no inner warmth.

Any woman would have worn such exquisite gems with pride, but Christina Atherton wore them with an indifference that was almost melancholy. People spoke to her, but it was as if she neither saw nor heard. Her smile was pinned to her face like a mask. He would not have dared give open expression to the feelings she aroused and this was because of something at once remote and detached in the attitude and icy façade of the dazzling beauty.

Lord Rockley was intrigued.

As the festivities got under way and proceeded in grand style, sensing she was being watched, Christina turned her head slightly, her eyes lighting on a man who had made no effort to present himself. He stood several yards away from her by one of the windows. With hands clasped behind his back, legs a little apart, he seemed to carry about him a kind of lethal charge—the air immediately about him held an indefinably vibrant quality that kept one at bay—like the bars around a panther's cage. The comparison was apt, for there was something very panther-like about him.

He had an air of careless unconcern as he studied her with unswerving regard. It was as if he had just landed there by chance. With his skin bronzed from seeing active service in foreign parts, he looked completely at odds when compared with the pink-faced, well-fed local gentry.

He was a man with thick, dark brown hair, which he wore drawn back, and was very tall with a lean, rangy look that gave an impression of dangerous vitality. He had the bold profile of a predatory hawk in the midst of a gathering of tame peacocks, which gave him a somewhat proud and insolent appearance. Even the slender brown hands emerging from the broad, embroidered cuffs of his frock-coat recalled the talons of the bird of prey, while the look in his silver-grey eyes was unnervingly intent.

He smiled a thin, crooked smile, revealing a lightning glimpse of very white teeth when he found her watching him warily, from her great, luminous, shadowed eyes. His own, boldly mocking and amused, did not waver. She gave him stare for stare, with a coquettishly raised brow of question.

Christina felt a vague sense of recognition and finally realised it was the same man she had met yesterday in the woods, the man who had called himself Simon. Her face turned crimson with remembrance and shock—and more than a little embarrassment when she recalled their kiss and the intimate content of their conversation—bringing a smile to his lips, which closed like a fist about her heart and a leap of gladness almost bowled her over. Voices around her drifted away into the depths of her mind, hidden where no sound could reach it, muffled noises and feelings that drove all feelings from her.

This man was a guest at Oakbridge and, despite his attraction, she had to mentally revile the air of authority he conveyed, which no doubt stemmed from a haughty attitude or perhaps a military rank. His imposing presence seemed highly inappropriate here at this time. She actually shivered as she saw him abandon his idle stance and come towards her.

Much as she wanted to take to her heels and run, good manners and the need to look into his eyes once more obliged her not to turn away. With sudden realisation, she knew this must be Lord Rockley, and as she watched him come closer she knew by his look that he was thinking of their encounter in the woods. What had he been doing there? she wondered. He had told her he was a stranger to these parts and finding his way about. How long had he been there, how much did he know?

Fear was heavy in her breast. Of what was he thinking when he looked at her? What was there in his eyes that made her feel afraid? His slow, appreciative smile made her feel somehow ashamed and alarmed, as though he were able to pierce through the bones of her skull and ferret out the secrets of her mind. She was uneasy— but why should she be? *To his enemies...he is...more evil than the Devil himself...* Her brother's words came back to her and her legs trembled. Outwardly everything appeared normal. There was no reason for him to suspect anything untoward. He wasn't remotely what she had expected. This man who had come here to seek out the highwaymen and destroy them was younger than she had thought, and unexpectedly handsome.

'So, Miss Atherton—for it is Miss Christina Atherton, is it not? We meet again—under different circumstances,' he said when he stood in front of her, politely inclining his head slightly without taking his eyes off hers. 'I hardly hoped you would recall me.'

At the sound of his deep, soft and mellifluous voice, Christina was transported and, for a moment, completely speechless. Try as she might, she could find no flaw in those wide shoulders, lean waist and long limbs. The impeccably tailored clothes were to be admired as much as the man who wore them. Yet on someone of less impressive stature, the froth of lace at throat and wrists, the waistcoat of ivory hue that matched his breeches beneath a midnight-blue coat might have lost much of their flair.

Her confidence was slowly returning. Something in his look challenged her spirit and brought her strength back in a surge of excitement. Far from being overawed by this man's presence and by the danger that lay in wait for her each moment, Christina was aware of release and a relaxation of tension in finding herself at last face to face with him. But she must not forget herself. She must be politeness personified with this particular gentleman.

Finding her voice, she said, 'I am Christina Atherton and I do remember you. How could I not? Our encounter was—momentous to say the least. How do you do?'

His dark brows lifted a fraction and he smiled suddenly, a slow, startlingly glamorous white smile. The electric touch of his strong, bare fingers grasped hers warmly and for just a moment too long before raising them to his lips and releasing them.

'Very well, Miss Atherton. It is a relief to know your name—although I did suspect who you were when I saw you receiving your guests. I am Lord Rockley—Simon Rockley.'

'Yes, I thought you might be,' she replied, 'since you're the only guest here I am not acquainted with— or should I say to whom I have not been properly introduced.'

'I hope you don't mind and that I will be forgiven if I have put you to any inconvenience.'

Christina felt as if she were being manoeuvred into a series of uncomfortable corners. She would have to be careful what she said to him. 'No, of course not. You are very welcome.'

'I was watching you a few minutes ago. I saw your expression when you recognised me as being the man you met in the woods yesterday.' Humour glinted in his eyes. 'I'm happy to know you did not forget me.'

Despite his open attitude, he was a guest in her home, and Christina was a little mortified that she'd let her feelings about him show so openly. Relying on the old adage that the best defence is a good offence, and deter- mined to keep tight rein on controlling her attraction to this beautiful man, she said very firmly and politely, 'I never forget a face, Lord Rockley.'

'Neither do I—and not when a face is as lovely as yours. When I saw you, I was completely captivated by you.'

'Really?' she quipped. 'I don't see why. You are a guest in my home, Lord Rockley. If I have any kind of feelings about any guest, including you, you would never know it because I would never let them show.'

'That's very reassuring,' he said softly. 'But I wonder how long you could keep up the pretence.'

'As to that, we will never know.' In an attempt to still her rioting nerves, she smiled brightly. 'You are most welcome at Oakbridge, Lord Rockley. We are honoured to have you as our guest. I hope you will be comfortable. You must forgive me if I seem surprised.'

'I must?' His face was no longer grave, but open and almost beguiling.

'When my brother told me you were to stay the night with us, I must confess to thinking you would be quite different.'

'But why should you have expected me to be anything but what I am?'

'William told me you were a military man, so I imagined you to be much older.'

His eyes sparked with amusement. 'I assure you I am quite old—thirty-one, to be exact—which is a great age to a young woman of such tender years and must make me a veritable antique.'

His words brought a reluctant smile to Christina's lips. 'No, indeed. My father always used to say that one is as old as one feels. You certainly don't look like an antique—and I'm sure you don't feel one.' She glanced at him obliquely. 'Your reputation precedes you, sir.'

He arched a quizzical brow. 'You have heard of me?'

'Who has not? You are the terrifying spectre that people use to terrify their offspring from disobeying their elders,' she said, a teasing gleam in her eyes.

'The bogey man?'

She laughed lightly. 'Something like that—more myth than man.'

His eyes narrowed on hers. 'Let me assure you, Miss Atherton, that I am all man.'

A crimson flush coloured her cheeks. 'I will take your word for that, Lord Rockley. My brother and I are honoured that you chose to stay at Oakbridge, when there are so many other noble houses in the district at your disposal.'

'It really doesn't matter where I stay. From what I've seen, Oakbridge is a splendid house.'

'I think so, and I know my brother does. I took over the running of it for my father when my mother died four years ago. Sadly, my father died a few short months after her. I am under no illusion that when William marries I shall have to move over for his wife.'

'You'll probably be married yourself by then.'

'I doubt it since William is to marry very soon.'

'I have noted that Oakbridge is somewhat isolated—though perfectly situated.'

Christina met his eyes. They were intent on her face and missed nothing. The warning there seemed to pierce her like a dagger's thrust. He seemed to be consciously searching for an answer in her face, as if she held the key to what he wanted to know. She knew there was an unusual colour in her cheeks—she couldn't help it, and she hoped she did not show how agitated she was. She tried to calm herself. Was she being unduly sensitive, or did his words hold a double meaning? Did he know? At that moment Lord Rockley's mere presence reminded her of the dangers in which they all lay.

'I—I think I should find my brother and ask him to introduce you to our guests. It's most unseemly of him not to have done so.'

'Do not put yourself out, Miss Atherton. I have already spoken to your brother and he has introduced me to several guests.'

'Then you will have seen for yourself that they are all amenable and friendly enough.' Lord Rockley's face was inscrutable, but something flickered in those piercing, silver-grey eyes that seemed never to rest. Christina thought that even when his back was turned, one dared not slacken one's effort, for, like the panther, he could turn and pounce in the blink of an eye.

'Whatever people appear to be in public, their private lives are often very different.'

'Yes—I—I suppose that is true.'

'An event such as this is the best way for me to become acquainted with those who live in the neighbourhood. I am grateful for the opportunity.'

'I suppose it is.' Knowing of Lord Rockley's reasons for wanting to familiarise himself with the local folk and reluctant to speak of it, Christina cast a sweeping glance over the chattering, happy throng. 'You will see it is not a formal party and that comfort and pleasure are our guiding principles. You have taken a glass of wine, I hope, and eaten from the buffet table. I can recommend the strawberries—they are quite delicious, freshly picked from our own gardens this afternoon…' She flushed, unable to still her tongue in her nervousness, but she could not seem to help it.

This was not lost on Simon and he smiled. 'I have

had some wine, but I have not yet eaten. Perhaps later—and when I do I shall be sure to have a dish of strawberries.'

'H-Have you come alone, Lord Rockley?' she asked hesitantly, sensing from the way he was looking at her that he was aware of the awkwardness in her manner and amused by it.

'No. My valet is with me. One of the servants has taken him to the rooms you have so graciously prepared.'

'I'm glad you are being looked after. I hope your stay at Oakbridge will be an enjoyable one.'

Looking at her lovely face and form, Simon could be forgiven any impure thoughts that crossed his mind. She really did have the deepest, loveliest blue eyes he had ever seen, and her lashes were long and dark and swept her cheeks when she lowered her eyes with a fresh naïvety, which he assumed stemmed from innocence. The bodice of her gown was scooped low—the white flesh lay like pearl against the ice blue of her dress. She looked away to acknowledge an elegantly attired woman, and his eye was drawn to the faint shadow beneath her jaw line, and the tendril of silken hair in her nape. He imagined that tiny curl around his finger, his hands at the back of her neck, just where the heavy mass of her hair lay above the lace of her gown.

Having to move to one side to allow a lady to pass, she brushed his arm. The action freed a delicate perfume, and Simon's attention was immediately riveted upon her tip-tilted eyes, and the full pink lips. She touched the corner of her mouth with the point of her tongue, which was pink and moist, wetting her bottom lip, and she smiled a little, as if at some secret thought. Sharply, he recollected himself.

'Unfortunately I am not here to enjoy myself, Miss Atherton,' he said in answer to her remark.

'No, of course you're not. I—I understand you are not from these parts.'

'No. My home is in Hertfordshire, so I imagine that I shall be regarded as a foreigner hereabouts, and be the object of suspicion.'

'Suspicion of what?'

The question and the forthright way in which Christina expressed it caused Simon to raise his brows. 'Of strange conduct—while I go about my business.'

'My brother told me you are here to investigate the increase in highway robbery in these parts,' she remarked, knowing the subject of his being in the area could no longer be avoided, no matter how she had tried to dance around it. She lifted one delicate brow and her lips curved in a smile, showing milk-white teeth, her eyes looking innocently into his. 'A military man turned thief-taker. It is an interesting occupation.'

'Not so interesting as necessary.'

'Then I wish you good fortune, sir. It is a great undertaking you have been set.'

'So it is, but it will have its rewards in the end. I am confident of that. Five years ago two highwaymen operating in this area were hanged at the Assizes. For a while there was relative peace on the roads.' He smiled wryly. 'There is nothing like a hanging to put the fear of

God into folk and to make them take stock of things, but then it started up again. Perhaps you can be of help.'

Christina stepped back and looked at him. His heavy-lidded gaze was speculative. She had expected arrogant self-assurance from a man with such handsome looks and military bearing. Instead, what she saw was wariness and an icy control. 'I'm afraid not, Lord Rockley. You see, I make a point of never travelling anywhere after dark.'

'No traveller is safe anywhere or at any time. It is as dangerous in busy towns as on deserted country roads, and noblemen or women with an escort are as susceptible to attack and robbery as a person journeying alone. But certain areas attract special reputation, and because robbers are on the lookout for wealthy men and members of the court driving down to Bath and to Bristol, this happens to be one of them.'

'Then I can see that when I visit my friends I shall have to go well guarded,' she uttered on a light note.

'Very wise, Miss Atherton.'

'Although some say that highwaymen, at least those of the gentlemanly sort, are popularly regarded as heroes.'

Simon's eyes hardened. 'That does not lessen their crimes, and I find it hard to grasp why they seem to have endeared themselves in that way. They are still criminals and must be caught. In reality, most highway robbers are unlikeable characters, violent, brutal bandits and sometimes murderers, all out for quick gain. Their purpose in life is to acquire enough money to enjoy the good life, and to do so at the expense of others who may have worked hard for what little they have.'

Apart from a slight fading of the flush from her cheeks, Christina's expression did not alter. Of course she had heard of people who had been harmed by robbers when they refused to hand over valuables, though these were only stories, but she had heard them and her heart beat faster as she remembered them now.

'Is there not forty pounds' blood-money paid for the capture and successful prosecution of a highway robber? Which must surely mean that the highwayman's greatest danger lay with bounty hunters and informers.'

'It is true that highwaymen are more at risk from betrayal by an accomplice or someone after the reward money than from retaliation by one of their victims. You are well informed, Miss Atherton.'

'Only in so far as what I hear, sir.'

'Forgive me if you think me impertinent, but I would be interested to hear more. Your co-operation would be appreciated.' He began to smile. His mouth curled at each corner and his charm, that which he used to capture the pretty ladies with whom he sometimes dallied, was brought into full play. 'You would not go unrewarded.'

The lovely sparkle in Christina's eyes was gone, leaving only frosted blue. 'I don't think so, Lord Rockley. If I knew anything at all that might help you with your enquiries, I would be reluctant to divulge it, for if the highwaymen you speak of are as dangerous as you say, then they would not take kindly to my turning informer.

Are—are you looking for anyone in particular?' she ventured to ask.

'Oh, yes, Miss Atherton. I am looking for the leader of a gang who has so far managed to evade the authorities, a man who has acquired a well-deserved reputation for exceptional viciousness. His robberies are carried out with a stamp of professionalism, I will grant him that, but he will not evade the law for ever. I have a way of discovering what I want to know. I have my instincts and they work well for me.'

'And the name of this individual, sir?'

'I prefer to keep that piece of information to myself for the present.'

'Then I wish you every success in your search for this man, Lord Rockley. The sooner he is apprehended and under lock and key, the more easily we shall all sleep in our beds.'

'I know what I'm up against. This particular band of thieves are no amateurs at the game—a highly lucrative game, I might add.'

'Yes, I imagine it must be,' Christina said.

'So long as it lasts,' Simon replied.

Christina felt that Lord Rockley was conveying a warning to her in what he said. She averted her face to where William was helping himself to a glass of wine. What could she do? she thought desperately. How she would like to tell this man everything, to have him go down the tunnel and arrest Mark Bucklow so they could be free of his terrifying intimidation, but she dare not. He would find some way of carrying out his threat.

Like the tolling of the funeral bell, she heard Lord

Rockley say, 'It will not be long. Sooner or later even the most cunning, clever criminal makes a mistake.'

'Yes, I am sure you are right—and I wish you every success. Now, please excuse me. Duty dictates that I have to speak to our other guests.' She smiled. 'You are welcome here, Lord Rockley,' she said graciously. 'My brother is honoured by your attendance. But as to your purpose here, I am afraid he cannot be of help. Please enjoy the festivities and help yourself to refreshments. We have an exceptional cook, so the food promises to be simply delectable. There is also to be a firework display shortly, which promises to be quite spectacular. I hope you enjoy it.'

He inclined his head. 'Thank you for making a complete stranger feel at home, Miss Atherton,' Simon replied. 'You are very kind.'

'It is my pleasure to be of service.'

Quite unexpectedly, he laughed. 'As it was mine yesterday,' he said quietly.

She flushed hotly on being reminded of the kiss they had shared. 'Please forget what happened, sir, I beg you,' she implored. 'You made me lose my head...'

His laughter stopped as suddenly as it had begun, as he stared at Christina with a gravity in which there was a challenging note. 'Forget that I kissed you? Forget that I looked into your eyes and saw them change colour? Forget the sweet taste of your lips? That is asking too much of me.'

Torn between a desire to hear more and fear of the feelings he would invoke, with her thoughts in turmoil she left him, not wanting one more word from him or glimpse of his handsome face or his overwhelming male presence to complicate her already muddled feelings. She realised she was trembling. She must not forget that Lord Rockley was their enemy and all the more dangerous because he was handsome and charming and because she felt that it was going to be impossible to hate him as she had been able to before she had known who he was.

Chapter Two

Christina paused to speak to Sir John Cruckshank, a short, stout gentleman, always amiable and with a warm sense of humour. He was also the local magistrate.

'I see you've met Lord Rockley, my dear,' Sir John said, his face overly flushed beneath his elaborately curled black wig.

'Yes,' she replied flatly, having already met the man with the rapier gaze, who possessed the instincts of a magician, the intellect of a genius, and the persistence of a blood hound. She pinned a smile to her face, giving Sir John no indication that this illustrious gentleman he spoke of had not impressed her in the least. 'He…is to be our guest for the night, his home being too far away for him to travel late at night. I understand he was a military man.'

Sir John nodded. 'He has seen much service with Marlborough in the Netherlands. He is highly talented in his field and politically astute,' he said, dabbing at the light perspiration on his forehead, the light powder of snuff stirring gently upon his person as he spoke.

And with arrogance by the bucket load, Christina thought unkindly, yet unable to quell the emotional detachment she felt for their unwelcome guest. 'You know him well, Sir John?'

'We are acquainted. Like his uncles and his grandfather, he made soldiering his career, but unlike your ordinary soldier he has plenty of money behind him. At thirty-one years old, he has an outstanding record and is highly thought of by Marlborough himself, who has expressed his regret at his leaving.'

'I have heard that he's acquired a fearful reputation—that there are those who liken him to the Devil himself.'

Sir John nodded. 'That is true. But in battle it is no bad thing for his enemies to fear him. The man's a legend.'

'Why?'

'A lot of reasons—his courage and exploits, some of which no one knows—to do with espionage and being able to flush out the enemy.'

'That's informative,' Christina said with a smile.

'You would have to be in the military to understand. Everybody expected he'd be made colonel in time, but that's not going to happen.'

'Why? What happened?'

'Nothing. Six months ago he decided to retire and live a life of ease.'

'I would hardly call taking on an assignment to

track down a gang of highway robbers a life of ease, Sir John.'

'Of course, you are right. Let us hope he can sort out this unsavoury business with these damned highwaymen—and then we might all travel in safety. Rockley isn't noted for his sweet nature, and I can't think of anybody who would understand the assignment better.'

Christina studied the little magistrate curiously. 'What is your assessment of Lord Rockley as a man, Sir John?'

'Well, he's a formidable opponent, for one thing, with a high-functioning intellect. If Rockley decides a man's guilty, he'll lock on to him and he will stay with him and nothing his prey can do will shake him off or sidetrack him. He will get him—and bring him down. And that,' he finished with a chuckle, 'is why he was given the assignment. Although he does have his own reasons for tracking down these criminals.'

'Oh?'

'About a year ago, the coach his brother and his wife were travelling in was apprehended by Bucklow—they had been visiting friends in Newbury and the hour was late. Their young daughter was with them. That was probably one of the worst crimes the highwaymen have committed. His niece and his brother were shot—the girl died outright, his brother was badly wounded.' He shook his head. 'Dreadful business.'

Christina stared at him in disbelief. It was such a tragic story. 'I'm sorry to hear that. Lord Rockley must have been badly affected by it.' She could imagine his grief, followed by the anger he must have felt at this direct attack on his family, and could well understand his determination to track down his niece's murderer.

'Absolutely, my dear.' Sir John looked towards the doors as people began drifting outside. 'Ah, I see the firework display is about to begin. Excuse me, my dear. I must find my lady wife. I promised to find her a prominent place where she can see them at their best.'

As Sir John bustled away, a beleaguered-looking William appeared by Christina's side. He was trying to put on a brave face, but she knew he was as afraid inside himself as she was and trying hard not to let the presence of Lord Rockley get the better of him.

'Go now, Christina. Go and see Mark. Tell him we have an unwelcome guest and to be careful. And don't be long. Rockley's eyes are all over the place. I doubt he will be enticed by the fireworks for long.'

Christina's heart sank when she looked at William, for his flushed face and the brightness of his eyes were evidence that already he was showing signs of intoxication. It was as if he could forget his fears and repression when under the influence of liquor.

'Does he suspect anything, do you think, William?'

'I don't know, so best be careful and keep our heads. Act guilty and we'll all be caught. I saw you talking to him. Keep your wits about you and say nothing to incriminate any one of us,' he warned. 'Rockley's a wily fellow—and clever. If he does suspect anything, he'll be like a dog with a bone until he gets to the bottom of it and has us all arrested. Now go, and hurry back.'

'I will try—and, William, please don't drink so much. I hate it when you do.'

She missed the glower he threw her when she turned to acknowledge a close neighbour, a young man who came to speak to them. Smiling and excusing herself, with no time to lose and with gathering apprehension, she slipped away, unaware as she did so of the man in the shadows, watching.

Simon had observed Miss Atherton's altercation with her brother in perplexed fascination. She looked agitated and her expression was, strangely, one of intense fear. She stopped speaking when a young blood on his way to the firework display approached to pay his respects. All signs of Miss Atherton's distress had vanished behind a flawless smile. Why, she was a consummate actress, he thought. Either that or she was a desperately frightened young woman.

His instinct told him that she knew something, something she was desperately trying to keep hidden. There was a certain naïvety about her that he couldn't quite reconcile to her being a conspirator in all of this. He could be wrong, but, having learnt to be an excellent judge of character through his work, he didn't think so.

Having heard of the magnificence of Oakbridge Hall and its fine estate, on his arrival he had been surprised by its run-down state. Either William Atherton had not been gifted with the same talent for management or astuteness as his father and his grandfather before him, or something had happened.

He frowned, unable to stem the feeling that there was something dangerous simmering in this house. It was tangible. He could feel it. While unable to say quite why he was troubled, the very quietness of the place now everyone had left to watch the firework display made him feel that an ill-defined something might happen.

Seeing Henry, his valet, hovering at the bottom of the stairs, Simon's eyes locked on to his, before quickly flitting to Miss Atherton, who was walking in the direction of the domestic quarters. Expressionless, again he looked at his valet. It was as if a silent language passed between them, for seeming to understand fully what his master asked of him, Henry nodded his head slightly and followed in Miss Atherton's wake.

Christina made her way to the domestic quarters where the entrance to the cellars was located. Servants hurrying about their duties found nothing unusual on seeing the mistress in the kitchens, although they might have raised a curious brow on seeing her don a shawl and slip through the door to the cellars. Here, casks and racks of wine were stored. Candles flared in lanterns fastened to the walls, should more wine be needed for the festivities. Lifting her skirts, she hurried on her way, wishing she didn't have to face Mark.

Few people ventured beyond the wine cellars, where a small, narrow door was located in the roughly hewn wall, unnoticeable to the eye unless it was known to be there. With every nerve in her body vibrating, Christina raised the iron catch and it opened without a sound on its well-oiled hinges. The ancient tunnels, unused for many years, were narrow, dark and dank. They had a tomb-like atmosphere and a deathly chill, as if a frigid breath of winter moved like an invisible spirit along the passageways. Having set a flame to the wick of a lantern, she held it high to light her way, the tiny flame dipping and dancing in its glass chamber against the draught that flowed towards her. She drew the shawl up close about her neck as her gaze tried to penetrate the total blackness beyond the meagre glow of the lantern.

Her nerves were stretched taut as she hurried along the twisting tunnel, stumbling frequently on the uneven ground. She hated being so confined, feeling as if the walls were closing in on her. She was relieved when she saw a vague, dim illumination some distance away and the muffled sound of men's voices. The chill of a draught invaded her clothing, the airy rush touching her limbs beneath her skirts, but she was scarcely aware of it as the light ahead of her became bigger and brighter.

Shaking with cold and her own apprehensions, she eventually stepped into the light, then halted, holding her breath. The tunnel opened into a large room with a vaulted ceiling. It was accessed on a low hillside in a thickly wooded area away from the house. It was secluded, the trees providing cover for horses and men. The room was stacked with boxes and chests of every description, full of coins, jewels and household treasures—for Mark did not confine his thievery to robbing vulnerable travellers, and house-breaking was a lucrative occupation.

He ran an effective intelligence system, and the time spent watching and listening in parlours and wayside inns and employing reliable spies was the best way to acquire information about which travellers to target and which to leave alone. All the spoils were to be taken to London and sold.

The son of a lawyer, it was Mark who had found out about the tunnels in some old deeds of Oakbridge kept in his father's office in Reading. Knowing they were the perfect place for him to expand his illegal operation and hide his ill-gotten gains, he had targeted the vulnerable and gullible young owner of Oakbridge, bringing about his downfall and honing in for the kill when he was ruined with an offer he couldn't refuse.

Christina focused her eyes on the scene before her, barely conscious of the flickering light of the lanterns or the pervasive chill of the tunnel. The air was thick with the fug of tobacco smoke and the unpleasant stench of unwashed bodies. About a dozen of Mark's loyal vassals were present, accomplished thieves each and every one. All except the leader were black-clad and each equipped with a brace of pistols. Some were seated on upturned barrels and boxes, while others squatted on the floor, idling the time away with a throw of dice.

Her sudden appearance surprised them and had them springing to their feet, their hands automatically going to their pistols. Their leader turned and looked directly at her and said with a note of mockery in his harsh, baritone voice, 'Easy, men. Calm yourselves. 'Tis Miss Atherton herself come to call. Although as to the reason…I can only surmise it is my own charming self she has come to see.'

Her look was one of intense dislike, but Mark Bucklow appeared not to notice. There was something about him that physically revolted her. She hated it every time she had to speak to him, to see the lust in his eyes and to hear the lechery in his sneer when he addressed her. As he threw off his cloak and swaggered towards where she stood with her legs trembling, she clamped her jaw, shrinking inside, realising it would gratify him too much if she showed her fear. Better to hold her ground, unpleasant as the next few minutes would be. He seemed to have the power to get right under her skin, and she hated herself for letting him.

A man who enjoyed the robust, earthy pleasures of life, he liked to cut a dash, did Mark Bucklow, and dressed in outrageously extroverted fashion. Tonight he was flamboyantly dressed in scarlet velvet and gold braid to draw attention to himself, a froth of lace at his throat and wrists. Two pistols were thrust into a gold sash about his thickening waist, and a dagger showed above the deep cuff of his boot. He was tall and stout with long and curling sandy hair. Some would call him quite handsome—not in a gentlemanly way, with fine chiselled features, but with broad, strong cheekbones and a wide mouth. Grinning his wolfish smile, he was the very picture of what her mother had taught her to fear.

Taking the lantern from her, he set it down, placing his hand on her elbow and drawing her away from the others, who had resumed their seats and once again began to throw the dice.

'I am indeed honoured that the mistress of the house should seek me out, Christina,' Mark drawled mockingly, 'and looking as pretty as a picture, too. I'd like to think it was for my benefit.'

'We are entertaining—on your say so for what can be gained from it. It cannot have slipped your mind,' she uttered with cold sarcasm, her eyes flashing irately.

Reaching out, he ran one of his heavily jewelled fingers down the curve of her cheek, laughing softly when she cringed and drew back. 'Ah, you show your claws, Christina,' he murmured. 'I like that. You are so adorable when you are angry. But enough of this,' he said on a sharper note, knowing it would have to be a matter of considerable importance for her to brave the tunnel. 'The evening is going well, I trust?'

'Yes, perfectly well—only...'

He cocked a brow, his dark eyes assessing and gleaming sharply. 'What? Do I detect a problem? Is something amiss, Christina?'

'William sent me to tell you—to warn you—that we have an unexpected and uninvited guest by the name of Lord Rockley. He has been appointed by the Lord Lieutenant to investigate the increase in robberies in the area.'

Mark stared. For a practised scoundrel who was never at a loss for a quip, he suddenly found himself with nothing to say. He kept his face expressionless through sheer strength of will-power. He didn't need to hear anything about Rockley. Mark had heard of him, though he'd never seen him in the flesh. Rockley was a powerful, ruthless man, whose exploits were talked about throughout Europe. Mark did not fear him—indeed, Mark feared no man—but he was fully aware of Rockley's strength. To take on such an assignment, Rockley had set himself against him as his full-blown enemy.

Undaunted, Mark was ready for the challenge. He would crush Rockley as easily as he would an insect.

Mark shrugged unconcernedly. 'The infamous Lord Rockley. What do I care? He isn't the first to come after us, and he won't be the last. If he interferes in what I do, he'll find himself food for carrion before the dawn. He will be dealt the same treatment as any man who tries to get the better of me—friend or foe.'

'Even those who work for you?'

'Especially those who work for me and attempt to double-cross me or shirk a hold-up—as I've made clear to your brother. Their weakness would render them an encumbrance—an encumbrance to be rid of.' He sneered as his eyes did a sweep of the men sitting around. 'You know the expression, I am sure—there is no honour among thieves. It must also apply to thief-catchers.'

With a complete contempt for authority, and pouring scorn on the law and its representatives, Mark wouldn't be unduly worried by the appearance of this particular thief-catcher, but after meeting Lord Rockley, Christina thought that perhaps in this instance he should be.

'Now that I have delivered my message, I must go back. How is Toby, by the way? I hope he was returned to you and is recovering from the injuries incurred yesterday.'

Mark nodded towards a corner where the little dog was sleeping soundly on a heap of sacking. 'Toby's like me. It will take more than a bramble bush to defeat him.'

'Yes—I'm sure,' Christina remarked tartly. 'I must

go. Soon the guests will be coming in from the firework display and I must be there to receive them.'

'What? You will leave me so soon?'

'Yes, I must.'

He growled in exasperation. 'Such cruelty, Christina, when all I want is to take care of you. Of all the women in the world that I could have, doesn't it mean anything to you that you're the one I want?'

'No, Mark, it doesn't.'

'Come away with me and you can have me and my money.'

'I don't want you or your money. I want you to move away from Oakbridge—to leave us alone.'

'And be reduced to poverty and penny pinching,' Mark sneered. 'I don't think so, Christina. That would never do for your precious William. He always did like the good things in life, which was what I noticed about him from the start. We have an arrangement. Oakbridge serves my purpose.'

'Only until the authorities catch up with you—as they will one day.'

'Me and your brother. If they catch me, I'll take him with me.' His eyes narrowed and gleamed. 'You can count on that, Christina. You won't come out of it unscathed either, I promise you.'

'And that doesn't bother you, I suppose,' she said scathingly.

Mark shrugged. 'Not in the slightest. I'm not moving from here. As I said, it suits my purpose.'

'And if we want to contact you for any reason, where can we find you?' William had told her he often used the Black Swan Inn at Wakeham for his meetings, but where he actually lived was a mystery to her.

He leaned forwards, saying for her ears alone, 'If I thought you might find your way to my lair to help me while away the daylight hours, I would tell you, but since you aren't too friendly and might take it into that pretty head of yours to turn me in, you're better off not knowing. Let's just say it's an out-of-the-way place where a man can come and go without any questions being asked of him.' He raised a speculative brow. 'Do you think you might come looking for me, Christina?'

'Never. I know too well what you are, and I want none of it.'

A gleam of anger flashed in Mark's eyes. 'It's too late for that. You're part of it whether you want to be or not, and should you take it into that pretty head of yours to hand me in, I swear you will pipe a different tune. But I am not the devil that you should show such hostility, Christina. You'd be better employed in being more like your brother and joining forces with us.'

'William wants no part of this business any more than I do, and you know it.'

'You're right. You're a proud one,' Mark said, with a quick, dangerous sneer, but he schooled it to a taut smile. 'Very well, Christina, elude me if you will, but you will submit to me. Not now. Not tomorrow. But you will, and you will no longer speak to me with such haughty disfavour.'

She stared at him, emotionless and defiant. 'Threaten me all you like, Mark, but you will never have me.'

He laughed, a horrible, brittle sound that bounced

off the rocky walls and caused the rest of the thieves to glance his way. 'Sweet, foolish Miss Christina Atherton.' His lips angled upwards in a confident leer as his eyes moved possessively over her body. She was, after all, such a tempting young thing. It would be a shame not to taste her. 'You claim to know my nature. Don't you see that the more you run away from me, the more lusty I grow for the chase?'

Picking up the lantern, she took a backward step, gripping the shawl at her throat with her free hand. 'Stop it. I don't want to hear it. I've said what I had to say and now I must go back before I'm missed. We don't want Lord Rockley becoming suspicious by my behaviour.'

'Oh, yes, the man whose exploits are talked of from here to China. He's earned himself an admirable reputation in his field—espionage, if I'm not mistaken. How convenient that he happens to be a personal friend of the Lord Lieutenant and that the work is within his professional competence. He is probably the best qualified man in England to attempt to track me down.'

'He may very well succeed.'

'Not if I can help it. Describe him to me so I shall know him when we meet—perhaps when I waylay his coach when he takes his leave. Where does he live so I know the road he will take? I shall take care of him myself.'

Christina paled, thinking it incredible that Mark would go so far as to try to rob the very man who was looking to arrest him. 'Lord Rockley's home is too far away for him to travel back tonight. He is to stay at Oakbridge overnight.'

Mark looked surprised and most displeased by her revelation. 'Is he, now? Well, if he becomes inquisitive and comes looking, there will be nothing to find. I'll make sure of that. In the meantime it is up to you to keep him amused so we can go about our business without interruption.' His eyes were appreciative as they caressed her face. 'Looking as you do, that shouldn't be too difficult. Tell me, is he young, this Lord Rockley?' She nodded. 'How young?'

'A-about thirty or a little older, I believe.'

Mark's eyes narrowed. The mockery had gone and his voice was purposeful, a man whose mind was already telling him that this Lord Rockley might pose a threat in more ways than his investigations into his criminal activities. 'And is he handsome?'

Christina knew her face had pinked when she recollected Lord Rockley's handsome looks, but she was unable to do anything about it. She stiffened, looking utterly wary. 'I—I suppose he is—passable.'

Mark's eyes were full of feverish suspicion. 'Passable? My instinct and the flush on your cheeks tell me his lordship is more than *passable*.' He grasped her wrist, his fingers closing like a vice. 'Have a care what you do, Christina—what you say. Informers can expect harsh treatment from me.' He released her wrist as quickly as he had grasped it. 'And don't forget your own interests are at stake.'

She tossed her head and glared at him in defiance. 'If it was up to me, I would have you gone from here and never see you again.'

Suddenly Mark's hand shot out and he caught her

roughly by the chin, cupping and squeezing her soft flesh and thrusting his face close to hers. 'Do not defy me, Christina. You would only regret doing so. A face such as yours does not bear well under a fist. It is too fine and fragile.'

'Your threats do not frighten me,' she hissed bravely.

'No? They should. I have ways to convince you,' he sneered, releasing his grip and thrusting her away. 'Now go. You can tell your precious William that I shall heed his warning and I thank him for letting me know, but nothing is changed. We have a busy night ahead, and make sure you get rid of Rockley in the morning.'

About to turn away, she hesitated, her chin still throbbing from his grip. 'There is one thing I must ask you. Will—will you promise me that there will be no bloodshed? Some of the guests are elderly and I hope very much that they will go unmolested.'

'I can't promise that. I'm not in this business to pick and choose who I will and will not waylay. If they become difficult, it's often necessary to—frighten them a little. Sometimes it's the only way to get them to part with their valuables.'

'I beg you not to,' she said, before turning and hurrying away. Knowing Mark was watching her and afraid that he would come after her and waylay her in the tunnel, with the sure-footed speed of a hunted animal she moved swiftly on, not stopping until that awful tunnel was behind her and she was back in the wine cellar, where she could hear the servants in the upper part of the house going about their business.

Slipping past the wine racks, she suddenly noticed the large, swarthy-skinned man who had just stepped out from the shadows. He was well within her sights and, judging by his stillness, he'd clearly been taking full advantage of that fact. She didn't recognise him and wondered who he could be. She approached him, determined to find out.

'I did not see you there. Are you lost? I don't think I've seen you here before. I'm Miss Atherton, Lord Atherton's sister.'

'And I'm Henry, Lord Rockley's valet, Miss Atherton, at your service. I've just been to the kitchen for my supper.'

'I see.' She noted that he was well turned out, despite having the appearance of a large hound, and had his deceptively sleepy eyes fixed on her—she suspected he was far from being the idle man he looked. 'I hope you were accommodated.'

'Very well, thank you.'

'This, as you see, is the wine cellar and some distance from the kitchens.'

'I know. I couldn't help myself. This is a fine house. I was just taking a look around.' He stepped back. 'Excuse me. I'll find my way back.'

Christina watched him go, wondering what he had really been doing in the wine cellar. How much had he seen? Never had she seen a valet who looked less like a valet. Servant he might be, but there was a single-minded determination in his face and in the set of his thick jaw that reminded her of his master. Most certainly he was just as arrogant, because he had not troubled to lower his eyes when he had spoken to her.

When she reached the hall, she was relieved that everyone was still outside watching the firework display, which was lighting up the night sky in a fantastic array of colour. Feeling the need to compose herself, she took refuge in her own cosy sitting room, closing the door behind her. The only light was from the fire, which she had insisted on being lit despite the warmth of the summer night. Drawing out this moment of quiet solitude, she sank into her favourite chair next to the hearth.

The fear her meeting with Mark had left in her heart was more than she could bear. She closed her eyes and his face appeared with such terrifying clarity she found herself trembling. The picture was so clear that she opened her eyes to make it go away, but they were misted with tears and she seemed to see him in the shimmering firelight, and even thought she heard him laugh.

Sensing she was not alone, she turned her head and looked in the direction of the door. The figure of a man was just visible outside the circle of light cast by the fire's glow. She saw a flash of shiny buttons on a coat front, and the hint of white neck linen, and he was tall. Her hands gripped the arms of her chair.

'Why do you cry?' a cool, drawling voice spoke suddenly. 'Are you hurt?'

It came to Christina that the face she had glimpsed in her mind's eye and taken for Mark was quite real. Alarmed, she brushed the tears quickly from her eyes to see the speaker more clearly. 'Who are you?' she demanded, surprise lending more strength to her voice than she felt. 'I am perfectly all right. What do you want?'

He moved further into the light and she recognised Lord Rockley. She rose, realising she would be at a disadvantage if she remained seated. Caution also dictated that she leave his presence immediately, but something else, something far less familiar, kept her rooted to the spot. It was as if the damp of the tunnel had seeped into her brain, making her forget everything save this man who was once again regarding her with bold, unguarded interest.

'Lord Rockley! You find me taking a moment's respite.'

'I can fully understand that.'

'You can?'

'You're a young woman with a large house to run, with many decisions to make. I imagine the responsibilities are vast.'

'Truth to tell, Lord Rockley,' she quipped, slightly irritated because he had intruded on her solitude, 'only one person dares to threaten me at this moment.' Christina had said it pointedly, leaving him in no doubt to whom she referred.

'Since I have never threatened a woman in my life, I can only think it is your peace of mind I threaten.'

'Maybe intimidation is a more appropriate word. Do you seek to intimidate me, Lord Rockley?'

'So you feel intimidated, do you, Miss Atherton?'

'No, I do not feel in the least intimidated by you,' she lied.

His smile was quick and disarming. 'If I ever do make you feel intimidated or threatened in any way, you can be assured you are misunderstanding my concern for your welfare.'

'Really, Lord Rockley! You do not know me, so how you can feel concerned is quite beyond me.'

'Why are you sitting with only the fire for light?'

'Because I like sitting in the dark. What are you doing here? Have you lost your way?'

'Forgive me for intruding. I have seen all I wish to see of the fireworks and sought a place where I could sit a while. I saw you enter this room and followed you. You weren't among those watching the display. I did wonder why you deserted your guests.'

His high-handed manner had an unexpected effect on Christina—her shock gave way to anger rather than fear. What did this man mean by telling her what to do in her own home? The fact that he should seek her out, knowing she would be alone, suggested that he had something more to say that would not be to her liking. 'I merely took the opportunity to make sure everything was going according to plan.'

'Then I hope everything was to your satisfaction.'

The tone was natural, but its very ordinariness struck terror into Christina, who thought she read into it the most dire threats. 'Yes, it was. Now please excuse me,' she said quickly. 'There are things I have to do. I have neglected our guests too long.'

'You are of a hasty nature, Miss Atherton. You make a custom of taking your leave unexpectedly.'

'Not really. As I said, I have duties to attend to.' She turned away but he was beside her. She could feel his warm breath on her neck.

'One thing I have observed about you, Miss Atherton—you have confidence in the way you do things.'

'As in most things.'

'And you are most gracious.'

She turned to find his gaze levelled on hers. 'I hope I am never ungracious.'

'No,' he murmured. 'I don't think you would know how to be, even though my arrival was both unexpected and, I suspect, unwelcome, because of who I am and the reason for my being here. Should any of your guests have connection to those I seek, my presence will be unnerving for them.'

'I can speak for most of the people here tonight, and I know they would not involve themselves in criminal activities.'

He nodded imperceptibly, his inscrutable gaze unwavering. 'Since you are a respected lady of the community I believe you, for I do not believe you would include disreputable villains among your guests knowingly. But it is the remainder of those present who concern me. Thieves are suspicious men. Is there no one you can think of who fits the description?' he pressed.

'No—but—one hears things—rumours—of robberies on the highways and house breaking,' she replied hesitantly. 'It is inevitable, you will agree, for it goes on all the time and not just in this area.'

'And you will agree that the villains need to be caught. Imagine how you would feel if they were to break in here and steal items you hold dear, family heirlooms that cannot be replaced. The stolen property will be sold and the more unusual the items, the more easily they are traced. If recovered, the property will provide valuable evidence against the thieves, who will otherwise be hard to identify. They may even be local men, but building a case against them…well—that is quite another matter. It is firm evidence I need.' He moved closer so that they stood just inches apart. 'Mark Bucklow, Miss Atherton. That is the name of the man I would very much like to find. I am sure you know who I mean.'

Christina's heart gave a lurch and alarm flared in her eyes. Her throat tightened so much she was afraid it would strangle her. He turned from her and moved away slightly, giving her a moment to digest the name he had unexpectedly thrown at her. Unable to think of an answer, she tried to spare herself embarrassment by pretending confusion. 'M-Mark Bucklow?' she whispered. 'I—I don't understand,' she said.

His deep voice was quiet, but his reply forbade further pretence from her. 'I think you do.'

Christina stared at him. In response he lifted his brows, waiting for her to reply. 'No, I'm not sure—'

He didn't like her continued attempt to evade the issue, and he made it clear by saying, 'You do know him, do you not? Or you will have heard of him. Are you saying you have not?'

'I didn't say that.'

He smiled at her continued evasiveness, a slow, strangely secretive smile that made his eyes gleam beneath their heavy lids. Christina was clever and sharp and noticed the nuances of that smile and she instantly sensed peril lurking behind it. It was the dangerously beguiling smile of a ruthless predator who wanted her to sense his power. She straightened her back, lifting her chin with a show of bravado. She had never allowed Mark Bucklow and the men who worked for him to see her fear—perhaps that was why they respected her more than her brother—and nor would she show this stranger that weakness.

'I am sure there isn't a person hereabouts who hasn't heard of him, since his felonious activities have given him a certain notoriety. I dare say you might tell me he is as civil a gentleman as one could hope to meet, but somehow I don't think so.'

Thinking of the crimes Bucklow had committed against his own family, he turned his head back to her. When told what had happened, Simon had felt his bones strain in his flesh, urgent with desire to hunt and kill the man who had killed his lovely young niece and shot his brother in the chest, leaving him a shadow of his former self. But he had been in Belgium at the time, and he had a duty to those he commanded. Vengeance had warred with responsibility, and most reluctantly gave way. He hadn't long to serve with the army. Until then, men depended on him; the job was his. He couldn't abandon it for the sake of a time-consuming personal quest. Bucklow could wait, but the longer it took, his hatred would increase a thousandfold.

'Do you know him, Miss Atherton?' He slowly walked back to where she stood, leaning forwards so that his face was only inches from her own, his piercing, knowing eyes, gleaming like hard, brittle stones, locked on hers. 'Is he the reason why you are afraid?'

Christina expelled the breath she hadn't realised she'd been holding. She felt as if he had just backed her into a corner from which she could find no escape. She had the horrible, guilty feeling that he somehow knew everything there was to know about what went on at Oakbridge. She considered telling a lie, but lying was not in her nature, and those disturbing eyes of his were levelled on hers.

'I do know him—though not well—and I fear no one. Mark Bucklow is a native of these parts. He is the son of a lawyer of some distinction in Reading, and it is no secret that Mr Bucklow has disowned Mark. You were correct in saying that there are few who have not heard of him hereabouts—though he is not often seen.'

'Perhaps that is because he is a creature of nocturnal habits, and unless one happens to be on the road after dark it's hardly surprising that he is rarely seen.'

'What he gets up to has nothing to do with me,' Christina said sharply, avoiding his probing gaze.

'Perhaps you think he is some kind of Robin Hood, who carries out his robberies courteously and happily disburses the proceeds of his robberies to the poor and needy.' His smile was scathing. 'He is no such thing, Miss Atherton. Mark Bucklow is little more than a ruthless cut-throat.' He lifted his brows and regarded her closely. 'I trust you managed to locate him yesterday to return his dog.' He watched the colour drain from her face and he smiled thinly. 'So, I was right. The dog did belong to Bucklow.'

'Yes—but I did not return it to him. One of the grooms did.'

'And you know where Bucklow can be found?'

'Mark Bucklow is as elusive as a shadow, Lord Rockley. No one knows where he lives when he is not holding up coaches.' As far as Christina was concerned, this was true. She had no idea where he resided when he was away from the cave. William had told her he could often be found at the Black Swan Inn at Wakeham, but he wasn't there all the time and only used the inn for his meetings.

'Then perhaps your groom could throw some light on that.'

In every respect, Lord Rockley was the most coldly rational man Christina had ever met. His forthright manner and questions broke through her wall of politeness and she attempted to curtail the discussion. Drawing herself up straight, she looked him straight in the eye.

'Sir, as you are aware tonight my brother and I have a house full of guests. I do not take kindly to being questioned in this manner about a subject that does not concern me. Your perseverance is beyond belief. If you came here to interrogate me, then however discourteous I may seem, I must ask you to leave. Either that or you will speak no more of robbers tonight. I find your manner extremely rude.'

Christina stood quivering, visibly struggling against

a growing anger that made her eyes gleam like two hard blue stones. Simon looked at her thoughtfully for a moment, touched despite himself by her obvious youth and scruples. At length he said in a more gentle manner, 'You are quite right. I have been unforgivably rude and I ask your pardon.' He held out his hand. 'You are upset, I can see. Come over to the fire now and sit a while before you return to your guests. There will be no more talk of highwaymen tonight.'

Christina eyed him warily. 'Do you promise?'

'I promise. We shall just—talk. Light-hearted conversation with an intelligent and extremely beautiful woman is almost a forgotten pleasure to me.' A definite note of cajolery lightened his voice as he added, 'I'll do all the talking if you agree.'

Christina hesitated, stunned to his reference to her as a beautiful woman, then she decided he'd meant nothing by it except a little empty flattery—although he had kissed her at the very moment of their meeting, and what she had seen in his eyes then went way beyond flattery. A few moments more without tension and fear was being offered to her, and her battered nerves cried out for relief. What harm was there in what he asked?

'Very well, then. I will sit for just a moment longer and then I really must show my face—if you agree to do the talking.'

He nodded, a lazy grin sweeping over his handsome face as he realised she was agreeing to favour him with more of her precious time, and the unexpected glamour of that white smile did treacherous things to Christina's heart rate. In an attempt to calm her emotions and put a safe distance between herself and this man, she crossed the room to the hearth.

Simon waited until she was seated in the chair she had vacated on his arrival before sitting opposite. He was silent as he gazed into the heart of the fire. Christina was struck by his stern profile outlined against the golden glow of the flames. She saw a kind of beauty in it, but quickly dismissed the thought. It was out of keeping with the unfortunate situation they had been thrown into by his sudden arrival. Suddenly he turned and looked at her. He was relaxed, his eyes as calm as the sea on a fair day.

The fire cast a glow on her, turning her hair to silver, and causing a shadow on her cheeks. Simon thought how young she looked, how innocent. With an openly gracious manner and a beauty charmingly enhanced by her ice blue gown, she truly seemed imbued with a radiance of her own.

Sitting back, he crossed his legs and nonchalantly tapped his fingers on the arm of the chair, his gaze doing a leisurely sweep of the dimly lit room. It was clearly Miss Atherton's domain. The large armchairs in which they sat were drawn up to the fire and embroidery and books littered the surface of a small inlaid side table. Picking up an open book, being careful not to lose the page, he read the title on the leather spine.

'*A Gentleman's Journey through France and Italy*. Very interesting. Are you reading the book, Miss Atherton?'

'Yes. Not only is the book interesting, but informative, too. Unfortunately, William is not a great reader.

He is a sporty type and enjoys being outdoors—horses and shooting and fishing and that kind of thing.'

'And he leaves you to run the house.'

'Yes, but I don't mind.'

'You are very understanding, Miss Atherton.'

Christina laughed to hide her confusion. 'I have to be. Whatever I do or say, William is invariably of a different opinion.'

He grinned. 'Brothers generally are. And you enjoy reading?'

'Very much. It is one of my favourite pastimes.'

'No doubt you enjoy reading books with happy endings—about love and romance, which is the sort of reading that suits most young ladies.'

'Some, perhaps, but not on the whole. Your remark is exactly the kind I would expect from a man.'

He chuckled low. 'And it clearly offends you.'

'Yes, it does. I think you are misguided like all men and arrogant in your presumption.' She thought he was about to protest, but he merely stared at her with amazement. Devilment prompted her to add, 'You're not used to having your attitude questioned, are you?'

'Not since my dear mother passed on.'

A smile softened her rebuke and her eyes sparkled with humour. 'To believe that ladies are satisfied with the banal and cannot understand the highest forms of art is simply not true. We have equal intelligence and are as capable of appreciating literature and poetry as any man.'

'And you, Miss Atherton, I believe you are a lady of that description.'

Somewhat dazzled by the warmth in his voice, Christina could feel a blush rising. 'I like to think so.'

'And I am thinking that I am lucky to be in such fine company,' he murmured softly.

Christina met his gaze. When she was in his presence, she felt as if she were walking on egg shells. She smiled nervously. 'Thank you for the compliment.'

'My pleasure.'

'I met your valet earlier, by the way—in the cellar.'

'Henry? We saw military service in the Netherlands together,' he said by way of explanation.

'Either he has a partiality for fine wines, Lord Rockley, or he was snooping.' And if so, Christina wondered, on whose orders?

Lord Rockley cocked an amused brow. 'Snooping?' He grinned. 'Now there's an interesting thought. Henry never snoops.'

'Then we must assume he has a partiality for liquor.'

'He has been known to take a drop,' he remarked, and left it at that.

Christina was not appeased by his taciturn reply and she glanced at him sharply. 'He seemed sober enough to me at the time. In fact, he seemed to me to be a man well in control of his faculties. Do you always leave him to his own devices—to go wandering about at will?'

'Always. Henry is his own man and quite harmless, I assure you.' After a quiet moment, he said, 'And you are content here at Oakbridge? Does not the London scene and all its frivolities beckon?'

'Not really. I have simple tastes and I am quite content

to remain here. But I do not remain at Oakbridge all the time. I have an aunt who lives in London and I often visit her—Aunt Celia. She's a dear and we are very close. When William marries—which will be soon, I think—I shall go and live with her.'

'But you will miss Oakbridge.'

'Of course I will. Oakbridge has always been my home—as it will become Miranda's.'

'And you have no wish to get in the way of that.'

'No. As newlyweds they will want to find their own way. I should hate to be looked on as some interfering sister.' Hearing a commotion outside the door and realising that the guests were returning to the house, she rose, smoothing down her skirts. 'I must go. William will be looking for me.'

Chapter Three

Simon followed her to the door. 'You are very much like your brother,' he remarked, reaching out for the brass doorknob.

'I am? How?' Christina glanced up at him to find he was looking at her strangely, as if he was preoccupied. She was bewildered by his mood and, caught up in a rush of irrational confusion, she looked away from him—she felt mesmerised, uncertainty flooding over her. He touched a lock of hair that was coiled on her neck, and she felt the brush of his fingers on her flesh. When they lingered, her heart beat erratically, a thrill of anticipation spreading through her. Brief though the touch was, his fingers left their imprint upon her flesh. She was conscious of the power of his masculinity. So great was the pull.

'The colour of your hair, I think.'

'We are of similar colouring, but that is where

the similarity ends. Our temperaments are so very different.'

He nodded slowly, his gaze holding hers. 'You are right. You are stronger, I think.'

'Sometimes I have to be,' she murmured somewhat absently. 'William is my brother and I love him dearly, but with me, he has a way of putting on airs when it pleases him—not that I take such nonsense from him, nor will I from any man. You're not married, Lord Rockley?'

He shook his head. 'Over time I've courted many winsome young ladies without making any lasting commitments. I think being in the army and constantly on the move had something to do with that. There was never time to think of settling down.'

'And where do you live when you're not residing with your brother?'

'In Hertfordshire. I inherited a house, Tapton Park, which belonged to my mother. Unfortunately it has been empty for a good many years and is in need of repair and refurbishment. An assortment of builders, carpenters and decorators have been working on the place for the past year. Hopefully they will soon be done and I shall have the house to myself.'

'I see. Sir John told me about what happened to your family. I'm terribly sorry. It must have been upsetting for you.'

'It was. Perhaps now you can understand how important it is for me to find Bucklow and bring him to justice.'

'You know for definite he was the one?'

'Oh, yes, Miss Atherton. I know.'

'And—will you be staying long with your brother?'

'That depends.'

'On what?'

'How long it takes me to ferret out this gang of thieves that is terrorising the neighbourhood.'

'You have a dangerous task ahead of you, although I suspect you have proved your worth fighting for the King. You must have killed a lot of men.'

'When I had to.'

'I often wonder what it must be like to confront someone whose intent was to run you through.'

He raised a dark brow. 'What would you do, do you think? Try to save yourself? Fight back?'

'I think I would fight back. I'm no weakling to run for cover. I think women are more resourceful than men give us credit for. Any one of us would kill to defend those we love. I'd not like doing it, but it would be a necessary evil.'

He smiled slightly. 'You remind me of Diana the huntress. I believe you have as much courage as any man. I suspect you would be a veritable tigress when roused. I can see I shall have to take care to tread carefully when I am around you, Miss Atherton.'

'Please don't mock me. I am perfectly serious.'

Placing his finger beneath her chin, Simon tipped her face to his. 'I do not mock you,' he murmured. 'I too am perfectly serious.'

His touch stole her breath and ignited a flame within her blood. The intensity of his grey eyes held her transfixed. The potency of his gaze was unlike anything she had previously experienced in her life. It made her feel things she had never felt before. No one had ever touched her like this or looked into her eyes with such vibrant ardour, holding her transfixed. His gaze lingered on her parted lips and they stood without moving, exquisite sensations speeding through her veins.

Then she was assailed by the memory of Mark Bucklow. Her flesh went cold, a dark fear channelling through her terror. She stepped back, causing Simon to drop his hand.

'I have to go. Please excuse me. I hope you enjoy what is left of the evening.'

Turning, she assumed he had moved away from her, but suddenly she felt his presence behind her, felt his warm breath caress the back of her neck, causing gooseflesh to prickle along her skin. And then his arm snaked around her waist, drawing her back to him.

'I did not lie when I said I was captivated by your beauty from the moment I saw you,' he whispered, his lips dangerously close to her ear.

Christina stood quite still, refusing to turn around, refusing to look into those silver-grey eyes and be swayed by what he wanted her to feel.

'Had we not met again tonight,' he went on, 'I would have carried away the memory of your beauty, while longing to turn back and seek you out, for beauty such as yours blinds a man to reason and is powerful enough to steal away his soul for ever.'

Christina firmly disengaged herself from his embrace and stepped away, wanting to cover her ears against this seduction that was proving too potent. Still she did not turn and look at his face. 'Please stop this before you embarrass us both. I think, perhaps, you have imbibed too much punch, Lord Rockley. Might I recommend you do not drink any more, and, if you do, a little water will make it less potent.' Without another word, she left him.

However, as the evening progressed, she found her eyes seeking him out. She watched him, surprised at the easy camaraderie he readily exhibited with the gentlemen, which left her much in awe of him. Whether they were business men, scholars or members of the local gentry, these men gave every indication that they thoroughly enjoyed conversing with him and felt totally at ease to reciprocate banter, leaving Christina in no doubt that if they knew of anything that would assist him in his investigations, he would draw it from them with perfect ease.

She also noted that some of the younger ladies were quite taken by his handsome looks and charming manners, as they simpered and giggled and fluttered their fans. Christina watched them with disdain. How silly some women could be when there was a handsome man about, she thought, telling herself that one should not concern oneself with such things as whether a man is handsome. Appearances could be deceptive, and it was always the woman who paid for her lack of foresight— but her own heart fluttered as she watched him leisurely circuit the room, while telling herself she ought not to.

Quickly she reined in her thoughts. There was no

place in her life for girlish daydreams and romantic notions, and to wish it were otherwise only added to her misery.

The guests departed from Oakbridge in a steady procession, each one praying for a safe and uninterrupted journey to their homes. Christina saw them on their way alone, since her brother had seemingly disappeared.

'Travel safely, Mrs Senior,' she said to an elderly lady, a close neighbour, who was being helped down the steps by her husband.

'I sincerely hope so, my dear, and that we aren't set upon by one of those pesky highwaymen. What is being done about the villains who hold up carriages and rob decent people of their possessions at the point of a pistol? Nothing, I tell you. Absolutely nothing. As usual, the forces of law are resting upon their considerable laurels.'

Christina smiled sympathetically. 'Unfortunately, that does seem to be the case, but you don't have very far to travel, so hopefully you will not be apprehended.'

'I wouldn't count on it. That Mark Bucklow is a confirmed scoundrel, and while he is at large no one is safe. I remember him as a youth. He was trouble then—thief, trickster and all-round petty criminal. Little wonder his father washed his hands of him.'

When the last of the guests had departed, Christina went to her room without seeking William out. Her heart was heavy with a physical pain of pity and guilt for those who would be the victims of tonight's thievery, and she felt sick with disgust of their assailants. It was too much to hope that every one of their guests would arrive at their homes unmolested, for she knew that Mark Bucklow and his gang would be waiting to do their ghastly work.

A great weariness stole over her. All night she had been living on a knife's edge. Lord Rockley's presence had much to do with that, and her terrifying ordeal of having to face Mark. She shuddered when she thought of him. How she loathed him. How she hated the familiar way in which he looked at her, his mocking smile and leering eyes. It was so difficult trying to behave as if everything was normal, and then to be forced to run a very narrow gauntlet. It was all so hopeless, she thought, dangerous, too, and she could see no end to it.

William had been drinking heavily, as he was wont to do when he was as troubled and anxious as he was tonight. Indeed, he was so irresponsible and reckless at times that it was difficult to believe he was her senior by seven years. Loathing himself for what he was doing to his friends and neighbours, but unable to see a way out, William tended to lose himself in drink and bury his head in the pillow to blot out what was happening, leaving her to take care of their guests.

As soon as she got into bed, she lay in that half-conscious state that hovers on the borderline of sleep, when anxiety and events of the day become a jumbled mass of confusion. It was always the same after their guests had left, and she couldn't bear to think of what might befall them on their way home in the dark. It was all so awful, so sordid.

* * *

It was during the early hours when she woke with a start, sure she had heard a sound and that there was someone in her room. The hairs on the back of her neck prickled and, with her heart thudding wildly in her chest and fear coursing through her veins, she sat upright, straining her eyes in the gloom. The dark shape of a man loomed large across the room. Suddenly a light flared and a candle was lit. The flickering light illuminated the room and Mark Bucklow's menacing face was behind it. He was standing quite still, devouring her with his eyes.

'You! What is the meaning of this intrusion?' she demanded, clutching the bedclothes to her chin, striving to keep her voice calm. She was unable to believe he would have the audacity to risk entering the house while Lord Rockley was staying and find his way to her room. 'How dare you come here? You have no business in my bedchamber. You have no right. Get out.'

'You are wrong. I have every right.'

In the shifting moonlight, he loomed large and menacing over his surroundings. His awesome presence filled the room, and Christina gave him the rapt attention a cornered mouse gives a stalking cat. 'I told you to go,' she said furiously. 'Are you deaf? If you do not leave this minute, I shall scream.'

'What, and have your guest come to rescue you?' He laughed low in his throat, his eyes mocking. 'That would never do, now, would it?'

'No doubt you have done your worst tonight. I can only hope that no one has been hurt.'

'It's proved to be a lucrative night, if that is what you mean. All's well now—and very quiet outside. So I thought it was time you and I got a few things straight. You are too eager to keep away from me, Christina. I am afraid that will not do.'

'I want nothing to do with you, Mark Bucklow, as well you know. I am tired of telling you.'

He laughed. 'Do you really dislike me so much, Christina?'

'I loathe you.'

He shrugged casually. 'Pity. I am drawn to you as to no other woman.'

'Your compliment disgusts me.'

'Come now, Christina. I was hoping for a better welcome than this. For a wench who is involved up to her pretty neck in what goes on here, you're high-minded all of a sudden.'

'Whatever arrangement you have with my brother, you have not been given leave to trespass inside his house.'

''Twill be more than his house I shall trespass on, Christina.'

'Thieves are not welcome in my room,' she fumed with an anger born of fear.

'No?' he said, sauntering slowing towards the bed, leering down at her as she edged away from him. 'What about thief-catchers, Christina? Are they welcome?'

'Lord Rockley means nothing to me. Like you, he is like a thorn in my flesh. I am just as eager for him to be gone from Oakbridge in the morning as I am for you to leave my room now.' When he closed in on her, putting the candle down on the bedside table, tiny shards of fear pricked Christina's spine while a coldness congealed in the pit of her stomach. 'Have you no decency?'

He shrugged. 'Your protests are seemly, but misplaced, my dear. Come now, don't be coy. Show me what you are hiding from me. It will be better for you if you don't fight me.'

With brutal force, he jerked the covers from her hand, whipping them back from her figure. Fear stopped her heart. Realising the danger she was in—in her bed, with no weapons but her own brain to oppose a man ten times her strength—and driven by self-preservation, before he could grasp hold of her, like lightning she rolled to the edge of the mattress and shot out of bed.

With the presence of mind to grab her robe as she went, she was across the room and out of the door before her assailant could draw breath.

'Go away,' she cried, when she thought he would give chase. 'Leave me alone.'

'Christina, you will come back if you know what is good for you,' Mark called after her, his voice reverberating along the landing on which Christina ran to escape him.

'Never,' she gasped.

Mark watched her go, determined to have her one way or another. She would be a delectable morsel in his bed. Possessing her would serve as sweet succour to his lonely nights. He had never had a woman the likes of her before, and he was heartily sick and tired of the jaded strumpets who eagerly made up to any man for a coin or two. As he slipped back into the shadows, the mere thought of bedding her kindled that part of him which harlots, with all their knowledge and experience, failed to do.

Fighting to control the shaking that gripped her body, her eyes darting wildly about her in the sleepy quiet of the house, like a ghostly shadow Christina ran for all she was worth towards William's room.

Slipping her arms into the sleeves of her robe, only once did she dare turn her head and glance behind her, just in time to see her assailant's dark shape slip silently down the stairs. Feeling a surge of relief, she slipped into William's room, closing the door behind her and resting her back against the hard wood. The curtains were only partly drawn across the window and the high, bright moon cast a silver glow about the room. Breathing deeply, she closed her eyes, taking a moment to compose herself before crossing to the bed. It only took a moment for her to see that the bed had not been slept in.

Panic assailed her. Where was William? Why was he not in bed? In frantic haste, she slipped out of the room, ran along the landing and down the stairs to the hall, which had been the scene of so much gaiety just a few short hours before. Above the modulated ticking of the long-cased clock, she was sure she could hear someone snoring. Seeing a light beneath the door of the library, she crossed towards it, hoping fervently that Mark Bucklow had left the house and was not waiting for her behind the library door.

Pushing it open, she stepped inside, feeling an overwhelming disappointment on seeing her brother slumped in a limp, disorganised heap on the leather sofa. His eyes were closed, his head resting on the padded back. His neck linen was loose, his clothes were dishevelled and the empty decanter on the low table beside him. A glass of brandy on the floor, as if it had fallen from his inert hand, spoke for itself. A low, drunken snore deepened into a rich sonorous sound, making her crushingly aware of her mistake in not having one of the servants see him directly to his room before she had retired. There was no sign of Mark Bucklow, so she surmised he had left the house.

But what was she to do with William? She was tempted to leave him where he was, but she didn't want the servants to see him in such a sorry state in the morning. Taking his shoulders, she tried shaking him to rouse him, but her efforts failed to interrupt his measured snores. Wrinkling her nose against the strong smell of liquor, hooking her hands under his armpits, she tried hauling him to a sitting position, but it was like trying to hoist a bag of rocks. Falling to her knees in front of him, she almost wept with her helplessness and the misery that engulfed her. Unless she woke one of the servants to assist her, there was nothing for it but to leave him.

'Can I be of assistance?'

The question, spoken by a rich, masculine voice, seemed to hang in the air, and then Christina's head spun round. Lord Rockley stood in the doorway, watching her. She had not heard him enter, and the strangeness of that was lost in the depth of her turmoil.

'Oh!' Christina gasped. 'You startled me.' The tremor in her voice could not be controlled.

'My apology. You seemed engrossed in your thoughts.'

Christina scrambled to her feet, appalled that Lord Rockley should find her clad in nothing but her loosely flowing robe and nightdress, while realising she was caught and could not escape with dignity. Conflicting thoughts raced around inside her head. What was he doing here, and how much did he know? Apart from having removed his jacket and loosened his neck linen, he was dressed exactly as he had been at the party. 'I'm sorry—but—you find me…' Her voice faded away. Her tongue seemed unusually clumsy, and she began to fear that it would stumble and betray her.

'With something of a problem on your hands, it would seem,' he stated, crossing towards her and sweeping a hand towards William. 'He's made quite a night of it.'

She shrugged helplessly. Now that Lord Rockley had seen William, it was best to be completely honest, since there was no other logical explanation. 'It is much of his own doing, I'm afraid. William imbibed too much last night, and I was trying to get him up to his room when you came in.'

Unbeknown to Christina, Lord Rockley had lingered in the doorway long enough to take in the situation. So engrossed had she been with her brother's predicament that he had taken a moment to peruse her at his leisure. Her slender figure seemed taller in the rosy glow of the candlelight. Her resplendent golden hair enveloped her in a sort of radiance, which suddenly made his heart ache. Her beauty was almost blinding, and he had a presentiment that she was one of those rare women for whom wars are fought, and who rarely bring happiness to the men who possess them.

Christina glanced at him quizzically. 'What are you doing downstairs at this hour? Is there something that you want?'

He shook his head and stood looking down at her. She was very pale, the pupils of her eyes dark and dilated, as if with some kind of horror. 'I'm a light sleeper. I heard a noise and came to investigate.'

'That would be William snoring.'

'No. It was something else. It sounded very much like voices raised in anger, followed by someone running.' He directed his words at her, watching her closely to see their effect upon her. She started—there was only the slightest flinch—but he had seen it. It was enough.

Feeling a crimson rush of embarrassment creep into her cheeks burning and confusing her, Christina averted her eyes, crossing her arms over her breasts. She felt that his eyes missed nothing—the fear she still felt from Mark's intrusion into her room, the trembling of her body beneath the fine fabric of her nightdress.

'I—I can't think what that could have been. I heard nothing myself. P-perhaps it was the wind you heard.'

'There is no wind tonight.'

'Then maybe you imagined it. This is an old house. Creaks and groans are heard all the time.'

He nodded, still watching her. 'Yes—maybe you're right and that's all it was. How did you know your brother had not gone to bed?'

'I went to bed without seeing him. I did not hear him come up and I was worried.'

'Is it usual for him to get in this condition?'

'No—I mean, yes—sometimes. Liquor affects him very quickly. It doesn't take much for him to get like this. I keep telling him not to drink so much—particularly when we have guests—but he doesn't listen.'

'Perhaps he's worried about something? Is he, Miss Atherton?'

He was watching her intently. 'I—I cannot think that he has anything untoward to worry about.'

Suddenly he grinned. 'Not now, perhaps, but he will have in the morning.'

Her eyes flew to his in alarm. 'He will?'

'Most certainly. His head will feel as if an army is marching through it. Why do you not simply leave him where he is?'

'I would prefer the servants did not find him like this in the morning. I have a reluctance to lend William to the ridicule that would surely follow.'

'Then we'd better see about getting him to his room.' Subdued amusement played on his face as he bent over William and lifted a limp eyelid. The snores continued undisturbed, and when Simon glanced at Christina, his humour had grown more obvious. 'Would you like me to try to carry him?'

'I would be most grateful—but I think he will be too heavy.'

With a quick and easy movement, Simon lifted William from the sofa. The fabric of his shirt stretched taut for a moment, revealing the flowing muscles across his shoulders and arms. The weight that Christina had been unable to move was casually laid over his shoulder. He glanced at her, strong white teeth sparkling behind a broadening grin.

'There. Nothing to it. Lead the way, Miss Atherton, and we'll soon have your brother tucked up in bed and sleeping like the proverbial babe.'

As she brushed past him to obey, a gentle cologne touched her senses with an acute awareness that left her almost weak. She hurried across the hall and ascended the stairs, her cheeks hot and pink as she felt her back almost smothered by his perusal as he followed close behind. Indeed, had she glanced behind and seen the admiring attention he paid to her gently swaying hips beneath the thin fabric of her robe, she might have had even more reason to blush.

Entering William's room and going quickly to the four-poster bed and folding back the covers, she then busied herself with lighting a couple of candles and watched Lord Rockley lay her brother down with a gentleness she had not expected from him, easing him on to the pillows, removing his shoes and drawing the covers over him.

Feeling vulnerable and very much alone, she had the feeling that had her brother been more like this man, she would have been able to cast off her unhappiness and all her difficulties. But it was absurd, a fantasy, and she must not allow her thoughts to run along those lines. She must not forget Lord Rockley's purpose for being here, and she was sure that even when he had left Oakbridge, it would not be the last they saw of him.

She bent over her brother and loosened his shirt. When she straightened, her heart quickened, for Lord

Rockley was standing much too close. Her senses felt dazed. Meeting his silver gaze, she observed that his eyes glowed with a warmth that made her heart beat unevenly in her chest. He really was extremely handsome, and try as she might, she could find no flaw in those wide shoulders, lean waist or long limbs. Mentally chiding herself for allowing her thoughts to run away with her, she stepped away and smoothed the covers over William's chest.

'I can't thank you enough,' she murmured, warmed by his solicitude. 'As you said, he'll have a bad head and be as cross as a bear in the morning.' She smiled up at him. 'I shall not go near him until he's recovered his temper.'

'Very wise,' he replied, handing her William's shoes.

Christina reached to take them and was almost startled when his fingers deliberately lingered on hers. A sharp thrill went through her, slowly shredding her nerves. Never had she been affected as deeply as by this casual contact. In an attempt to calm her emotions and put a safe distance between herself and Lord Rockley, she crossed the room and placed the shoes on the floor beside a chest of drawers before turning to look back at him.

'Please don't let me keep you from your bed. William will be all right now, but—if you don't mind, I would rather he didn't know about this. He—would not approve of you being here alone with me—dressed as I am.'

Simon looked rakishly across at her, boldly appraising

her as she turned her head and looked at her brother, his eyes touching her everywhere. The pure white night-dress showing beneath her parted robe flowed in fluid lines about her body, moulding itself against her as if reluctant to be parted, showing the womanly round-ness of her firm breasts and the graceful curve of her hips. The pale light illuminated her profile like a cameo against the shadows of the room. He noted the delicacy of her features, and the tilt of her chin. She was very young, he thought, and frightened.

'Heedless of your brother's opinion, Miss Atherton, I do approve most heartily.' He moved towards her, stand-ing close and capturing her eyes in her upturned face. 'Is there anything more that I can do for you?'

She shook her head, tearing her eyes away from that penetrating gaze, noticing how her heartbeat had quick-ened its pace with the knowledge of his presence. The sudden warmth in her cheeks and the way her fingers shook as they drew the belt of her robe tight about her small waist gave testament to her nervousness.

Aware of her unease and unable to resist this lovely young woman, vulnerable and so very innocent in her night attire, Simon lowered his head near the curling mass of gold-lit fair hair and closed his eyes as her fra-grance spiralled through him with intoxicating effect, snaring his mind and his senses.

Christina felt his nearness with every stirring fibre of her body, with every shivering wave that washed through her. Her eyes remained downward as the warmth of his breath touched her ear, and she stared in fixed attention where his shirt gaped open, partly revealing a firmly muscled, darkly matted chest. As he moved closer, her nerves jumped and she placed a cautious hand against that firm chest, taking a step back, but the contact was explosive. It caused her heart to beat even faster.

'I think,' she stated breathlessly, 'that you should leave now, Lord Rockley.'

He smiled down at her. 'Does my presence unnerve you, Miss Atherton?'

She gazed up at him, feeling more powerfully drawn to him than ever, her body reacting in that age-old way a woman responds to a man. 'Yes—if you must know, it does,' she answered honestly. 'It is not my habit to be alone in a bedroom, dressed in my night attire, in the early hours of the morning, with a gentleman who happens to be a virtual stranger to me.'

'Worry not, Miss Atherton,' he murmured, taking pity on her confusion and moving away from her. 'A young woman's reputation is such a fragile thing, and I have no intention of taking advantage of you. I promise that whenever we are together, I shall be a gentleman personified.'

Christina cocked a brow at him, conveying her distrust. 'A gentleman who takes his liberties seriously.'

'How else would I take them?' he teased gently.

She laughed softly. 'I think the sooner you go to your own room, the better. I really do not think I am safe in here with you.'

'Come now, Miss Atherton. Will a man ravish a woman in whose house he is a guest?'

'If he's desperate enough,' she replied skittishly.

'Desperate?' His eyes caressed her face and there

was a smouldering darkness in their depths. 'I am that. I would like to take things further, but if I want to gain your trust it is not the way for me to carry on.'

'You are right. Trust is important in any relationship.'

He looked at her speculatively. 'Would you not like me to escort you to your room?'

Christina was certain as he spoke that there was more than a conventional offer in his words. What did he know? What had he heard? Did he guess at the possible danger that might lurk in her room? 'I shall be perfectly all right now. Thank you.'

'There's no reason to thank me. I am glad I was able to help.' He crossed to the door. 'Goodnight, Miss Atherton. I hope you sleep well.'

She watched him go and listened to him walk along the landing towards his room before blowing out the candles and going to her own, her mind still occupied by their guest. Gingerly she pushed open the door and stepped inside, recalling Mark Bucklow's earlier invasion. It was funny how fear could disappear, only to return and terrorise you once more.

Christina rose early, when the air was still and the grass drenched with dew and traces of a thin chill vapour lurked beneath the trees. Quickly donning her riding clothes, she slipped noiselessly along the lightening gallery and down the stairs. From there she let herself out of the house and made her way to the stables to saddle her spirited chestnut mare without encountering a living soul. Anyone who saw her would have thought she had a definite secret object, but she had nothing on her mind other than riding out over deserted countryside.

She knew the area well and there was no lane or pathway with which she was not familiar. She always avoided the place where the entrance to the tunnel was located, having no wish to come upon Mark or any of his villains. Giving her horse its head, she delighted in the sharp morning air on her face as it rushed by.

When she entered the woods, the air was hot, clammy and oppressive. She rode on, relieved to see the river ahead, thinking that she might sit a while in the shade and dip her feet in the cool, flowing water. So engrossed was she in her thoughts that she was unprepared for the sight that sprang upon her. A horse was nibbling the lush green grass that grew along the river bank, its owner about to plunge into the water. Her eyes widened and her mouth formed a silent O on recognising Lord Rockley.

As she was hidden by the dense foliage, Christina gazed across the narrow stretch of land that separated them and did an admiring appraisal of him as the sun beat down on his almost naked form in shimmering waves of heat. A narrow cloth covered his loins and provided the minimum of modesty as it moulded itself to his manhood. As a respectable young woman, she knew she should avert her innocent eyes, but, eager to see more, she carefully parted the branches. She froze when they rustled slightly. Holding her breath, she paused, not wishing to be caught looking. Lord Rockley remained facing the river, and she was thankful that he seemed unaware that he was being observed—but she failed to see the knowing smile that played about his lips and that his eyes were dancing with silent laughter.

Completely mesmerised, the heat crept into her cheeks at the sight of him standing on the river bank like some bronze-skinned statue. Suddenly he turned in her direction, and for a moment she thought he had seen her, but he merely looked about him, brushing his hair back from his face.

No detail on his magnificent, finely honed body was obscured by the distance that separated them. Lean of waist and hip, his shoulders were broad and rippled with muscles. The light furring on his chest dwindled into a shadowed line as it trailed down his flat belly. His legs were long and straight and corded with muscles.

An ache of suppressed passions began to spread through Christina, stirring a quickness in her blood. Her eyes followed as he turned and strolled closer to the water's edge, lowering to the flexing buttocks as he waded out to deeper water. Arching his back, he plunged further out with a clean dive. He swam into the centre of the slowly flowing river, his arms stroking the water relentlessly.

Christina could sense his need to exert himself, to wear off some of his pent-up energy by pitting his body against the current, and she was aware of an ache in her own body. How she wished she could wear out her frustrations in such a way. Knowing she was in danger of being seen, she reluctantly turned her horse and headed in a new direction to continue her ride.

She hadn't ridden far when another rider suddenly

appeared behind her, galloping hard. Reining in her horse, she waited for him, recognising Lord Rockley. Riding towards her, he seemed in total control of his horse's movements, yet he did it with such ease, the pair flowing together as one.

His sudden appearance disturbed her train of thought and try as she might she could not dispel the sight of his splendid, naked body as he had plunged into the river. She had thought about him more than she ought throughout the night, and to have seen him practically naked and to have him suddenly appear provoked a confusion of emotions. She felt the blood rush to her face in sudden embarrassment. How could she face him after last night and with this fresh memory disturbing her thoughts? How could she appear before him calm and unconcerned when she could remember only how he had carried her brother to bed in a drunken stupor— and she clad only in her nightgown?

As he drew closer, he subjected her to the same sort of intense scrutiny he'd focused on her the night before, and she found it just as discomforting and overly personal. She was drawn to him, insofar as she knew him, but there were things about him to discourage a deeper acquaintance. The sooner he was gone from Oakbridge, the better it would be for her peace of mind.

He pulled his horse to a halt beside her—a magnificent black stallion, the white blaze on his nose creamy in the sunlight. Christina held her breath when she saw the beast bunch his muscles. He reared up, pawing the air, and was superbly controlled by his rider. She gasped, fearing Lord Rockley would be thrown, but he remained firmly in the saddle, his teeth gleaming white in a devilish smile, as his horse's hooves hit the ground with a bone-jarring force that would have unseated a less-experienced rider.

'Good morning,' he murmured, looking across at her, his voice like a gentle caress. As he had ridden to catch up with her, he had thought she was like a fresh spring breeze. His eyes warmed in appreciation of her dazzling beauty and he smiled into her radiantly glowing face, knowing perfectly well that it was more than the exertion of her ride that was responsible for the pink that warmed her cheeks and that caused her to lower her gaze.

He leaned forwards, better to see her face. 'Did you like what you saw?' he asked, in a lightly teasing voice.

Christina raised her eyes and looked at him, the colour in her cheeks deepening when she saw the sparkling gleam in his eye. 'I don't know what you mean.'

A roguish grin readily showed the contrast between his dark skin and white teeth. He was enjoying every second of her discomfiture. 'Yes, you do. Don't play the innocent. I know you were there—at the river.'

'Oh—yes—I—I'm sorry. I just happened to ride that way. It's rare I see anyone at this time. I—I beg your pardon if I interrupted your swim. I didn't want to intrude, so I rode on.'

'You did not disturb anything,' he replied briefly. 'However, I can well imagine your confusion at the time, which sits charmingly on such a lovely face.' It was not so much a compliment as much as a calm and sincere statement of fact, which caused Christina's heartbeat to quicken. 'However, you need not have remained hidden. You could have joined me—or at least stayed long enough to have a paddle.'

'I don't think so. I shudder to think what the servants would have to say if I went home with my hair dangling wet around my ears.'

He grinned. 'You could have sneaked into the house when no one was looking.'

'No, I couldn't. The servants at Oakbridge have eyes everywhere.' An ardent admirer of good horseflesh and eager to turn the conversation in a different direction and not dwell on his handsome looks and the way his damp hair curled about his head, Christina was unable to restrain an appraising smile. 'I do not pretend to be knowledgeable about horses, but he is a splendid animal.' She watched as Lord Rockley ran his hand over the stallion's sleek neck, keeping him on a tight rein to control his prancing. There was a glaze of moisture on Lord Rockley's brow from his exertions, but he was clearly enjoying the ride.

'I salute your good taste,' he answered, meeting her gaze. 'I hope you managed to get to sleep after your disturbed night.'

'Yes, thank you, I did. And you?'

'I slept well enough, though I am used to rising with the dawn.'

'I imagine that is a consequence of being a soldier.'

'Something like that. How is your brother this morning? Hung-over, I don't doubt.'

'I'm sure he is, but I haven't seen him. If he runs true to form, I'll not see him before midday.'

'I'm afraid it is partly down to Henry. When all your guests had departed, your brother allowed my valet to lure him into making a night of it.'

'William does not usually take any luring into a game of cards or taking a drink. I consider it a complete waste of time.'

'I agree with you,' Simon replied. 'There are so many other more interesting things to do than drink— such as discussing the state of the nation, world affair, politics—'

'All of which are completely boring topics that would be of no interest whatsoever to William,' Christina interrupted, laughing lightly, unable to imagine her brother sitting down to discuss matters of such a serious nature,

'I am sure he has an extensive knowledge of local matters. He would probably enjoy discussing that.'

Christina gave him a dubious glance. 'Is Henry from these parts?'

'No.'

'Then I hardly think local matters could possibly be of interest to your valet.'

'You'd be surprised. Henry has a wide range of interests,' he said, in such a way that made Christina wonder just what William had discussed with Lord Rockley's valet when he had been in his cups—and how much that clever valet had managed to glean from her brother. 'For what it's worth, I'm sorry he was worse for wear.

It can't be easy for you having to deal with the guests on your own,' Simon went on.

'I'm used to it—and you needn't feel sorry for William. It is entirely his own fault that he imbibes too much. Like a lot of men he will ruin himself with anything he has a taste for. Unfortunately, in his case it is strong liquor. Hopefully, with advancing age will come the wisdom to avoid excess.' On a sigh, she looked at Lord Rockley and smiled as he cocked a dubious brow. 'I know you are probably thinking that this is rarely the case, but I live in hope.'

'Then I, too, hope he sees the error of his ways and begins to think about you for a change. You deserve better than having to deal with an inebriated brother. It's a fine morning. Do you usually ride alone and so early?'

'Why should I not?' Christina retorted, but her tone was mischievous rather than affronted. 'I ride on our own land and I am perfectly capable. I am used to riding in all weathers. They are generally solitary pursuits— unless William is not engaged with other matters or suffering the effects of a hangover. But I don't mind being on my own. Actually, I enjoy it.'

'Then I hope I am not intruding. I could ride in the other direction if my presence offends you.'

She smiled. 'Of course it doesn't. You are our guest, after all. You are welcome. Perhaps we can work up an appetite for breakfast.'

'Will you be joining me?' His brow arched questioningly, but it seemed more like a plea than an enquiry.

'Of course. It would be ungracious of me to let you

eat alone.' A smile slowly spread across his face, showing his even, white teeth. 'I am sure you will want to be on your way directly afterwards.'

'I'm in no hurry.' His grin widened as he looked ahead. 'A wager. If I beat you to those trees in the distance, you will allow me to stay for luncheon. If you beat me, I promise to be on my way after breakfast.'

'Then you leave me with no choice but to throw the race.'

'How so?'

'It would be most ungracious of me to set you on your way when you clearly have a desire to prolong your stay.'

'Then the wager is pointless, for should I win, it will look for all the world like I've invited myself.'

'Which would be true, I suppose, but you are most welcome to stay for luncheon. Might I suggest that we simply ride for the pleasure of riding, for the thrill of it, and we both go all out to win.' Without waiting for his reply, she kicked her horse into gallop.

Chapter Four

Admiring the spirit in which her own wager was made, Simon laughed loud and gave chase with no intent to lose, knowing that his own horse, with its fierce temperament and lightning speed, his muzzle drawn back over his teeth as he scented the air, would outpace the smaller chestnut mare.

Already several lengths ahead, Christina careered over the land towards the trees in the far distance, exhilaration speeding through her veins as she urged her horse faster. She could hear Lord Rockley's horse thundering behind her, closing in on her, but by exerting all her skill, she managed to keep in front. Ahead of her, a fallen log lay across her path. A less experience rider would have skirted round it, but Christina knew her capabilities; without slackening her pace, she urged her horse over it. Now, with their destination close, she truly thought victory would be hers, but like a lightning bolt, Lord Rockley, who had held his stallion back so that he could admire her skill, sped past her, his lips stretched in a broad smile of triumph, reaching the trees first.

Christina slowed her horse to a walk. She was breathing heavily and her face was flushed. 'A good ride, Lord Rockley. The race is yours—although I never thought I could win. I would be a fool to rely on my weight and stamina against a man on a horse of such superior strength. He is a superior animal.'

'He certainly is and he's got me out of many a scrape, but against such a very lovely opponent, I concede defeat.'

The admiration in his voice made Christina's heart pound faster. 'You are gallant, sir, but you are the clear winner. Come, let's have a steady ride back. I can promise you a hearty breakfast.'

They traversed a winding lane, looking over fields where a small herd of cattle grazed, and nearby was another field of ripening corn. They rode on leisurely for a while, then, passing a wooden copse, they halted near a large oak that dominated a knoll beside a rippling stream. The tree's widely spreading branches furnished abundant shade.

'Let's walk a way,' Simon suggested, dismounting.

Christina did likewise, and side by side, leading their mounts, they strolled along a path that twisted and turned through the trees on the edge of a wood that overlooked the rich vale of Oakbridge, with its wide river and water meadows. Christina stopped to take in the view, familiar with every aspect. She breathed deep of the earthy forest scents, conscious that she was not alone in this secluded leafy spot. The pale trunks of ash, beech and oak lifted their foliage-draped limbs to the sky, guarding like sentries the pathways winding about their feet.

Just as appreciative of the view as she was, Simon said, 'How pleasant the countryside is here at Oakbridge. I cannot imagine that you would ever want to leave it.'

'It is so beautiful,' she breathed, as the trees seemed to beckon her with their timeless mystery, drawing her closer, pulling her into their dark, whispering company. 'I shall hate to leave it, but I know I cannot remain here for ever.'

'It is so different from London, where I've just spent several weeks.'

'So it is,' she replied, turning to look at him with sparkling, humorous eyes, 'if you can ignore all the frightening rumours of highwaymen and the like. People complain about them all the time—how they rob the rich and break into their houses, no matter how hard the magistrate tries to calm their fears by promising to hunt them down.'

'I thought we promised not to speak of highwaymen,' he remarked, reminding her of their conversation the previous night.

'So we did,' she replied, beginning to saunter on, 'but that was last night—and you were far too inquisitive, as I recall.'

'I have to be if I am to bring the offenders to justice.'

'And what did you expect to find at Oakbridge, sir?' Her delicately boned chin raised a notch as a smile flitted across her lips, and she met his gaze with a brow pointedly raised in a challenging mode. 'Highwaymen hiding behind curtains and under every bed?'

'In truth, I did not know what I expected, but certainly not that.' He grinned sideways at her. 'Nothing so easy.'

'We hear rumours of the villains being seen here and there, but the best William and the magistrate have done has been to catch a poacher on our land snaring rabbits.' She turned her head and looked at him gravely. 'Was it wise to reveal yourself and your mission? Aren't spies supposed to work—undercover? I believe that is the correct word.'

'I am not a spy.'

'No, I suppose not, but isn't there a danger of the thieves going to ground until you give up and return to wherever it is you came from, having failed in your mission?'

'I did think about that, but unfortunately your magistrate has a loose jaw. My decision to accept the Lord Lieutenant's request was well broadcast before I reached the area. I'm not unduly worried. Mark Bucklow is so confident that I don't think he will allow my arrival to upset his routine. I find it curious that no one seems to know very much about what he does—where he goes during the day—or perhaps those who do know are reluctant to say in fear of reprisals. No doubt he has some snug retreat where he can stay hidden until nightfall.'

'Do you know anything about him at all?' Christina dared to ask, wondering what he would do were she to tell him she might know the exact location of the snug retreat he spoke of.

'I know he is an astute businessman and that he's developed a fast and profitable turnover from his life of crime. What he receives from his thieves is taken to his receiver in London. He is known to be handy with his fists, skilful with pistol or sword, and to possess a powerful presence. Therefore few people give him trouble and he enjoys a widespread respect. As with most of his counterparts, I intend to see that his career will end predictably in a one-sided meeting with the hangman.'

'It is a nicely balanced gamble you play, Lord Rockley. Are you not afraid, working alone as you do, that you yourself will become the victim?'

'I'm used to gambling, Miss Atherton, and I'm very good at it. I risk all to gain all, and I work best when I am alone.'

Despite herself, Christina smiled. 'I admire your confidence. Even if it leads to the most dangerous difficulties. You seem to enjoy it, but would you enjoy it quite as much if there weren't the risk?'

'Do you suggest that I do this for my own enjoyment?' He seemed genuinely angry for the moment, then he smiled. 'I think you are determined to make me see the worst in myself.'

'No, not at all. I am merely warning you of the danger.'

'I thank you for your concern—if that is what it

is—even if I cannot heed the warning. I confess I do enjoy what I do sometimes. In this instance, I am personally involved,' he said quietly, looking into the distance, 'which makes me determined to succeed in catching these criminals and bringing them to justice. If they know I am on to them, it might make some of them nervous. That is when they make mistakes, and if they do, you can be assured I shall be watching closely.'

Simon looked at his companion and smiled, utterly charmed by her. Watching her as she walked beside him, with her cheeks pink from the exercise and her glowing blue eyes, he had no wish to become embroiled in another discussion about highwaymen with her. However, there was another aspect to the matter. He found himself becoming increasingly attracted to Christina Atherton. He did not want her to be hurt by anything that happened and he feared that was highly likely if she had anything to do with Mark Bucklow. He truly hoped she was not involved in any way. A young woman, tender hearted—how could she not be hurt and distressed by such things?

Christina glanced at her tall, long-limbed companion, conscious of his presence and how handsome he was. And then she remembered with a sudden stab, as if a knife had been thrust into her heart, that his only reason for being here was to find Mark and his cohorts. William was one of those, and his very life was in danger from either side.

Her face must have paled and her eyes clouded. As if he read her thoughts, Simon paused and said, 'You know, Miss Atherton, if anything is worrying you, I want you to know that you can trust me.'

His voice was urgent and compelling. Standing in front of him, she peered up at him through long silken lashes, giving him an enigmatical smile. 'Why, Lord Rockley, should I believe I am in danger?'

A well-defined eyebrow over gleaming eyes jutted upwards. 'Of the worst possible kind, I fear.' His gaze settled on the softness of her mouth and his lips curved in a slight provocative smile.

'I presume you mean from the forces of evil at work in these parts?'

'What else?'

'What else is there?'

'Me.' He moved closer to her. Taking her hand, he lifted it to his lips and kissed the pale fingers while his eyes warmly probed the depths of the deep blue orbs, finding there a myriad of emotions.

Nervousness was taking the place of Christina's usually natural calm. 'What are you doing?' she asked when his hard hands took her upper arms and his long, lean body pressed itself close to hers.

'I'm going to kiss you.'

Christina paused to let that sink in. He was very sure of himself and he had a clever approach. But they were alone in the woods, which, she realised, made her extremely vulnerable to his whims. She was overpoweringly aware of his strong hands clasping her arms, and her bosom pressing against his broad chest. When his arms went round her, she tried to twist free, acutely conscious of the brush of his hardened thighs against her own and the manly feel of his body branding her through her clothing as he held her in an unrelenting vise of steel-thewed arms.

'But—you can't be serious.'

'I am very serious.'

'You have a sly way of getting what you want, Lord Rockley.'

A devilish grin slanted across his lips. 'Where you are concerned, Miss Atherton, I can be downright devious.'

'Are you sure you want to?'

He nodded silently.

'You've probably been in situations like this many times, but it's completely new to me.'

'I thought it might be. But I am still going to kiss you—to see if your lips really are as sweet as I remember.'

It hit Christina for the first time that, despite his teasing attitude, he was very serious. She tried to steady her confused senses, while he continued to hold her close, towering over her, his broad shoulders blocking out her view of anything but him. 'Absolutely not,' she said. 'The very idea is insane.'

He chuckled. 'I like being insane.'

He was laughing, but he wasn't merely serious, he was resolute. She could hear it in his rich, too-hypnotically deep voice. The mere thought of getting so close to him—of kissing him, of exposing herself emotionally as well as physically—made her cringe with panic. 'Please don't,' she said achingly. 'Please don't do this. We—we are strangers.'

'What better way is there for strangers to get to know one another?'

'But—I—don't want to be kissed—not by anyone.'

Christina pulled back, but his powerful arms tightened about her. 'You'll have to tell me why—or I won't take no for an answer.'

'It would change everything. Let things stay the way they are.'

'That's not good enough. Try something else.'

Trapped by his nearness, her body and all its senses alive, she lowered silky lashes, wondering if her yearnings were so visible as she said softly and without conviction, 'I wouldn't like it.'

'You had no objections before. Besides, how will you know if you don't try?'

With a mixture of dread and helpless anticipation, she lifted her eyes and met his steady gaze. 'I just do.'

'I think you would.'

His powerful, animal-like masculinity was an assault on Christina's senses. Somehow at that moment she found it impossible to be afraid of him or even to fear what he might do. It seemed to her that they were alone in a world that had no substance or reality. She felt her bravado crack for a split second, and reality nudged through the opening—along with something else that was completely alien to her. Against her better judgement, she allowed her captivated senses to become engaged, and, with an inner smile of surrender, she realised that Lord Rockley was still adamantly determined to kiss her. She also realised that she wanted him to. Very much. The suddenness of that yearning surprised her.

The instant Simon saw the sparkle in her glorious eyes and the pink, embarrassed tint mounting in her cheeks, he knew he'd won.

'You are awfully sure of yourself,' Christina remarked.

He lifted his brows and arrogantly declared, 'I am.'

'And I suppose you're good at kissing.'

'I've never had any complaints.'

His deep voice abruptly became husky, and Christina felt it like a sensual caress. Her eyes became focused on his mouth. 'I cannot believe this conversation,' she murmured.

Neither could Simon, but it had got her where he wanted her.

'In fact, I am quite shocked.'

He gave her a grin closely reminiscent of a leer. 'If you could read my mind, Miss Atherton, you'd be doubly shocked.'

A dimple showed in the corner of her mouth. 'It is evident your thoughts don't need stimulating, Lord Rockley.'

'Not as long as I can hold you in my arms. All I need to do is gaze at you and my aspirations—and other things—come to the fore.'

Raising her eyes shyly to his, she emulated a thoughtful vein. '*Other* things?'

A dark eyebrow angled roguishly upwards as the silver-grey eyes gleamed back at her. 'You're teasing me,

Miss Atherton, and I'm wondering for what purpose. I think a private demonstration is called for.'

So saying, he pulled her more firmly into his arms and held her there, lowering his lips to hers. At the first touch of his mouth, Christina went rigidly still, her breath indrawn, though Lord Rockley hadn't any idea if it was fear or surprise that paralysed her. At that moment he didn't know and he didn't care. His only desire was to hold her, to savour the sweet feelings swelling inside him and to share them with her.

'Kiss me back,' he urged, telling himself not to push her, not to force her. 'Kiss me, Christina,' he coaxed, using her name for the first time, his warm breath caressing her lips. His mouth was firm, yet tender and persuasive as his lips urged hers to respond, to open, and Christina, in her naïvety, hypnotised by those passionate silver-grey eyes and feeling her body begin to melt, needed no urging and yielded her lips to his.

When she obeyed and leaned into him, crushing her parted lips to his, Lord Rockley groaned aloud with the pleasure of it. The kiss began as a gentle questing, with his mouth moving slowly upon hers, but the fires ignited like dry kindling in a blaze of passion. It sparked and flared ever brighter beneath his scorching demands, turning Christina's mind upside down and uncovering a need in her that she had not known existed. She moaned softly, moulding herself more intimately to his body.

Backing her against the trunk of the nearest tree, Simon kissed her with all the persuasive force at his disposal, his mouth slanting over hers, his tongue teasing and provoking, his hands sliding down her arms and then around her narrow waist. Her body became pliant against his as he stroked her back and sought her breasts, taking her nipples between his fingers and forcing them to tighten into hard buds beneath the soft fabric covering them. He pressed her closer to him, his mouth plundering hers, his tongue tormenting.

To Christina, what he was doing to her was like being wrapped in a cocoon of dangerous sensuality where she had no control over anything. Particularly herself. Somehow her hands had crept up to his shoulders and around his neck. Her fingers were tangling in his hair, tugging him closer, and when a groan leaped from her throat, she felt him smile against her lips.

'Now that's what I like to hear. Enjoy it, my sweet.'

'But I think we should stop,' she whispered breathlessly against his mouth.

'Shh,' he murmured. 'Be quiet.'

Subdued by his authoritative tones, Christina fell silent and was still against him. She had neither the desire nor the strength to do so, as once again his mouth seized hers in a possessive, wildly erotic kiss that was astonishingly personal. Pleasure shot through her like an arrow, and she stared with dazed eyes at the face above her own. The urge to push him away, to stop this madness now, still remained, but with each touch, each kiss, it was growing fainter. The world around them seemed to melt away, leaving only Lord Rockley and herself locked together in a charmed circle against which dull reality crumbled away.

Christina was a little frightened by the violence of the passion that had so suddenly been unleashed in her.

She had never felt before this wild longing to be near, to touch a creature of flesh and blood. Clasped in his arms, pressed against his hard chest, she shivered from head to foot. Lord Rockley's bronzed skin was damp with fine sweat and he was breathing hard, the sound filling his willing captive's ears. Their kiss seemed to go on for ever, becoming more passionate, arousing Christina's blood to madness. She was no longer aware what Lord Rockley was doing. He unfastened her bodice and it was not until his lips left hers and he buried his head between her warm breasts, that she found she was half-naked in his arms. But the sight of her own flesh, rosy in the sun's light, did not embarrass her in the least. It was as though she had been created for him alone, for his pleasure and happiness.

Lord Rockley evinced a remarkable vigour. His quick, masterful caresses were those of a soldier for whom every second counts. And yet, in this violence of his that robbed her of all will to resist, Christina found an extraordinary gentleness. In a few seconds, the old Christina, who had met the passionate advances of the local young men with such cool composure and indifference, turned into a passionate woman for whom a man's admiration had suddenly become the whole meaning of existence.

Finally Simon released her lips and drew back a little. With his palm still on her breast, he could feel her heartbeat, feel it slowing, her body still languid with pleasure, her eyes still dazed with passion. For a moment all was quiet around them, and then with a sudden jolt, Christina's heart began to pound and her body stiffened, and

Simon knew that memory had returned. And with it realisation.

Christina felt horrified with the returning knowledge and hastily fastened the bodice of her gown. *What have I done?* What madness had possessed her to do something that was wild and completely against her nature? How could she have been so foolish? Both wretchedness and self-recrimination beat at her like hard fists. Had she not learned her lesson from her association with Mark Bucklow? She had managed to evade that highway robber so far. She remained free. At least that was what she told herself over and over again. Until she almost believed it—until she had met Lord Rockley.

What was it about the man that made her so pliable with him? He was handsome, no one could deny that, but there was a quality of manliness that very much appealed to her. She had allowed herself to fall into his arms without a thought. He was practically a stranger and she had allowed him to touch her and kiss her— worse, she had revelled in it. At the time, nothing else had mattered. Never in her life had she felt like this. It was as if her body were awash with feeling, alive with need. What she had just done complicated everything. Without looking at Lord Rockley she gently pushed him away. Her chest ached, but she held tight to her self-control.

'That should not have happened. I think we should go back now.' When he opened his mouth to speak, watching him as if she half-expected him to pounce on her and tear her clothes off, she quickly silenced him. 'Please—do not speak of it,' she burst out. 'And I am not your sweet, so don't you *ever* call me that again. You have no doubt charmed many women out of their virtue. I only hope I do not find myself a victim of some ploy you've construed.'

'Worry not. I play no games with your heart.'

Slowly, deliberately, Simon reached out a hand to touch the cheek of the beleaguered girl, relieved when she did not draw back. Her skin was warm and soft, and he wanted more of her. But she would not allow it and he would not allow himself to force her. There was a bittersweet triumph in his self-denial. It was not often he denied himself a woman.

'Are you afraid of me, Christina?' he said, quietly and carefully, using her first name with a familiarity that had come with the kiss.

'No, of course not. You seem to forget that you are our guest at Oakbridge. You take too many liberties, Lord Rockley,' she reproached to hide her confusion and roiling emotions, which were in danger of getting out of control. 'I should certainly not be here alone with you, and I should have known better than to allow it. We will forget this moment, I promise you. We will put it behind us and never speak of it again.'

'Aye, we will never speak of it again—if that is your wish,' he said. 'Everything will go on as before we kissed—but if you think you will ever be able to forget it, then you are a fool.'

'I will forget. I must,' she whispered fiercely, with more conviction than she felt. 'I—am not ready for this yet.'

Simon's hand lifted her chin, and his fingers slowly stroked her throat as he stared into her eyes.

'I want you, Christina,' he breathed in a husky murmur, the pulse beating in his temple making her aware of his needs, and he saw the confusion in her face. She shook her head in an almost pleading gesture of denial, mutely appealing for mercy, but he pulled her close and she stared with helpless entreaty into those smouldering silver-grey eyes as his face loomed above her own. Again his mouth lowered, opening and slanting before covering hers.

Murmuring words of endearment and passion, he pressed fevered kisses upon her throat and cheek and lightly touched the delicate eyelids that flickered downwards to receive the featherlike kisses. When he found her lips once more, his kiss was deep and filled with passion, and then he raised his head and released her.

Their eyes met and held. Hers so blue and his of a paler hue, entwined, touching hidden places, remembering. She had spoken a lie when she had said she was not ready for any of this just yet—they both knew it, and she was all too aware of the loneliness that would settle down upon her when they were parted. There was no denying that Lord Rockley had fascinated her from the moment she saw him. Though she wanted to hold him at arm's length for her own good, she was becoming increasingly aware of him as a man. Her spirit was nurtured by his nearness and the comfort he could bestow, and she wanted to draw succour from his strength and his caring attention.

The truth was that she would not forget his kisses—

they were the first she had experienced, and she desperately wanted him to kiss her again, to feel his hands caressing her naked flesh—and more—and the sad thing was that he knew it. Abruptly she glanced away, denying the truth, and grasped the reins of her horse. Placing his hands on her waist, Lord Rockley lifted her into the saddle as if she weighed nothing at all, before mounting his own horse.

As she was about to ride on, he reached out and touched her knee, halting her. She looked at him, meeting his gaze, waiting for him to speak. On a more serious note, he said, 'I meant what I said earlier. I want you to feel that you can trust me. I speak in all seriousness.'

There was no mistaking that he was in earnest, and Christina felt a sudden warmth in her heart at his kindness. After what had just transpired between them, the offer was so unexpected, the tone of his voice so inviting, that it would be so easy to tell him all, to unburden herself completely and put all her trust in him. His mere presence gave her a feeling of safety and security. And yet it was all an illusion. He was the danger, and it was danger of a different kind to the danger Mark Bucklow posed. Nevertheless, even though she knew it to be the truth, her heart could not credit it.

It was Mark she feared, Mark who terrified her, while there was something about Lord Rockley that made her feel that as long as he was there, she was safe. She desperately wanted to tell him of Mark Bucklow's threat to William, to them both—of how he terrorised them and had threatened to kill them if they did not comply with his wishes—but she was much too afraid.

Lifting her head, she looked straight ahead, drawing her body upright in the saddle. 'It is indeed kind of you to think of me, but I assure you, Lord Rockley, that should anything be amiss—which there isn't, I hasten to add—then I have my brother to turn to. Besides, you will soon be gone from Oakbridge and it is unlikely we shall meet again.'

His eyes narrowed and he shook his head slowly. 'Don't bet on it. I shall make damned sure we do.'

Urging her horse into a gallop ahead of Lord Rockley, Christina gave herself a mental shake. She had been an utter fool back there, being drawn to Lord Rockley and romanticising, simply because he was tall and handsome and because she was an idiot, a spineless idiot who was disgustingly and helplessly attracted to him. The sooner he was away from Oakbridge and her—before her weak will and fragile moral fibre crumbled in the face of his dangerous appeal—the better.

When they rode into the stable yard, it was clear as soon Christina set eyes on Tom that all was not well. He was subdued, his expression a mixture of anger and distress. Gently she placed a hand on his arm as he snatched the reins from her and turned to lead her horse to its box.

'Tom? What is it? What ails you?'

The groom hesitated and looked warily at Lord Rockley standing behind her. He cleared his throat. 'It's serious, Miss Christina, but…'

'It's all right, Tom. You can speak in front of Lord Rockley. Tell me what has happened.'

'It's Mr and Mrs Senior. Their coach was held up when they were on their way home last night.'

Christina paled visibly. 'Oh, no. This is simply dreadful news, Tom.'

'Aye, well—like you say, but the ordeal was too much for Mr Senior.'

'What can you mean?' she whispered, her heart heavy with dread at what he might tell her, 'Tom, what are you saying? Was he hurt?'

'He's dead, Miss Christina. Mr Senior is dead.'

She stared at him in disbelief. 'Dead?' she gasped. 'You—you mean those who held them up killed him?'

He shook his head. 'From what I've heard, it was some kind of seizure.'

Christina was numb. Mr and Mrs Senior were two of the most liked and respected people in the district. The manner of Mr Senior's death would upset and anger a lot of people. All at once, the full consequences of what they were doing swept over her in a sudden tide of apprehension and despair. Sometimes she felt it was all too much for her and that she couldn't go on, but she had to. There was nothing else for it.

She was aware of Lord Rockley standing close to her and knew he was watching her intently, but she dare not look at him, so she was oblivious to the hard gleam that had entered his eyes and his clenched jaw. Feeling that in some way she had colluded in Mr Senior's demise, Christina was utterly overcome with shame and guilt.

'Mrs Senior must be beside herself. I must go to her at once.'

'Those thieving...' Breathing deeply, not wishing to let his anger get the better of him in front of Lord Rockley, Tom regained control of himself. 'They still took their valuables—not that the good lady had many. They took Mr Senior's watch and chain from his dead body and left him.'

Christina touched his arm sympathetically. 'You're upset, Tom, and rightly so. Have the carriage made ready while I change my clothes and I'll visit Mrs Senior right away.' She turned to Lord Rockley. 'I'm so sorry. You'll have to breakfast without me, I'm afraid. I really must go and see Mrs Senior.'

'I understand, but I insist on you having breakfast and then we'll go together.'

Christina stared at him. 'Together? But—you don't have to concern yourself with this.'

'You seem to forget that it is my concern,' he reminded her brusquely, taking firm hold on her elbow and leading her towards the house. 'The villains who waylaid them have to be caught. I'm sure Mrs Senior managed to have a good look at them, so she might be able to give me a description.'

Christina stopped and stared at him, appalled by what he was suggesting. 'I hardly think this is the time to question her. The poor lady will be traumatised enough after everything that has happened.'

'That can't be helped. It has to be done while the details of the event are still fresh in her mind.'

'Still fresh in her mind?' Christina repeated sharply. 'I hardly think the events of last night will fade in a hurry.'

Simon's eyes narrowed and he said coldly, 'You have no objections to me accompanying you, have you, Christina?'

Christina had plenty, but kept her mouth shut. She hid what she was feeling, or hoped she did, as she walked beside him, bluffing before those hard, sharp eyes that were cleverer than any she had known. She had no appetite for breakfast, but she managed to eat a little fresh fruit. It was an awkward, silent and hurried breakfast. She kept her eyes downcast, well aware that Lord Rockley often glanced at her.

Escaping to her room to change as soon as she had finished and dressing hastily, she was surprised when an anxious and hungover William sought her out, making no apologies or even a mention of how he had got to bed. His fair hair was tousled and he had a night's growth of beard on his chin.

'William, what are you doing here?' Christina demanded, more sharply than she meant. 'You look dreadful. I can't tell you how disappointed I am in you. Why did you have to drink so much? I understand you and Lord Rockley's valet imbibed together when everyone had left. I cannot think why you would take such a risk by sitting up half the night drinking with a man who I am sure is as big a snoop as his master. I sincerely hope you didn't give anything away.'

'I didn't divulge anything that might incriminate us, I assure you, Christina,' he grumbled. 'I do remember that much. I want to know what happened when you went to see Mark last night. It makes me devilishly nervous having Mark at Oakbridge with Rockley nosing around. Did he abandon his plans?'

'No, he didn't. He would not allow Lord Rockley's presence to change anything.'

'Is Rockley still here?'

'Yes, and as master of the house, William, you should be entertaining him, not me,' Christina reproached crossly. 'He accompanied me on my ride earlier. I left him having breakfast.'

'I'm glad you're getting on with him—you spent a good deal of time speaking to him last night. He's a handsome devil, don't you think?'

'He's—very attractive—in a dangerous sort of way.'

'My sentiments exactly, which is why I want him gone from here as soon as possible.'

'I couldn't agree more.' In too much of a rush to spend time dressing her hair, Christina twisted it into a knot in her nape.

'He's watching us—he's watching all of us. It's my belief that he's been snooping about for a while. He misses nothing. He's looking for evidence, possibly against us, and if it exists he'll find it.' William looked at her in alarm. 'Has he given you any indication that he suspects us?'

'No—oh, I honestly don't know, William,' she answered wearily. 'He's looking for Mark—he did tell me that much. He means to find him.'

'Then he'll have to look hard. Mark's a slippery customer. He lives on his wits and he's managed to evade capture so far.'

'I wish he would be caught,' Christina said fiercely. 'He—he came to my room last night.'

William's eyes opened wide. 'Why did he do that?'

'Why do you think?' she snapped, all the indignation and horror she felt on Mark invading her privacy coming to the surface. 'To pester me. Not content with using this house for his illegal purposes, he has his lust-filled eyes turned on me. If he is thwarted now, you can be sure he will make us both pay. I couldn't bear it if—if he...'

'Christina—don't upset yourself. Mark wouldn't—'

'And you are certain of that, are you, William?' she flared. 'Any kind of relationship between me and that man is impossible and too loathsome to contemplate. In the eyes of those who know me I would sink beyond social and moral redemption. I will not have it. I will not have Mark Bucklow entering my bedchamber when the whim takes him. I will not have him entering this house at his pleasure. He—he could have bumped into Lord Rockley, and then where would we be? Because when he is finally caught, you can guarantee no one will believe you took no part in his crimes and you will be condemned alongside him.'

'Indeed, Christina, he has overstepped himself.'

'In future, I will lock my door. But you are to speak to him, William. You must make him realise that he is not to enter the house again. We simply cannot go on like this—and to add to our worries, something dreadful happened last night.'

'What?'

'Mr and Mrs Senior were stopped on their way home.

Whoever it was that held them up frightened poor Mr Senior so much that as a consequence he collapsed and died.'

This news had the power to arouse William and he looked quite shocked. 'Mr Senior—but—dear Lord, Christina, that is the worst thing.'

'Yes, it is.'

'He was attacked?'

'Apparently not. It was some kind of seizure. I'm going to see Mrs Senior now.' She paused in what she was doing and looked at him hard. 'This has to stop, William. We have to get out of this hold Mark Bucklow has over us. I don't care how it's done, but we have to.'

'Don't you think I want that? But it cannot be done, Christina. We are in too deep. He needs Oakbridge. You know what he will do to us if either of us even thinks of betraying him to the authorities.'

'I know, and I shudder to think what Father would make of all this. I'm glad he isn't here to see it.'

'So am I,' William replied, somewhat shamefaced. Even as he said it, he imagined that he could see his father's eyes looking at him reproachfully for not standing up to Mark and his threats and felt a shiver down his spine.

'Miranda will be coming back from London very soon,' Christina reminded him. 'If her father gets so much as a whiff of your involvement in any of this, he will call the betrothal off. He will never agree to an alliance between his precious daughter and a criminal—for that is what you will be.'

'Miranda? It must not happen. Miranda is one of the finest things that has ever happened to me. I couldn't bear to lose her.'

'I know, William. We'll do all we can. Hopefully it won't come to that.' He loved Miranda. She saw the truth in his eyes, in the sudden quiver of his mouth and by the softening of his expression. 'Her father is eager for the match to go ahead—to have his daughter become a proper lady. We'll think of what is to be done about Mark later, but right now I must go to Mrs Senior. Lord Rockley insists on accompanying me and there's nothing I can say to put him off.'

'I should come with you.'

'Yes, you should, but you're in no fit state and I don't have time to wait.'

With his glazed eyes fixed on hers, William struggled in his blind belief in his sister to make everything right. After a moment he gave a jerky nod and turned away.

Christina closed the door behind her, leaning her head against it and closing her eyes. If only she'd been born a man, she would not have let this happen. She feared Mark Bucklow and loathed him for what he was and what he was doing to them both, but she was fully aware of his strength. He would crush her as easily as a snail beneath his boot if she opened her mouth, she had no doubt of that. But she would find some way out of this misery—she must.

Chapter Five

Christina found Lord Rockley pacing the hall.

'I apologise for forcing my company on you further,' he said harshly. 'I promise that as soon as I have spoken to Mrs Senior, my valet and I will be on our way, leaving you to do whatever it is you do—although my business is far from finished here.'

Christina thought this a strange thing for him to say and she wondered what could be behind his words. She would be relieved when he had left Oakbridge, but she felt a strong tug of regret. She could not understand her own feelings, yet she felt a curious reluctance about him leaving. She felt it strange that she did not fear him. She had never felt entirely comfortable in the company of men, and she had expected it to be no different with Lord Rockley. But it was. With him she felt safe, protected, and deep down inside her she did not want him to go away.

* * *

They had travelled the mile and a half in comparative silence. Simon had much to think about. His contemplation on his conversation with Christina the night before, and her furtive manner when he had raised the subject of Mark Bucklow—how much more suspicious it all seemed after what had happened to Mr Senior. And according to Henry, who'd been out and about early, his ear to the ground, Mrs Senior's conveyance wasn't the only coach to be stopped and the occupants robbed after leaving Oakbridge last night.

Simon had been suspicious about Oakbridge all along. Christina's familiarity with Bucklow's dog, the voices raised in anger during the night, one of them a woman's voice—Christina's he was sure—and that when he'd queried it and she had nervously tried to assure him that there was nothing amiss but her brother's drunken snores, all added to his suspicions.

A deep silence hung over the Senior household. Servants glided about like shadows. Ever since Mr Senior had been brought back to the house with news of the robbery, Mrs Senior's grief had filled the house with alarm and dread. The old lady sat dwarf-like on a sofa. With her daughter beside her, she was in a terribly distressed state.

Such grief as this made Christina feel deeply ashamed. She sat beside her and took her hand. 'I am so very sorry,' she said.

Mrs Senior raised a piteous grief-stricken face towards her, eyes red-rimmed from weeping. 'I know, my dear. It is good of you to come. I—I cannot believe what has happened. It was quite—quite dreadful. We should never have attended the party last night. Mr Senior wasn't well—but I told him it would do him good to socialise—and I was so looking forward to going to Oakbridge—it would remind me of the old days, when your grandfather—' She broke off and looked down at her hands. 'Those thieves showed no mercy. They—they even robbed his dead body—my poor, poor husband. I should never have made him go.'

Mrs Senior buried her face in her shaking hands and began to sob again so piteously that Christina leant across and put her arms about the old woman's shoulders. She had listened to her account of what had happened through a misty haze of pain and tears, remembering that her last memory of Mr Senior was one of laughter and a smiling face. Now there was nothing left.

'Dear Mrs Senior, please stop torturing yourself. You have nothing to blame yourself for.' Christina glanced at Lord Rockley, who had taken up a stance by the window.

He moved towards them. After expressing his condolences to Mrs Senior and her family, in a voice that was suddenly sympathetic and understanding, he said, 'Forgive me. I do not mean to add to your grief, but I would be grateful if you would try to answer one or two questions.'

With gentle tact he questioned her about the assailants. She was willing to answer his questions, but could not give a clear description of them—two of them, as she recalled, who insisted on them parting with their valuables.

'I am sorry I can't recall anything more that may be of further value to you, Lord Rockley,' she said, dabbing at her eyes. 'One ruffian looks just like another in the dark—and I was too concerned about Mr Senior to take much notice. I'd like to think the villains are unlikely to show their faces in the area again, but I won't be satisfied until they're caught.'

'And it is my job to see that they are,' Lord Rockley said.

After handing Christina up into the carriage, Simon settled himself into the seat facing her. Christina felt tension and guilt weighing on her spirit. Lord Rockley's lips had tightened into a thin line, then, grimacing with suppressed anger, he said, 'This cannot go on. There must be an end to it—and soon.' The level grey eyes settled on Christina. 'This is Bucklow's work. One way or another I will find him.'

Christina looked at him, her face shadowed with an immense sorrow. 'Yes, I know. I—I hope you do.' She averted her eyes, and for several minutes neither of them spoke. She stared at the passing scenery unseeing, silent and withdrawn. She could not rid herself of the remorse that she had forsaken her pride, and she suffered regret that she had allowed this to happen. A coldness came over her face. She must act. She felt she could bear no more. She could not pretend any longer. She was too frightened.

'I am not blind, Christina, nor am I a fool,' Simon

now said quietly. When she turned her distressed eyes to meet his own, he felt an overpowering tenderness. 'Earlier I asked you to trust me and I meant it.' Christina's eyes must have clouded suddenly, because, as if he read her thoughts, he said, 'I know you are afraid and I would like you to tell me why. You are too young to be involved in some of the things that have become a part of your life.'

Christina knew exactly what he meant, and she averted her eyes, raising her chin mutinously. 'I do not comprehend what you mean. I really have no idea.'

'Do not play with me, Christina. Listen to me.' His voice was urgent and so compelling that Christina had the urge to confess all. 'I know Bucklow is no stranger to you, and I would not like to discover that your brother is in some way caught up in his criminal activities.' When Christina opened her mouth to argue the point, he held up his hand for her silence. 'Wait. Hear me out, for I believe there are things about Bucklow that you and your brother are not aware of.'

Something about his tone of voice made Christina look at him more closely. She was too curious about what Lord Rockley had to say not to ask, 'Things? What kind of things?'

'The Bucklows are of the Catholic faith. Are you aware of that?'

'Yes—but then so are many others of our acquaintance. Does it have any significance?'

'Mark Bucklow is a Jacobite.'

A sudden chill crept into Christina's heart. 'Oh, I see. But—what has that to do with anything?'

'Are you aware of what Jacobites are, that they have been on the move ever since James II's Court was exiled?'

'Yes, of course I do. They are people who would like a Catholic king to succeed Queen Anne, since she is childless and has no heir.'

'James the Third.'

'I do know that. I am not stupid. Are you saying that Mark Bucklow is a spy or something?'

'No. He is not a spy or a conspirator. He is merely an ardent and extremely active supporter of the Jacobite cause. Are you aware that he lived in France when James II's Court was exiled there? He was undoubtedly involved in plans to bring James back to the throne— just as he is involved in installing his son.'

'And you know Mark Bucklow's character well?'

'His character doesn't interest me. A man is defined only by his actions.'

'So, if he isn't a spy or a conspirator, what is he?'

'The money he makes from his thieving he sends to France to help finance the Jacobite cause. There is nothing he would not do for James Stuart. There is talk of rebellion, and if that is indeed the case, then they will need money to fund it. So, if you count him among your friends, Christina, you do yourself no favours.'

Deeply offended by his remark, she stiffened. 'He is not a friend. If he is what you say, then when he is caught he will be charged and convicted of treason.'

'That is right. *If* your brother is involved with him in any way, by his collusion it will be assumed that he is a defender of the Jacobites and will be charged with the same. You will not escape, either, Christina. The taint of popery will hang over you and you will probably never shake free of its deathly grip. The Jacobites seek to put James—who they believe is the rightful king—on the throne before a successor has been chosen.'

'But that is not possible—not while the Queen still lives.'

'Precisely. Queen Anne is in poor health, but she could live for a long time. Who knows? I don't think they are prepared to wait.'

Still reeling from the discovery of Mark Bucklow being a Jacobite, Christina stared at Lord Rockley in horror as she realised what he was saying. 'You mean they would kill her?'

He nodded.

Christina, her face ashen, felt panic rising. This was worse than she could have imagined and she would have no part of it. Suddenly Mark Bucklow's thieving had taken on a whole new meaning and she realised the depth of William's and her own involvement—but to force the rightful monarch from the throne—to kill her...

'I can hardly believe it possible. William would not knowingly involve himself in anything of a treasonable kind.'

'I believe you. He would be a madman to associate with Bucklow at all. What the Jacobites intend will never happen. They have neither the money nor the men—no matter how many carriages Bucklow intercepts and robs. James will never be installed upon the English throne, and the rich Jacobites here become poorer every time they throw their money into the

Channel, believing it will wash ashore on France and entice James to England.'

'You are extremely knowledgeable about such matters.'

'I have friends in high places—Marlborough, who is one of Queen Anne's most trusted advisers, is one of them. I cannot stress hard enough the misfortunes that will fall on your family if your brother is merely suspected of treason. The circumstances will blight your whole lives and subject you to the worst kind of dangers. William is to wed Miss Miranda Kershaw. Her father is a wealthy wool merchant in Cirencester.'

'You know him?'

Simon nodded. 'Vaguely. He is a man who will make quite sure that his daughter will marry a person whose family connections will withstand the most scrupulous examination.'

'But—I told you, it is arranged. Miranda and William are to wed very soon.'

'But not soon enough. When I have Bucklow in my grip—which I am certain will be sooner rather than later—his entire network of thieves will be blown right open. I think you know what I am saying, Christina.'

Christina sat tense and still. She met his gaze, knowing he was issuing a warning and that she would ignore it at her peril.

'If you know where Bucklow can be found, it would be in your best interests to tell me.'

Christina called upon the sturdiest reserves of her self-discipline. 'I cannot do that—and—I wish you would talk to William about this. Tell him what you have just told me. If he has anything to say that might help you in any way, then I am sure he will do so. But— why are you telling me this?'

He looked at her for a long moment and Christina fancied there was a strange expression on his face she had not seen before. 'Because of what has happened to Mr Senior. Be wary, Christina. Let me help you.'

She felt his words like a douche of cold water, her brain racing as she tried to think of a way out of this hole, this trap into which she had fallen. 'There is no need,' she said, conscious as she spoke of the dismay in her voice. She felt he was unconvinced and added quickly, 'There is nothing you can do to help me.'

'So still you will not trust me.'

Having arrived at Oakbridge, the coach pulled to a halt. Tom was dropping the steps and Christina rose to get out, saying as she did so, 'It isn't that. It's just that I cannot.'

Christina did not turn her head or look at Lord Rockley as he walked behind her up the steps to the house. Not until they reached the door did he lean forwards to breathe in her ear, 'I understand and I would not force you, Christina. I sense your fear, and, should you find yourself in danger, will you promise to come to me? I will help you. I promise you.'

Christina paused to look at him. He was sincere, that she knew, but what could she say without betraying them all? She nodded and quietly said, 'Thank you.'

William was waiting for them when they arrived back at Oakbridge, and he greeted Lord Rockley with almost fawning enthusiasm. Christina felt a pang of relief to see him bathed and shaved, his attitude more cheerful, although she did wonder what had brought about this change.

'How was your visit to Mrs Senior? How was the dear lady?' he asked.

'Mrs Senior is extremely distressed, and with good reason,' his sister informed him.

'I am sincerely sorry to hear it. It's a dreadful business. I'll make a point of riding over to pay my condolences myself later.'

'I'm sure she would appreciate that.'

'It's almost time for luncheon. You will eat with us, Lord Rockley?'

Christina looked at her brother apprehensively. 'I believe Lord Rockley has to be on his way, William. Is that not so, Lord Rockley?'

Simon readily accepted William's invitation, which drew Christina's gaze to him. She could already tell that he wasn't going anywhere just yet if he could help it, and that he was already rethinking his strategy. 'A spot of luncheon before going on my way would be most welcome.'

'Splendid,' William enthused. 'It should not delay you too long.'

When they were seated in the dining room, Christina looked at the two men over the glowing expanse of white tablecloth and gleaming plates and cutlery as they ate a collation of cold meats left over from the night before. She spoke very little as, with relief, expansively William played host to Lord Rockley. Their conversation was mainly about horses and local matters.

When she had finished eating, Christina excused herself, giving Lord Rockley the opportunity to discuss with William what he had talked to her about in the carriage. She sincerely hoped so. With the newfound knowledge of Mark Bucklow being a Jacobite intent on removing Queen Anne from the throne to install the Catholic James III, the full horror of what he was mixed up in would hit home and he would indeed consider throwing himself on the mercy of the authorities.

When Lord Rockley was about to leave, Christina joined them in the hall to bid him farewell. She noted how William hung back. His eyes were cautious, anxious, as if he was uncertain about what to do next, which gave her reason to think he was troubled by what Lord Rockley had divulged.

She walked towards Lord Rockley, who was standing by the open door pulling on his gloves. Henry was waiting in the drive with the horses.

'You will be going to your brother's house, will you not, Lord Rockley?'

'I have not yet decided. I half promised Sir John Cruckshank I would call on him when I left Oakbridge. There are matters we have to discuss.'

'Whatever you decide, I wish you a pleasant journey.'

He cocked a questioning brow, his silver-grey eyes holding hers. 'You want me to go?'

'I—think you should.' She faced him, forcing herself

to meet his eyes, wanting him to understand that she meant what she said. It was partly because she was afraid of what he might uncover if he remained at Oakbridge any longer, but also because of the havoc he was creating in her heart. Here he was too close, too compelling, and even when he was gone it would be impossible for her to thrust him out of her thoughts for longer than a moment, for a situation was developing between them that must not be allowed to go further.

He stared back at her, his gaze caressing her features, delving into her brain. 'I understand only too well, and I know my valet and I are a nuisance, imposing ourselves upon you in this manner. Methinks I have been a soldier too long and have forgotten how to behave in civilised society.'

Christina was embarrassed that he should think she wanted rid of him. 'Oh, please don't think you are a nuisance. You are not—but...'

He held up his hand to silence her. 'Please don't explain. There is no need. I know I am outstaying my welcome. I understand exactly what you are trying to say.' Unexpectedly he took her hand, drawing her closer to him. His eyes searched her face, which was pale, she knew. She avoided his gaze, wondering what he was seeing, what he was thinking.

Simon sighed. 'I want to take the fear out of your eyes, Christina. Why will you not tell me what is wrong so that I can help you?'

He would help her? It was as if a warm, soft light had pierced Christina's sense of aloneness that had begun to engulf her. A sudden desire to weep misted her eyes.

'How can you help me?' she asked him, her voice husky with emotion. Afraid of what he might read into her reply, she summoned her self-restraint and a wobbly smile curved her soft lips. 'As I said, there is nothing you can help me with.'

Simon leaned in so close to her that his breath warmed her face. 'And I do not believe you, Christina. You cannot hold yourself responsible for the problems you are thrust into.'

How Christina wished it were so. But he did not know her. She sighed. 'Things are not—easy at Oakbridge just now. You must have seen for yourself that the house is somewhat—run down. Things are not what they were when my father was alive. I learned when he died that I must be strong for my brother as well as myself.'

Their eyes met. Christina saw no particular reaction in Lord Rockley's, but he must know William's love of the gaming tables in London had brought them to this.

'You know, Christina, you are a complete contradiction to me—in fact, in everything.'

'Why, what can you mean?' she asked with a puzzled look.

'Because one minute you look delicate and weak and very vulnerable, and the next you are strong and determined and more than a little obstinate.'

She smiled slightly. 'Oh dear! Is it that bad, Lord Rockley?'

'I'm afraid so—and my name is Simon.'

'But you hardly know me,' she uttered reasonably.

He shook his head, his fingers caressing hers, sending

a wave of heat through her body. 'You are mistaken, Christina. I need only to look into your eyes and I know everything I need to know about you. I know your beauty, your pain, your strength and your courage.'

Tears filled her eyes, and she bowed her head. Security seemed an almost tangible substance whenever he was close to her, and somewhere deep within her a yearning grew, as if her soul commanded her to speak. 'You cannot know,' she whispered. 'You cannot possibly know what my life is like.'

'I believe I do—more than you realise.'

There was a caressing note in his voice. Christina felt a sudden quiver run through her and a quickening within—as if something awakened that had been dormant until he had kissed her. Never had she wanted to be as close to a man as she wanted to be close to this man, never had she allowed her mind to be subjugated by her feeling in a situation such as this. It had always been too dangerous—and now more so than it had ever been.

Simon's face became very serious as he raised her hand and lightly placed his lips on her fingers. 'Take care, Christina. I shall come and visit you very soon. You can count on it.'

William came to stand beside her and together they watched Lord Rockley ride away with his valet. When they were no longer within their sights, they drifted into the drawing room.

'He said he'd be back,' Christina whispered. 'I'm sure he will be.' She looked at her brother. 'I was surprised you invited Lord Rockley to stay for luncheon when you wanted him gone from here. Was there a reason for this?'

William's mouth quivered and his eyes filled with tears. 'I had a letter from Miranda earlier. She is to leave London shortly so we should see each other very soon.'

So, Christina thought, it was this that accounted for the change in him. 'I see. If her father brings her to Oakridge, then it will be difficult keeping what happens here from them—unless we can put an end to it before they arrive. Lord Rockley spoke to you about Mark, didn't he?'

A thoroughly worried man, William nodded. 'Good Lord, Christina! I had no idea—not the slightest inkling that the man was a Jacobite. You must believe me.'

'I do, but Mark was so determined to use Oakbridge that it would have made no difference.'

'I always knew there was something—but this! It's incredible that I didn't suspect him of being a Catholic.'

'He pulled the wool over both our eyes. Did you divulge anything to Lord Rockley?'

'No, but by God I wanted to.'

The stoical gloom of the early afternoon was keyed to the sombreness of William's dour temper. Christina took no notice of it. Her brother sulked like a punished child and went to the decanter to pour himself a brandy.

'This is the worst thing, Christina. The very worst,' he complained, gulping the amber liquid down. 'That Mark and his kind are prepared to kill the Queen to achieve their ends is abhorrent to me.'

This knowledge cut mercilessly into Christina's heart with the precision of a surgeon's knife. It forced her to see William and herself and their motives clearly, as if for the first time, and she was ashamed of what she saw. If facing Mark was the only thing which could save them from a future that terrified her, then they would have to do it. She signified as much to William, and her icy resolution astounded him.

'I agree, which is why we must go and see Mark and tell him we want nothing more to do with this business.'

'I can't,' William said with a rising panic, shaking his head and pouring himself another drink. 'I can't, Christina. You know what he will do. He will kill me.'

She sighed, knowing it really was beyond her brother to stand up to Mark Bucklow. She wanted to hide herself away somewhere and give way to her sudden and appalling dread. She wanted to have someone take this burden from her, for she already had enough to carry as it was. She wanted someone to tell her what to do, as her parents had once done, as William had once done, but now her brother was waiting for her to be the decisive one.

'Then you leave me with little choice but to confront him myself.'

William's eyes flared. 'No, Christina, I forbid it.'

'Then do it yourself,' she argued angrily, unfairly, because deep down she was deeply concerned for William's safety. That he remained safe and alive was paramount to all else, and she knew that, to Mark, William really was dispensable.

William averted his eyes and shook his head dumbly, his hand trembling as he drank some more. 'He will kill us, I know it,' he said, placing the glass down noisily. 'We will never be free of him.'

'We won't if we don't do something about it.'

'There is nothing we can do and he knows it, damn him.'

'I will bribe him—offer him money—anything to get rid of him.'

'But we don't have any money.'

'This house still has objects of value we could sell to raise some money. If he is so desperate for money to fund his cause, then he might listen to me. We could sell the few jewels I have left—or some more paintings— or even some of your precious horses,' she said drily, thinking of the splendid horseflesh Mark had presented him with in the early days to buy his loyalty before William had become wary and afraid of his association with a criminal and wanted out and before Mark had issued brutal death threats against him. 'I'm sure they'd raise a goodly sum.'

'No, Christina, not the horses,' William uttered, crestfallen. 'You know how much they mean to me.'

'You have to be prepared to make sacrifices if we are to raise some money to pay Mark off.'

Feeling the pressing burden of a mountain she was finding impossible to climb, Christina turned from him and went to the door. Her conviction was born of self-preservation, and in her heart that instinct had taken firm root. She believed that if Mark Bucklow didn't shoot him first, William would hang if she did not pay heed to it, and her distaste for such an outcome meant she did not take long to linger in deliberation. Her course of action was clear. 'The way I see it, there is only one thing for it. It's up to me.'

'Christina, you can't. Think about it.'

'I don't want to think. If you think too much, you never do anything at all. I've made up my mind. I do not want to live like this any longer. I've decided it is time to put words into action. The time for secrets and reticence is past. As I see it we have no choice but to confront him—and failing that,' she said, looking back at William, 'I will go to Lord Rockley and tell all.' Whatever else he might be at this blackest of moments, Simon Rockley was a strong, unwavering gleam of hope for her to cling to in the darkness.

William paled and stared at her in disbelief. A silence dense and solid fell between Christina, enclosed in a steely resolve, and her brother, who was shocked by what she had said. 'Are you mad? If you want me to hang then that is a sure way to go about it, for I will never be able to convince him I am not involved with Mark.'

'That is a chance we will have to take.'

William's frightened words echoed in Christina's head as she went out without giving him time to protest further. Usually at times like this, she would think of something comforting to say, but for once her bright, clever mind was blank, her tongue silenced, and she realised she was as frightened as William. When she came to any decision she always acted upon it at once without stopping to weigh up the pros and cons.

Everything depended upon her now. She wasn't sure she was up the task, but she had to try. She was alone against the evil of Mark Bucklow.

As Simon rode away from Oakbridge, Christina was very much on his mind. From the first moment he had met the beauteous young woman and had found himself staring into her darkly lashed blue eyes, he had known that his life would be lacking a most important substance without her in it. His emotions were unmercifully churned.

Their earlier intimacy had taught him to see beyond the outer layer of the lovely, vibrant young woman and to read the true depth of the person hidden within. He realised with some surprise that for all the pleasure he had derived from their shared passion, some deeper, richer emotion was taking root in his heart. It had a quality that was outside his realm of experience. As yet, he could put no name to it, but it was satisfying knowing her feelings ran along the same lines. But while his hopes for the future blossomed, his fears at the same time ran as deep as a bottomless pit.

William Atherton had been non-committal when Simon had had the same conversation with him that he'd had with Christina in the coach earlier. As soon as he'd mentioned Bucklow's name, the young man's expression had become shuttered and he'd given no indication of his own involvement, but he'd been unable to hide the fear in his eyes when Simon had divulged Bucklow was an ardent Jacobite. That Atherton was somehow involved with Bucklow he had no doubt, but how he had become mixed up with such a ruthless individual, and involved his sister, he had yet to find out.

He had to save Christina from Bucklow. He had to protect her, even if she didn't want him to. Even if he wasn't here at Oakbridge, he had to be in a position to protect her.

Having ridden some distance from the house, something—an instinct, and he always trusted his instincts, told Simon to stop and wait. Was it coincidence or a stroke of luck for him when Christina and the groom he had met earlier galloped full tilt away from the house? Hidden by the thick foliage of the trees on the side of the road, he watched them ride by.

'Now where does she go to in such a hurry, do you think, Henry?'

Henry shrugged. 'Wherever it is, she's in a hurry,' he replied.

'Then I think we should follow. I think, Henry, that we shall find it interesting. In fact, it is possible that Miss Atherton is about to lead us to Bucklow.'

Christina rode swiftly, her determination only a little stronger than her fear. She was heading for the Black Swan Inn at Wakeham in the hope that Mark would be there. If he wasn't there, she would have to return to Oakbridge and wait until he came.

Unaware that Lord Rockley followed like a shadow keeping a close surveillance, and with Tom keeping close to her, she followed the winding river for a couple of miles until the land began to rise above the river bank and the road veered off in another direction. The road became a narrow lane, eerie and hemmed in by dense woods. Seeing no one, she followed it a while, then, turning a bend, she saw the Black Swan Inn.

It was an ideal spot for highwaymen. She doubted very much whether any constable would put himself at risk by coming out here. It was now mid-afternoon and, apart from a dog which sniffed and licked around the yard, there was little sign of life around the inn. Telling Tom that she would enter the inn alone in the hope of finding Mark there, instructing him to keep out of sight and ignoring his angry objections, she dismounted and handed him the reins.

Pushing open the inn door, she took a step into the smoke-and-liquor-smelling public room before letting the door rattle shut behind her. She took a close look around. The inn was small in comparison to some, and run down, catering to a shady clientele. The ceiling was low, but the room was wide, crammed with a crude assortment of grease-stained tables and benches. A few of these were occupied with a motley collection of drinkers—all strangers to her—and two men leaned against the bar, talking to the heavily bearded landlord.

On seeing Christina, he stopped what he was doing and cast an eye over her. She looked highly respectable, not at all the type of woman who usually frequented the Black Swan Inn.

Through a doorway at the back of the bar Christina could hear the clatter of pots in what she took to be a kitchen. She scanned the faces of the men at the tables who watched her. They were a disreputable lot, and they did not look away when her gaze touched them. Trying not to show her nervousness, she moved towards the bar. Gathering her courage, she enquired about Mark Bucklow.

'If he is here I—I need to speak to him,' she said, looking the landlord straight in the eye.

'And you know this is where he might be, do you?' the landlord said gruffly.

Christina stiffened her spine, determined not to show weakness. 'I was told this is where he can be found. Is he here?'

'He might be.'

The landlord looked her over with some scepticism before bidding her to wait until he found out if the gentleman was available and he had informed him of her presence.

Trying to shut herself off from the many pairs of inquisitive eyes directed at her, she listened to the landlord stomp up the wooden stairs that led to the first floor.

'Perhaps the lady would like something to drink while she's waiting,' one of the men at the bar said to the other.

Christina looked at him and hesitated. She was hot and thirsty after her long ride from Oakbridge, but she was in a hurry to get her business with Mark over and done with and to be on her way. A moment later the landlord came heavily down the stairs.

'He'll see you. Says to go on up.'

'Oh!' she uttered, hiding the relief she felt that he was indeed at the Black Swan. 'Will he not come down?'

'He says you're to go on up. His room's right at the end of the landing.'

His room! So he did reside at the inn after all. With nothing else for it, Christina gingerly climbed the stairs. She was not easily frightened, but it took some courage to walk deliberately into the lion's den. The door to Mark's room stood partly open, and as she drew near the entry and peered inside, it was evident he was in the process of shaving. He was standing over a bowl of water, looking into a mottled mirror on the wall as he scraped away at his chin covered with a thick lather of soap. A towel was draped across his naked shoulders. On seeing her in the doorway through the mirror, he removed the towel and wiped the soap from his face.

'Come in, Christina. As you see, you take me by surprise.'

With quaking heart and Mark's recent intrusion into her bedchamber still at the forefront of her mind, Christina pushed the door open further and went in. His hair was wildly tousled as if he'd just risen from his bed.

'This is an unexpected honour. How did you know where to find me? That I spend some of my time here is known to just a chosen few.'

There was that mocking note in his voice that always made Christina shudder. 'I made it my business to find out.'

He nodded, a wry smile twisting his lips. 'I always did consider you to be brighter than your brother. You came alone, I hope?' His suspicion of trickery showing, he crossed the rough-hewn planks to the wide-open window and looked down into the inn yard. 'Were you seen?' he demanded sharply.

'I don't think so. One of the grooms accompanied me. He's waiting for me downstairs.'

As he sauntered back to her his smirk was unpleasant. 'You must really want to see me to risk coming here. I'm honoured.'

There was something humiliating and degrading in the way his dark, bold eyes blazed down at her, travelling over the gown covering her breasts, where it lingered overlong. Christina was grateful her square, lace-edged neckline was demure or she might have found herself blushing. Whereas Lord Rockley's perusals evoked a sensuality within her that was hard to ignore, she was highly insulted by the brazenness of this man's scrutiny. To her, he seemed the epitome of everything that was bad, and she didn't care to confront him on any terms, let alone now when she had no one but an aged groom to serve as her protector.

'Don't be. I'm here to ask you once again—and I hope for the last time—to leave Oakbridge. You must find somewhere else to store your ill-gotten gains.'

'Is that all? And I was hoping it was my own charming self you had come to see.'

He was taunting her as he invariably did, and it was with a combination of anger and nervousness that she said, 'I have made it plain to you what my feelings are. I am here to discuss a way out of this mess for William and me. Nothing else.'

Mark looked at her with some amusement and not a

little impatience. 'And you think I might have softened
between last night and now, do you, Christina? Think
again. If you imagine that I'll simply pack up and go,
then you are mistaken. I meant what I said. I'm going
nowhere. I will see your precious brother dead and in
hell first.'

'Please, I implore you. William is not one of the other
poor fools you have inveigled into this mad, dangerous
venture—this Jacobite scheme which can only end in
death. To do all this, to risk death, for a king you have
never seen.'

'You know nothing of Jacobite affairs,' Mark snapped
in anger. His expression became ugly. 'Until my business is finished, I'm going nowhere.'

'Not until you have supplanted Queen Anne and
installed James on the English throne.'

He smiled thinly, his hooded eyes darkening. 'So, you
know about that—not that it matters. How do you know
that I am a Jacobite? How do you know, Christina?'

'Lord Rockley told me,' she said, her voice quivering with desperation, 'and we want no part of it, do
you hear? Especially after what happened to Mr Senior
when his coach was held up by you or another of your
gang of thieves last night. You terrified that poor man
to death.'

Mark chuckled at her rising ire, not in the least concerned by the death of one of his victims. 'That was
unfortunate, I grant you, but he was old anyway. His
death is hardly a loss.'

'You would complain if you were the wife of that
man. You are evil,' she accused. 'Evil. William is

risking everything by letting you use Oakbridge for your treasonable activities—everything, and it cannot continue.'

Mark shot her a dark look. 'Treasonable? Be careful how you bandy that word about, Christina. It will go ill for the man—or woman—who betrays us.'

'And you don't care how many people you hurt or kill in your aim to succeed, do you?'

He shrugged, growing tired of the discussion. 'The end will justify the means, so they say.'

'So you intend to go on stealing indefinitely.'

'Out of necessity—until I have what I need. I had to have a great deal of money to accomplish my goal, and there was no way I could earn it honestly. I became a thief, yes, but I only rob the rich, the gentry, lifting baubles from empty-headed women who won't mourn their loss. Some jewels are valuable, but their value decreases drastically when I take them to the fence— the best fence in London, I might add. A few more jobs and then I will retire and go to France.'

Becoming silent, he reflected on the beauty of the woman. Always cold to him, he likened her to an ice maiden. There were times when he was tempted to break through that thin barrier of ice and have his way with her. One day in the near future he fully expected to reap the rewards of his patience—but then, why wait? She had come here of her own volition. She was alone and must have known the risk she was taking.

'We will give you some money if you agree to leave,' Christina offered in desperation, moving towards him, her face eager with her decision.

His look was one of contempt. 'Pay? What with? As far as I am aware, your brother has precious little money to bandy about.'

'We would consider selling off some land...'

'Land?' He laughed, shaking his head, as if what she had suggested was the most ridiculous thing he had ever heard. 'I don't think so, Christina. Sell it by all means and give me the dues, though it will not persuade me to leave.'

Suddenly he moved closer to her, bending his hateful face close to hers. His eyes devoured her with greed in his ruddy face and a repulsive smile twisted his lips. He noted the moment when she shuddered in revulsion. His laugh was scornful as his gaze roamed over her and he seemed to enjoy the fear he saw in her face. 'You know what I want, Christina. There is a way William can eventually be free of me. His sister only has to be nice to me.'

'No,' she choked through her fright, stepping back. 'No! You'll never have me! Never!'

Mark laughed in a terrifying way and Christina braced herself to flee and made to dart past him, but he was quick and caught her round the waist, dragging her writhing, kicking and with arms flailing about in an attempt to claw him or do him some injury. Pressed against his naked chest, heavy with the flab of good living, Christina continued to struggle, but his arms held her in a bone-crushing grip that made her breathless and made movement nigh impossible.

'Let me go.' Sick with revulsions, her voice was little more than a desperate whisper.

'So, my beauty! So we're showing our teeth, are we? Don't want to give me me my bit of fun, eh? I have different ideas. I plan to have you, so there's no reason why you should fight me. I'm a strong man. I do enjoy force if that is what it's to be, but I prefer willingness.'

Terror shot through Christina when he lowered his head to hers and she realised her mistake in seeking him out. She cursed herself for being unable to free herself from the trap she had set for herself. He laughed again as she tried to turn her face aside, but he dug his fingers into her jaw and, with his tongue, ravished the depths of her mouth. Holding her with one muscular arm about her slender waist, with the other, just where the point of her collar ended, he ripped open the bodice of her gown.

Unaware that they were being observed by Tom hidden from view among the trees, Simon and Henry surveyed the Black Swan Inn into which Christina had disappeared.

'What are you planning?' Henry asked the stern-faced Lord Rockley. 'Do you think Bucklow is inside?'

'I would bet on it,' he replied, knowing they were dealing with a dangerous man. 'The man I saw looking out of that upstairs window at the end of the building I would swear was Bucklow. We must proceed with caution.' Hearing the gentle whinny of a horse close by, he rode towards the small thicket. Before he reached it, Tom came out, leading Christina's horse.

'Where's your mistress?' Simon demanded. 'Did she enter the inn alone?'

Tom nodded. 'Aye, she did. I wanted to go with her, but she told me to wait here.'

'Would I be right in saying she has come here to see Mark Bucklow?' When Tom stared at him mutely and shook his head, Simon snapped impatiently, 'Answer me, man. I have no time to waste.'

Bending to the other man's authority, Tom nodded. 'She came to see him—even thought I tried to talk her out of it. But he might not be here.'

'He's inside all right—and we don't know how many of his cohorts are in there with him.'

'Should we summon more men?' Henry asked.

Simon nodded. 'Cruckshank assured me he has men standing by should I need them. You know where he lives, Henry, and fortunately it's not too far away from here. Ride hard and tell him to get here without delay.'

When Henry had ridden off, Simon surveyed the inn a while longer. Taking note of Tom's agitated state and afraid that Christina might be in danger, he decided not to wait for Henry to return and approached the door with Tom close on his heels.

His eyes did a quick sweep of the men drinking at the tables before he turned his attention to the landlord and demanded to see Mark Bucklow. At first the man's manner was furtive and defiant, but when Simon made him aware of his identity and his purpose for being there, and that more men sent by the magistrate were about to descend on his inn at any moment, reluctantly he directed him to the stairs.

As those present seemed to melt into the shadows,

staring up the stairs, Simon felt the hackles prickle on the back of his neck. A chill seemed to penetrate his inner soul and he had to shake himself from the spell of it before he began to climb.

Chapter Six

No matter how hard Christina fought Mark in desperation, it was no use. He flung her on to the bed and himself on top of her, pinning her down. The weight of his sweaty body was so heavy that she wondered if her ribs could stand the pressure without cracking. The fact that she was being held against her will by this loathsome man, and the looming possibility that she'd soon find herself a victim of his lust, was not only thoroughly frightening to her, but immensely revolting.

His lips sank to her throat, moving on to her bosom. She winced in pain as his sharp teeth bit the tender flesh, and a sick feeling of nausea rose within her when his questing hands lifted her skirts and fondled the bare flesh of her thighs. She continued to struggle with every measure of resolve she could muster to gain her freedom, until, no match for Mark's brute strength, she felt her own strength leave her and she lay pliant beneath him. The utter helplessness of being a woman totally at the mercy of this man struck her with full force.

Then, invaded by a nameless terror, she lay perfectly still, her gaze suddenly riveted beyond Mark to the open doorway. She had to bite her lips to stop herself crying out in horror, for she saw who stood there. It was Simon Rockley. His tall, broad-shouldered figure blocked out the light and seemed to fill the whole room.

Sensing a change in her, seeing her stricken face, her eyes wild as she stared at the doorway behind him, Mark raised his head and looked towards the door. The smile of triumph on having Christina pliant beneath him froze on his face. With an angry snarl, he leapt to his feet. He would have rushed the intruder, but seeing him holding a sword pointing directly at him in one hand and the glint of a pistol in the other, then eyeing his own pistol out of reach on the table beside the bed, he backed off warily.

Christina shrank against the pillows. The blood left her face and rushed to her heart, which seemed to have stopped beating, leaving her suffering as she had never suffered before. Her eyes never left Lord Rockley's eyes, which were wide and savagely furious as he looked at her in murderous silence, his lips curling with disgust as he absorbed the scene. Such a transformation had come over his features that she recoiled before the change. All that had ever been controlled, attractive and good-humoured had given way to hot fury and positive revulsion. The silver-grey of his eyes seemed sheathed in ice, and anger fixed his mouth into a straight line.

'My compliments to you, *Miss Atherton,*' he

emphasised contemptuously, 'on your duplicity and your dishonesty.'

With a wildly beating heart, she stammered, 'S-Simon...' She longed to run towards him and explain that the scene was not at all as it seemed.

His eyes threatening to explode on finding the woman he wanted for himself inextricably entwined with the villain he now had every reason to believe was her lover, Simon looked at her. His gaze took in her hair, a mass of disordered curls about her head, her clothes creased and in disarray, her bodice torn. Despite her ravaged appearance she looked glorious and he hated her for it—for bestowing her favours on Bucklow so soon after leaving his arms. Rage ran through him.

'Be quiet,' he ordered. 'This is a matter for Bucklow and me and I order you not to interfere.'

'But it isn't what you—'

'I told you to be quiet,' he hissed, his eyes blazing, refusing to yield an inch. 'I don't want to know what is between you and this—this scurrilous villain. I've more important things to consider.' His gaze shifted to Mark. 'If you make any forward move to get away from me, I'll blow your head off. Do you understand?' He hesitated until Bucklow replied with a hesitant nod of his head. 'Now carefully pick your weapon up by the cylinder, place it on the floor in front of the bed and slide it very slowly over here to me. If you make one quick or unnecessary movement, you will be the one to pay for it. And it you don't think I have it in me to kill you, you are mistaken.'

Simon met his opponent's gaze and, reading the

simmering anger in his eyes, knew he was dealing with a dangerous man. As instructed, Bucklow took the pistol from the table and laid it on the floor and pushed it out towards him, then gave it a light shove, sending it sliding slowly across the floor. Without taking his eyes off Bucklow, Simon gently kicked it back to the doorway and Tom.

'Take it,' he instructed. He waited until his order was obeyed before handing his own pistol to Tom. 'Keep it aimed on this villain, Tom. There's no telling what he might do.' Holding the sword in his right hand, he waved it at Bucklow. 'I'll allow you to get your shirt on. Though Miss Atherton may prefer your present state, I'm sure there are other ladies who will be unduly shocked if you go out wearing only your breeches.'

As Mark reached for his shirt and thrust his arms into the sleeves, Christina quickly rolled off the bed and stood quivering at the side of her attacker. She was still furious from being manhandled by Mark and at Simon's mistaken assumption that she had been enjoying it. Her hair was streaming all over the place, and the bodice of her dress was parted down the middle, which she hastily pulled back together—but too late to hide the plump flesh of her breast and shoulder.

Knowing how this must look and the look on Simon's face telling her he was quick to judge, her dominant self-respect flared into life. His manner infuriated her. Angry and humiliated, her eyes sparkled wrathfully and her look clashed with his like steel on steel. They glared at each other for a moment, like two fighters measuring each other up, the one tall and haughty in the doorway, the other like a young fighting cock refusing to lower her gaze.

Simon's eyes passed briefly and with withering contempt over her, before discarding her and moving on to the man who stood beside her.

'So, you are Bucklow. On one black day of despair I vowed to kill you.' He took a step forwards, and when he spoke again his face had a look of such implacable hatred it transformed his features. 'Listen to me carefully,' he said, in a voice where anger simmered just under control. 'I had a niece—she was the most beautiful child—who never did anyone any harm. But you shot her down like a dog. You killed her, you bastard—and wounded her father, my brother. Not a day has gone by since that I haven't cursed you, Bucklow, and I swore to hunt you down and see that justice is done. And don't insult me by denying what you did or that you don't recall the incident.'

There was so much fury and anguish in Simon's voice that Christina's eyes filled with tears. What Mark had done to Simon's niece was too cruel to be borne, and the destruction of that world of love which had grown up around that young girl's death was too brutal.

Mark gave a casual shrug, his action compounding the crime. 'Aye, I remember. It was unfortunate, but I haven't lost any sleep over it.'

'I wouldn't expect you to.' Simon's lips curled with contempt as his eyes did a quick sweep of the room. 'I presume this is where you spend your days skulking away from the authorities.'

'And you're the ferret employed to seek me out,' Mark

growled, eyeing the tall and powerful, good-looking man warily, bitter hatred in his eyes. He remembered the girl he spoke of, how she had tried to run away when he had stopped their coach; when her father had run after her he had shot them both. He spat in disgust on the floor, measuring this man and the threat of his sword. 'The only thing about weapons is that one can never be quite sure of the other man's abilities. I have heard that you are a dangerous man to tangle with, Rockley. You may be good,' he sneered, 'but are you good enough? I know how to keep myself safe and out of the reach of your kind.'

'Clearly not,' Simon said, moving further into the room while Tom looked on, fearful for his mistress. 'It's been no difficult task running you to earth. Perhaps now you will learn that stealing other people's property doesn't pay.'

'I have a cause to fund—but then being the thorough investigator that you are, you will know all about that.'

'I know that you are an active Jacobite and that the money you receive from stolen goods goes to fund the Jacobites in France—a cause that is doomed to fail. Despite being a Catholic, your father is a respected lawyer without a stain to his character. Unable to condone your Jacobite sympathies, it is no secret that he kicked you out. Forced to fend for yourself you turned to crime—to highway robbery.'

A derisive chuckle came from Mark. 'And why not? I'm good at what I do. My grandfather was a highwayman, so it must be in my blood.'

'By all accounts he was hanged for his crimes—that, too, is in your blood, Bucklow. If you took money from your own kind to fund your cause, I would not take such a harsh view, but to terrorise others, to steal from them and often resort to murder when they resist, convinced me you had to be caught. So, by the authority of the Lord Lieutenant of this county, I am here to arrest you and order you to accompany me to a place of incarceration. You will then be taken to London, where you will be tried at the next sessions of the Old Bailey, where you will be called upon to answer for your crimes—among them your involvement in a plot to kill Queen Anne, a treasonable act.'

'Like hell I will,' Mark retorted, roughly pushing Christina away from him.

Simon looked at her mockingly as she gripped the wooden bedpost to stop herself falling. 'I owe you my thanks for having effectively detained this villain, Miss Atherton. My instinct told me that if I lingered around Oakbridge for long enough you would lead me to him eventually. How convenient for me that you kept your lover abed until I got here.'

'Lover?' Christina's temper flared anew.

'You!' Mark showed his teeth in a savage snarl and threw an accusing stare at the young woman who just a moment before he'd been attempting to rape. His eyes flared with rage as he spat, 'Bitch. You told them. You dared betray me.'

'Betray you!' She stiffened with alarm, for she had indeed intended doing just that if he refused her request to leave Oakbridge. 'No, Mark, I didn't. Lord Rockley must have followed me here. I swear I didn't tell him—I swear I didn't.' No one listening to her could miss the note of desperation in her voice or in the expression on her face.

'He isn't surprised to find you here.'

'I told you. Only because he followed me.'

'It must have been a shock to his sensibilities bursting in on us and seeing what we were about. When you came to me all dewy eyed and soft lipped, little did I know we would be interrupted in our loving pursuits. Then, of course,' he sneered as his gaze appraised the other man's handsome looks, 'I can see how he will appeal to your sex, my dear, and why you might have betrayed me with him.'

Christina uttered an indignant cry. 'Betrayed you! You lie.' Unable to hear any more and beside herself, she stepped towards Simon, desperate for him to understand what Mark had really been trying to do to her. 'Don't listen to him! He's nothing but a mischief maker—a wretch who uses people to serve his own interests. Love, he called it. How dare you call it that?' she flung at her assailant. 'The barbarous way you treated me? Is that what you call love, you—'

'Silence,' Simon ordered. 'I know what I saw and there was no resistance on your part. But enough. How and where you conduct your affair is your business, not mine, and I would appreciate it if you would keep the sordid details to yourself.'

Christina closed her eyes. She felt sick with anger and despair. She seemed to be caught in a web of half-truths more damaging than any insults. She realised how it must have looked to him. What he'd seen was corroborative evidence.

Simon's voice rang out. 'Will you place yourself in my custody, Bucklow, or must I take you by force?'

Mark bunched his huge fists, his eyes threatening to explode. 'Attempt to take me anywhere, Rockley, and I'll slit your throat,' he bit out between his teeth. Hearing the clatter of horses' hooves down in the inn yard and raised voices, he looked from Lord Rockley to the window as he considered his escape.

Christina remained stricken and frightened, seeing the rage running through Simon's eyes as Mark sprang forwards, bitter hatred in his. All of a sudden, Mark staggered back when Simon sidestepped quickly and pressed the muzzle of his pistol against Mark's chest.

'Not so fast. Don't do anything hasty. You'll not escape, Bucklow. I believe those are the men sent by the magistrate I can hear below. There will be enough of us to deal with you as I would like, so I advise you to give yourself up. Do not give yourself up to death deliberately.'

Mark half-closed his eyes so that they gleamed like bright slits. 'I think not, Rockley,' he hissed. His next move was like lightning as he hit out with his fist and knocked the pistol from Simon's hand.

Simon reacted with equal vigour and immediately seized Mark by the throat and slammed him against the wall. Christina fell back into a corner as Simon pounded Mark with the full force of his body behind his fists. She was shocked by this manifestation of violence from a man she had assumed was the very epitome of self-restraint. Mark was white with anger and fury and his anger gave him added strength. The two men fell upon each other, landing on the dusty floor where they became engaged in a desperate struggle. Their furious grunts were like those of wild beasts fighting for their lives and they moved so swiftly, Christina found it hard to follow their movements.

Punches were thrown and furniture sent clattering across the room. Mark fought like a man with no time to lose, tight-lipped, his face a mask of fury. Simon was constantly on the attack, but he was unprepared when the fight took them to the open window. Before he could be overpowered, Mark threw himself out just as the men who had come to take him prisoner could be heard clattering up the stairs.

Cursing fiercely, Simon grabbed his pistol and hung out of the window, taking aim.

Christina stared, round-eyed, then with a shriek and careless of her own safety, blindly she threw herself forwards. 'No, No more! Please don't kill him,' she cried, throwing herself forwards and knocking Simon's arm to distract his aim, unable to understand why she did so apart from the fact that she hated killing in any form.

Simon, surprised by her intervention, lowered his arm and looked at her, and in doing so allowed Mark to pick himself up, dust himself down, and with a mocking salute disappear into the woods. Cursing savagely, thrusting Christina away and calling her a crazy fool, Simon strode to the door where he barked orders to the men on their way up, telling them to scour the woods for Bucklow and any of his cohorts who could be found, before he turned to Christina.

'You crazy little fool. You should not have done that. You should have stayed out of it.'

The air was hazy with dust as she stood there, numb and immobile. 'I—I couldn't let you shoot him in cold blood. Enough harm has been done.'

'Bucklow deserves no better. Still, it is done now— and thanks to you the scoundrel has escaped. Follow me down,' Simon told her, breathing heavily and wiping blood away from a cut on his lip, his fury reduced to a dangerous calm. He handed her a small cover from a nearby chair with which to conceal her torn gown, earning from her a quiet, 'Thank you.' He averted his gaze, allowing her a moment to cover herself, before going on ahead of her.

Sure that right was on her side, Christina followed him down the stairs and out of the inn. She was too proud to make excuses for herself, let alone implore his forgiveness. She had calmed down and now adopted an attitude of icy composure. Taking a deep breath, she tossed back a lock of hair and asked, 'What are you going to do with me? My brother must be suffering great anxiety on my behalf. I am sure he would like to know—even if it should be the worst. Are you going to arrest me?'

Simon did not answer immediately. Christina could not know that if he refused to look or even speak to her, it was only because he did not feel in control of his emotions since first laying eyes on her in Bucklow's arms. Added to this was the humiliating fact that Bucklow had outwitted him. He was in the grip of a white hot fury unlike anything he'd ever known, turning his mind into a boiling volcano of rage. Parading before his eyes were visions of a bewitching young woman in his arms, laughing up at him, yielding him her lips, such a short time ago. He cursed himself for his stupidity in trusting her.

'While we search for Bucklow, you are free to go home,' he said at length. 'I will come to you there shortly.'

'And William?'

'He has committed a crime of such seriousness, I cannot ignore it. Your brother was foolish and gullible and basically weak. I will spare him if I can, but I promise nothing. You will tell him not to leave Oakbridge until I have spoken to him. Is that understood?'

Knowing how it must look to those gathered around outside the inn, Christina stood upright, clutching the cover tightly about her shoulders, enveloped in clouds of hair, which blew wildly about her in the strong wind that had risen, heralding the end of the hot and humid weather. As she walked towards Tom, who was holding her horse, she scornfully ignored the comments—some flattering, some impudent—that her predicament and her beauty brought from them.

She was aware of all these eyes looking her, but what angered her most was that Simon Rockley, believing her to be as guilty as Mark Bucklow, made no attempt to defend her.

As Mark fled from the Black Swan Inn, after escaping that arrogant, meddling lord, he'd dashed into the woods, frantic to make good his escape. Circling back to the inn where he dragged himself on to his horse, the rapidity of his flight was evidenced by the sound of the mount's hooves clattering out of the inn yard. He never halted until he was confident that he had lost his pursuers. Only then did he begin to breathe more easily. He did not much care that his plans had gone awry, but he had reached the point where he was tired of what he did, tired of being in England, and was impatient to go to France, where he would fight the Jacobite cause close to the young King James.

He was angry at being thwarted and made the fool this day, but there would be another day, and he would not forget Christina's betrayal in a hurry. He vowed silently that he was not finished with her.

William was not at Oakbridge when Christina got back. Apparently he had left the house shortly after her own departure for the Black Swan Inn. According to one of the servants, he had been in a state of agitation. And, no, the servant said when Christina enquired, he hadn't said where he was going.

Christina was deeply anxious about her brother. Simon Rockley would assume that because Mark Buck-low ran his criminal organisation from Oakbridge, he must do so with William's permission and that would make him just as guilty in his book. She knew she would have to face what this would do to him and to his standing in the community when it came out—if Mark didn't find him first and kill him. Her brother would be censured and condemned as a traitor and looked down upon by the very people who had been his friends, those same friends who had once been so proud to be associated with the illustrious Atherton family.

With a terrible dread she waited in a state of jarring tension for the inevitable moment when Lord Rockley would come. Her trembling had finally ceased, but she kept playing Mark Bucklow's terrible attack over and over in her mind, remembering the loathsome feel of his hands on her innocent flesh, and then her feeling of absolute relief when Simon had stormed into the room, his face a mask of cold fury. She would be for ever grateful for his timely arrival and relieved that he had dealt with Mark, but she was deeply saddened that he had misunderstood the situation.

It was dark when he finally arrived at Oakbridge, dressed entirely in black. His arrival would be followed by grave consequences for its owner and his sister. As soon as Christina saw him enter the house, reluctant to come face to face with him, she left the window and sat down on the bed to await being summoned.

She didn't have long to wait. As soon as she was confronted by his presence, she realised the maid had not exaggerated when she said that Lord Rockley was in a dangerous mood.

Christina was pale and quietly dressed, her hair was drawn severely back from her face, accentuating her high cheekbones and large eyes. Simon did not even turn round when she closed the door behind her. He stood looking out of one of the windows into the courtyard. He had his back to her and his hands clasped behind him. Without moving, he bit out, 'Bucklow escaped us. No doubt you will be overjoyed to know that. But wherever he has gone, his criminal activities are over. You and your brother can say farewell to all the schemes you have hatched out between you. I have been told your brother is not at home. Is this correct?'

'Yes,' Christina replied.

'And his whereabouts?'

'I—have no idea,' she replied with faltering truthfulness.

'I find his absence disturbing and rather curious. I ask myself what kind of man is it that allows his sister to do his dirty work. You have been brought almost to ruin by his ill-considered actions, and with suspicion hanging over him, he has left his sister to face the music, while he cowers elsewhere like the spineless creature he is.'

Christina's face flamed with indignation at the injustice of his remark. 'I object most strongly—'

'Object all you like,' he snapped. 'When I issue an order to someone I expect it to be obeyed.'

Only a few hours before this tirade would have reduced Christina to quaking submission. But now it left her unmoved and angry. 'You are not in the army now, Lord Rockley,' she said, reverting back to formal address despite him asking her to address him by his Christian name. 'My brother and I are not your subordinates. If you cannot speak to me in a civil manner, then I will take my leave of you.'

Simon whirled round to face her. His face wore the same glacial mask it had displayed earlier. Indeed, it was so expressionless it might have been carved from stone. 'Be careful what you say,' he uttered harshly. 'And don't be misled by the fact that just a short while ago I showed myself indulgent in my dealings with you.'

'One might almost say more than indulgent!' Christina retaliated with calculated insolence. 'I remember when I attracted you and you desired me. I was almost ready to surrender myself completely to you without shame or remorse—to let you make love to me. You see I no longer felt as if I belonged to myself. Why do you look at me like that? Are you afraid of me—of what I make you feel?'

He looked at her directly in the eyes. 'Afraid? No, I'm not afraid of you or your blandishments. Do you really suppose you can fool me with pretty speeches? They trip so smoothly from your lips that one would have to be mad to believe them.'

Despite her intention of keeping her temper, Christina found herself provoked beyond endurance. To have her feelings spurned and vilified in this manner was intolerable. Earlier, on their ride together, she had ventured much too close, and without warning had suddenly found her heart hopelessly ensnared. Those mesmerising silver-grey eyes had the strength to weaken her knees as well as her wit and will and she realised the folly of having lowered her guard. How quick he had been to reject her, so quick to accuse her of being Mark's mistress. How harshly and contemptuously he had cast her from him. The insults he had flung at her seared and scorched her heart, but she would not be bowed.

Raising her chin proudly, she glared at him. 'Believe

what you like. It is nothing to me. As I said, I will leave now since you clearly find my presence displeasing. If you feel inclined to do so, you can wait for William to return from wherever it is he has gone. If not, I bid you good day.' She was turning towards the door when his voice rooted her to the spot.

'Don't you dare walk out on me. You will stay here and explain yourself.'

Christina paused and looked at him once more. Disappointment in him wrenched her heart. The image of the man she had erected had been too perfect, too handsome, too noble and too admirable to have been realistic. Now, seen through new eyes, she could not find a trace of gentleness or kindness anywhere in his tough, chiselled features. There was a ruthlessness stamped on his handsome face, implacable authority in the tough jaw line, and a cold determination in the thrust of his chin. Inwardly, she trembled at the hard cynicism she saw in his eyes and the biting mockery she heard in his voice when he spoke. It did not rise above its usual low timbre, but she was not deceived. He wanted answers and he would not leave until he had them. He came to stand in front of her, looming over her, his eyes glacial.

'Last night, when I heard voices—it was Bucklow leaving your room, wasn't it?' he said, his tone biting, demanding.

'Yes, it was,' she answered. Having done nothing to be ashamed of, she had no reason to deny it.

His blistering gaze sliced over her with absolute contempt and his face took on a look that to Christina appeared positively satanic. 'I thought so,' he went on, her look telling him all he needed to know. 'You are lovers.'

'That, my lord, was unworthy of you,' she protested in outrage. 'And as you said, it is none of your business.'

'It is for me to be the judge of what is or is not unworthy. And let me advise you to moderate your voice if you wish me to hear you out.' There was a pause in which he scrutinised Christina's pale face. 'And now,' he went on, 'now you will explain yourself. You will give me a complete and truthful account of everything. Do you understand? No more lies. No more deceit. I want the truth, and the whole truth. You would be unwise to attempt any more falsehoods. I read you too well.'

Christina dug her nails into the palms of her hands to keep them from trembling. The pang of misery that shot through her was unbearable. But not for anything would she have given him the satisfaction of seeing how deeply his words had hurt her. Bravely she lifted her head and stared very steadily into his eyes. In a voice devoid of emotion, she said, 'You wish to know everything. Very well, I will tell you. And I swear that it shall be the complete truth.'

She began her story, speaking haltingly at first, forcing herself to find words that would be simple and convincing. She told him of how, when their father had died, William had gone to London and met Mark Bucklow, how he had lost a fortune at the gaming tables and how Mark had loaned him some money to help pay off his creditors. She told how, to raise money for their everyday living, they had sold items of value out of the house, and how things had taken a more dangerous, sinister turn when Mark suddenly appeared and began using the chambers beneath the house for storing his ill-gotten gains. When William asked him to leave, he had refused.

'At first neither of us realised what it was all about. It was only when we met some of Mark's men that we knew it was something very different and no gay-hearted adventure. But through it all, even though we were aware that Mark is of the Catholic faith, we knew nothing about his Jacobite activities. You must believe that.'

During all this time, Simon did not interrupt, but as she talked Christina saw the tightening of his jaw and the ominous steely glint that came into his silver-grey eyes. When she had finished speaking, she met his eyes squarely and said, 'You know it all now. I swear to you that everything I have told you is true.'

'You knew what was happening. You are implicated in the crime. And Bucklow?'

'What about him?' Suddenly she became aware of what he was thinking. 'You really do think that we are lovers, don't you? You think that?'

'Your word is a frail defence against overwhelming evidence. My eyes do not lie.'

'If you will only let me explain—let me tell you—'

'No, Christina,' he said icily. 'No more. I have heard enough. I know how little your pretty speeches are to be trusted. I remember how you evaded the issue when I asked you about Bucklow. When I asked you if you knew his whereabouts, you told me you didn't. That was a blatant lie—for when he wasn't at the Black Swan Inn, he was here at Oakbridge, making use of your house for his criminal activities. At every opportunity your deception has got in my way. How you must have laughed when in good faith I asked you to trust me. I was a fool. You are to be congratulated, Christina. You have at artful tongue and great powers of persuasion that would put all the deviants I have ever known to shame.'

Christina backed away from him. She placed a shaking hand on the back of a chair as if needing support, but her eyes met his proudly with a look as cutting as steel. He had, in those few, brief moments, become a total stranger to her. An impenetrable barrier had been thrown up between them, without doors or windows, one she would never break down. She smiled contemptuously.

'You have it all worked out, don't you? Very well. I have nothing to say to you in my defence since I see little point in wasting my breath on someone whose ears and mind are closed. Please go now. No doubt you will be back to speak to William. Anything further you have to say to me, you will communicate through William.'

'Do not worry, you will not be questioned further,' he said, striding towards the door. 'After this I do not care a damn where you go or whose bed you occupy. You have a highly refined sense of survival and I have every confidence you'll land on your feet wherever you go. No doubt you'll join up somewhere with Bucklow. Wherever he is, Bucklow has an equally good sense of survival—but he cannot run for ever. I am sure the two of you will find a nice little hovel to roll about in somewhere.'

Unable to believe he was saying these cruel things to her, Christina's face went white with anger and her eyes glittered. 'How dare you?'

With his hand on the door handle Simon paused and looked back at her. 'But I do dare, Christina. You, my dear, are a born courtesan if ever there was, and you don't set too high a price on your charms.'

His words effectively destroyed Christina's last shreds of self-control. Nothing could have more blatantly underlined her wretched status in his eyes. 'For pity's sake—what have I done to you that you should treat me so?'

'What?' said Simon sarcastically. 'You need me to spell it out? That you could happily climb into bed with Bucklow only hours after leaving my arms? Who knows? Perhaps you were acting under instructions, and it was your way to wheedle information out of me while I was in the throes of passion. Congratulations. You drove me out of my senses for a time. I shall have to put it down to the fact that I haven't met whores as attractive as you, and now my senses are fully restored I see you for what you are.'

Mad with rage now, forgetting the passion he had awakened in her, Christina stalked with clenched fists to where he stood. 'I think, Lord Rockley, you should apologise to me for that.'

'Apologise? To Bucklow's whore?'

He spat the word at her. At this cruel attack she saw

red. The whole gentle interlude they had shared had turned into a humiliating farce. It was no use arguing, she realised, because this man was blinded and deafened by fury. She was about to turn from him when a sudden surge of pride made her lift her elegant head and fix scornful eyes on him.

'One day,' she said coldly, 'you will go down on your knees before me and beg my forgiveness for what you have just said to me. But I will not forgive you. You will get neither pardon nor mercy from me.'

As she turned from him his hand shot out and grasped her arm. In a soft, bloodchilling voice as he loomed over her, he said, 'Those are words you will *never* hear from me. When this is over I shall forget you as if you had never been. The next time we meet will be in a court of law when you are convicted. Be prepared to see your lover hang, and after that...'

Christina threw back her head insolently. 'You have cast me in the role of villain without granting me the courtesy of a hearing. No rightful magistrate in the land would dare convict a felon without a fair trial.' She gave a cold, mocking, maddening little laugh of contempt. 'If you were sitting on the judge's bench, you would joyfully have had me strung up beside Mark by now.'

'Aye,' he growled. 'You and your brother both—'

He would have gone on, but his furious diatribe was interrupted when Christina, beside herself with rage and indignation, dealt him a resounding blow across the face. The sight of the shock and surprise followed quickly by absolute rage that entered his eyes did not cause her the slightest twinge of regret. He had insulted her basely and she felt obscurely happy at having been able to inflict pain on him.

Mechanically, Simon raised a hand to his cheek, which was turning red. To all appearances it was the first time such a thing had happened to him and he was rendered speechless. Realising this, Christina threw her head back proudly and contemplated him with satisfaction.

'Forget me if you can, my lord, but after that I doubt you will be able to.'

When he'd gone, Christina stood staring at the closed door for a long time, her chest heaving with anger. Gradually she felt her strength leave her, to be replaced by a terrible pain in her heart. Would she ever see him again? What did it matter? What did his fury matter to her now? He had inflicted a cruel wound on her. What had happened was irrevocable. He scorned and despised her, and all because of a misunderstanding that she was too proud to clear up, and he was too stubborn to learn the truth.

He had wanted proof of her innocence, if he were interested in her at all, which she was now convinced he was not. When she looked at it from his side, she had not defended herself because she was guilty. What other excuse could she have had?

She closed her eyes, willing the tempest to calm inside her, and when she opened them again she took a deep, determined breath. Where was William? Where was her brother? She must go and look for him.

* * *

Simon left Oakbridge to ride to the magistrate's house. Tomorrow he would take a look at the chambers beneath Oakbridge where Bucklow had stored his stolen goods. In a state of anger and frustration, he rode his horse hard in an attempt to put his thoughts into proper perspective. He always found it diverting to race across the countryside on the back of a stallion without regard for speed or the terrain. Following his meeting with Christina, he wasn't in the mood to care, not when he wanted to take his mind off the cold, dark emptiness that had settled on his heart.

He rode past the place where he had kissed her, but the memory of that blissful time—was it just that morning?—darkened his mood further, for it brought to mind the difference a few hours passing could bring to a man's life. Could a woman who had so ardently yielded to his embraces, and still warm from those embraces, then turn so completely about face and callously give herself to another? If she was truly innocent and what he had witnessed was Bucklow taking advantage of her, why had she failed to defend herself? Was it because she had not wanted to add another falsehood to the list, adding further proof of her guilt?

When William had failed to come home that night, Christina's worries for his safety increased. Morbid images of him in serious peril assailed her relentlessly. As the hours of the morning ticked away and still he did not return, spurred on by a sharp goading fear that he had left because of his deep-rooted fear of Mark, after donning her riding clothes, she went to the stables.

Her mare seemed to sense her mistress's urgency, for when Christina touched her heels to her flanks, she leapt into motion. Soon they were racing down the lane towards their nearest neighbour—the first of many that she would visit that morning to enquire if they had seen William, but without success.

After two hours of riding about the countryside and having run out of ideas of where to look for him next, she turned for home, hoping that in her absence he would have returned. Peering up at the sky, she felt her heart sink and new fears congeal in her chest. The winds she had relished earlier had strengthened, bringing with them a roiling mass of black clouds that snuffed the last of the rosy glow from the horizon. Even as she started towards home, a jagged steak of lightning tore across the sky in a sizzling display of the storm's power. Droplets began to fall, first in a light sprinkling that washed the dust from the air and brought the sweet scent of rain, and a moment later she was being pelted by stinging rain as a torrential downpour marched across the land.

A groan of despair slipped from her as she urged her mare into the shelter of the trees and out of the punishing rain. The horse responded readily, quickening its pace, but even the trees offered small relief from the torrent of rain unleashed upon them. Floods of water poured down upon the earth, blurring the outlines of everything around her. Christina could barely see, and in no time at all her clothes became so thoroughly soaked that they clung to her like second skins.

Suddenly, to the side of her, a dark shape flitted through the trees. With her heart thumping in her breast, gazing over her shoulder she peered through the pounding rain. Nothing stirred and yet she could not shake off the feeling that someone was out there. Uneasy, she urged her mare forwards.

Looking around for better shelter, she suddenly realised that she was close to the entrance to the chambers beneath Oakbridge. Being surrounded by a thickly wooded area on all sides, they were well concealed. She was loathe to enter, but at least they would provide shelter from the storm. Long before she reached the chambers she was shivering and utterly miserable in mind and body. Dismounting, wind billowed beneath her wet cloak, sending a piercing chill through her as its frigid breath touched her soaked gown. Leaving her horse beneath a lean-to close to the entrance, she stumbled inside, taking a moment to adjust her eyes to the gloom.

Inside it was cold and damp and very still. Lighting a couple of candles, she sank down on to a pile of sacks. Peeling off her dripping cloak, no sooner had she done so than she became aware of someone outside. Watching the entrance in horror, terror seizing her heart, through a curtain of wet hair covering her face, she looked at the figure that pushed its way inside. His long cloak streaming with water, his face invisible under a wide-brimmed hat, she knew it must be the person she had glimpsed in the wood.

At first she thought it might be a member of Mark's gang of thieves who was not aware that the game was up, that his leader was being sought and that he should give their base a wide berth. Then she felt suddenly cold. It was not until he removed his hat and lifted his head that she saw it was Simon Rockley. If he was surprised to see her, he gave no sign of it. Those eyes of his, which she had only yesterday seen softened by tenderness, were hard and he held his head in just the same arrogant way.

Chapter Seven

'Well, well,' he said, and there was a touch of irony in his mocking tone. 'I thought Bucklow's gang of thieves would have deserted this place as fast as rats deserting a sinking ship.'

Christina looked at him, the cut on his lip and bruising on his face brutal evidence of his encounter with Mark's fists. Uneasy about being alone with him, she was conscious of the sudden tension and nervousness in her. She was uncomfortably aware of their last encounter the night before, and the scene flashed into her mind with all its searing pain and bitterness. Scrambling to her feet, she drew herself up, trying not to think of her uncomfortable, clinging wet clothes. The image of Mark Bucklow rose between them, intangible but strong, and an unexpected sense of pain filled Christina's heart.

With an effort, she said, in the coldest and most

condescending manner, 'Good day, Lord Rockley. I needn't ask what brings you in such haste to this place.'

He raised one thick, well-defined eyebrow, watching her. A faint half-smile played on his lips as if he knew exactly what was going on in her mind. 'No,' he replied, his gaze doing a quick sweep of the large chamber, noting the chests and sacks of stolen goods still stacked against the walls, before coming to rest on Christina once more. 'While I was out hunting a wild animal of the human kind, I glimpsed you in the woods. I took you for one of his cohorts and thought if I followed you you would lead me to his lair. As luck would have it that is precisely what you did. With a bit of luck he will return to it and be caught red-handed.'

'There are no wild animals in these parts, Lord Rockley, as you choose to call Mark Bucklow, only men trying to evade the law,' Christina retorted with sudden impudent defiance, resenting his effect on her, the masculine assurance of his bearing.

The flowing cloak accentuated the long lines of his body, and she noticed again how incredibly clear his eyes were in the flare of the candles, the flames wavering and setting strange shadows dancing around them. She was conscious of an unwilling excitement, seeing him arrogantly mocking and recklessly attractive. Here they were, just the two of them, together in this deserted place where only the elements ruled, in an atmosphere bristling with tension.

'If you think Mark will come back here then you are

in for a long wait,' she said belligerently, fiercely. 'He is clever and cunning, not stupid, as you seem to think.'

For a fleeting second the intensity of Simon's silver-grey eyes seemed to explode. An expression she did not understand flashed through them, then it was gone.

He smiled sardonically. 'And as I expected, I take note of how quick you are to defend him,' he remarked coldly. 'And you? If you are not here to meet up with Bucklow, what are you doing here?'

'Just in case you have not noticed, my lord, it is raining,' she uttered sarcastically. 'I am here for no other reason than to seek shelter.'

'It is foolhardy to be out riding in such weather.'

'It wasn't raining when I left the house. I was looking for William—he failed to come home last night and naturally I am anxious as to his whereabouts. As soon as the rain shows signs of abating, I will make my way back.'

'But you don't have to do that. You could return by way of the tunnel that connects the chambers to the house—as you did on the night of the party.'

'I could, but my horse might not take kindly to being dragged along a dark and narrow tunnel. Besides, it is locked at the other end, the key inside the house.'

Hands on hips, Simon glanced around. 'Then it looks as if we're stuck here together until it stops raining. We might as well make ourselves comfortable while we wait,' he said, removing his cloak and sitting on a large crate.

Christina's eyes struck sparks of indignation. 'You

are conceited if you think I welcome your company. My desire is for you to leave me be.'

'You would have me go out in this weather?'

Her trembling chin raised to a lofty angle as she eyed him coldly. 'Yes, if it would relieve me of your detestable company.'

He looked back at her coldly and sprang to his feet in one quick, effortless movement. 'You'll be rid of me soon enough, I promise you. Meanwhile, I'll take a look around.'

Christina cast her eyes around the chamber. 'What will you do with the things that are left here?'

'I shall inform Mr Cruckshank of what this place contains and he will see to it that the stolen goods are returned to their rightful owners.' He looked at her, noting as if for the first time that she was soaked to the skin. Her snarled, glistening hair was tangled around her head and shoulders, and her dark eyebrows and lashes were shocking streaks across her pale, wet face. Taking pity on her wretched state, he said, 'You really should go back to the house. You'll catch your death. I have a dry redingote rolled up behind my saddle. Shall I get it for you?'

The softening in his voice stung her to attention. His concern was the last thing she expected or wanted from him. Just when she had hardened her heart against him he had to appear anxious for her well-being. Remembering the door he had brutally slammed in her face, she glared at him mutinously.

'Spare me your concern. Keep your gallant offering, Lord Rockley. I have no use for it, and after your condemnation of me last night, I find it in poor taste.'

Simon arched a brow as he peered at her. 'Are you trying to convince me how foolish you are?'

'Foolish or not, I will not wear it.'

At first Christina thought he would insist, but then he shrugged and turned from her, and said, 'Suit yourself.'

With her cheeks and hands icy cold, Christina watched as he prowled about the chamber, contemplating several packages in thoughtful silence. She thought he had forgotten all about her, but after a while he turned and looked at her pointedly.

'I imagine you are concerned as to Bucklow's whereabouts. Fear not. If we fail to locate him, he may yet escape the scaffold—but I very much doubt it.'

'You do not understand—you will never understand,' Christina burst out before she could stop herself.

'I can understand only too well, but don't worry your lovely head—he may well come back to you, one way or another before he is captured—as will your brother when he deems it safe to do so.'

Christina's hands clenched so tightly that the knuckles showed white, her mouth tense with astonished rage. 'Now you go too far. How dare you?' she hissed, all fired up. 'Who are you anyway, to come here insulting me and my brother—you, who are not even good enough to lick William's boots. You aren't worth a tenth of him—you—you cold, arrogant, callous monster. Why don't you go away and leave us alone?'

His eyes met hers in fearless, half-challenging

amusement. 'Now it is you who goes too far. Licking boots is not my stock in trade.'

Christina struggled impotently for the last vestiges of thin control, feeling it crack under the strain as he studied her, unabashed. He stepped closer, and all at once, in her weakened state, she found his presence threatening. Their eyes met and held for a long moment, the retired military man and the English gentlewoman, and although neither abated their dignity, or their unspoken opposition, the attraction between them was almost palpable.

Christina had a strange sensation of falling. He was so close. She raised her hands to push him away, and at the same time a blast of cold air broke into the solitary world, bringing reality with it. She both hated and desired this detestable, beautiful man. So many conflicting emotions swirled inside her, fighting for ascendancy. All night long she had told herself to put him from her mind, to forget him. But now, as he stood close to her, he was more attractive than ever, more desirable, and the urgency to be even closer to him was more vivid than before.

Suddenly Simon caught her to him and, lifting her head, Christina stared straight into his eyes. Her face seemed to swell and become hot with mingled anger and desire.

'Will you please leave me alone? Let me go.'

'Why?' he said, moving closer still, ignoring the warning that told him to put some distance between them. Raising his hand, he gently brushed the gentle curve of her cheek with the back of one finger. 'Are you afraid of what you will do, Christina?'

'No, of course not,' she replied with less force, weakened by the gentle caress of his finger and making no move to resist.

His next move was less tender. His hands gripped her arms, his fingers hard as they dug into the flesh beneath the sleeves of her gown. 'It's time you forgot anything that you feel for Bucklow.'

'I'll scream if you don't let me go!' She struggled futilely against the strength of his arms that closed round her.

His hands abruptly caught her head. 'Will you, Christina?' His mouth swooped on hers so she couldn't breathe, and he kissed her with a bruising, passionate strength.

Christina fought against the rising passion within her as if her life depended on it. But soon she knew she would no longer resist. She no longer wanted to resist.

He kissed her throat, her cheeks, her mouth, talking now in a hoarse, almost inaudible voice. With his lips close to her face he was murmuring passionate endearments mingled with insults, only stopping to cover her mouth with his own. She forgot everything, her rancour and the awful things he had accused her of, and abandoned herself to him completely. Her skin warmed with colour, and, unable to resist him, eyes closed, she turned to meet his kisses with her own, instinctively slipping her arms around his neck.

When he dragged her down on to the sacks, she felt a bolt of excitement and fear explode through her belly as he raised her skirts and pried her stiff thighs apart. She shuddered when she felt his hand glide up her thigh and search out the centre of her womanhood with sure mastery. Never would she have suspected that a man's hand on that part of her body could give her such fierce pleasure, or that she would respond so wantonly—a wantonness that disguised her innocence.

'Who would have guessed you had such fire in you?' Simon whispered in a ragged voice close to her ear while he paused to unfasten his breeches and settled between her thighs.

His hands were urgent as they slid under the soft, full curves of her bottom and lifted her to meet him. Having no idea what to expect, Christina gasped, but found an extraordinary gentleness in his touch.

'Christina,' he murmured, his breath warm against her cheek. 'Tell me that you want this.'

Christina groaned as his rigid manhood probed boldly at her with urgent intensity. 'I want you.' When he thrust home, she arched her back and gasped with the sheer violence of it. She turned her face away to hide the pain she knew had crossed her features as he buried himself fully in her silken warmth. And then, as her pain gave way to a burning, aching need, the miracle happened. It struck like a spark from the collision of two people created for each other. Christina's whole being seemed to burst into flame as he drove into her more forcefully, giving her a woman's ultimate pleasure, and taking his own as he took her mouth with another devouring kiss.

Sensations she had never imagined overwhelmed her,

and she knew a joy that effaced everything. Apart from Mark's assault on her the previous day, she had no real intimate experience with men, especially one as powerful as Simon Rockley, and she was lost. Suddenly there was no cold, no rain, no resistance, only the burning of Simon's lips on hers, on her body, and the power she felt beneath her hands as they gripped his shoulders. Completely beyond himself, he held her down, letting himself go as he thrust over and over, deep inside her.

Christina's mind knew she should have resisted, but she wanted him to take her. Her traitorous body had a life of its own, making her realise just how vulnerable she was to this man. Still it responded, time after time in explosions of lust, meeting his passion with her own, her demands the same as his, shuddering with pleasure and pain as he held her wrists pinioned on either side of her head, until in the spiralling rapture there were no thoughts, only a union beyond time.

And then the wave of passion was over. The climax sweeping over Simon made him feel he was falling into a red-hot haven of pure sensation. Christina was left spent and motionless on the crude bed, the hot, spiralling world that had caught her in its grip slowly beginning to fade. They were both breathing heavily, and when he lifted himself up slightly and she felt him gently pull away from her, she opened her eyes and looked up at him. He was staring down at her, and behind the confusion she saw in his eyes, mirroring her own, was desire. Hot, burning desire mingled with shock. She shared it—it was the shock of strangers meeting one another naked. Her eyes flicked away.

What Simon saw when he stared down at her shook him to the core of his being. It jolted him back to the here and now, and out of whatever fantasy he had just strayed into. It was only then that he came to his senses, reminding him of the inevitable consequences of what he had just done. He knew he should move away from her, but he didn't want to, for the effort of doing so would be immense. Now he understood what the warning deep inside him had been about, realising too late that he should have heeded it.

Christina knew it, too. Her eyes clouded as they gazed into his. She was trembling from the lovemaking, but his fingers suddenly closed around her wrists and he pried her arms apart, away from his neck, away from him, and he was drawing away from her. Without the warmth of his body, the chamber was cold, but just thinking about what had happened between them was enough to make her warm.

Standing up, the metallic shade of his eyes was dim as he adjusted his clothing, trying not to look at her. The slender, writhing creature who had lain beneath him bore no resemblance to the remote lady who had graced the party at Oakbridge just two days ago. He was aware of an edge of frustration. He had taken without the chance to explore the soft flesh, to tease and tempt her into a state of heightened passion. Where had his mastery gone? His self-control had deserted him. And now, as he looked at her once more, he wanted her again.

'Forgive me,' he uttered hoarsely, clearing his

throat, the anger having deserted him. He looked uncomfortable. 'Are you all right?'

'Please—I am all right.'

'I am relieved to hear it.'

'Do not distress yourself on my account.'

'I did not mean to do that. It should never have happened. You will keep this between us if you wish to keep your brother's respect.'

Abruptly Christina sat upright. Stunned, stricken and dumb, she slowly got to her feet, cautiously testing her weak legs to ensure they could support her weight. He was about to turn from her, but she stopped him, laying a timid hand on his arm.

'Simon,' she murmured in a low, trembling voice, 'yours is the only respect I care about—and you are right. It shouldn't have happened—but it has, and there is nothing either of us can do about it.'

Acutely embarrassed now by what she had done— unable to believe what had just happened, what she had allowed to happen—flushing hotly, Christina avoided looking at him as she fastened her bodice with shaking hands. Not until she had covered herself did she look at him again.

Simon turned his head away, possibly to escape the soft bewitchment of those lovely, imploring eyes, and then, furious with himself and afraid that his resolve was about to weaken further, he moved away from her. Pausing in his stride, he turned very slowly, almost regretfully. He opened his mouth to speak, but no sound came.

Christina's eyes followed him for a moment as he

walked towards the entrance. His normally firm walk seemed strangely hesitant. And then he had gone. Simon had no idea as he left her of the immense joy that radiated through her whole being. In that short time they had been together she had known such happiness that her fear of everything that threatened her had been forgotten. If only Simon hadn't left her. It hurt her deeply to think that perhaps what they had done hadn't meant as much to him as it had to her. She had given herself to him because of deeper feelings she didn't quite understand, while he had forced himself on her and taken his pleasure of her, for instant gratification, to be forgotten and discarded.

Some would say that she had given herself to a man who would scorn her and that she was now a fallen woman, dirtied and corrupted and beyond forgiveness. Whatever the truth of it, she could not deny that she had sacrificed her virtue, her principles and her morals, and now she would have to live with it, but she felt no shame in what she had done.

But she was confused. She had meant what she said about having Simon's respect, but what they had done had complicated that. How would she ever look him straight in the eye again? How would she ever be able to turn to him with ease and trust? How could he ever look at her without remembering how she had turned into a wanton in his arms? It was as if a caged creature she had not known existed inside her had been set free. She had never felt like this before. It was as if her body was awash with feeling, alive with need.

Her body was limp and aching and still throbbing

with a strange sort of tension. Draping her cloak over her shoulders, she went outside. The rain had passed and the sun was warm now. Wincing with considerable discomfort, she mounted her horse and rode out of the dense woodland before coming to the path and following it to the house. On reaching the stables she saw Tom rubbing William's horse down. So, she thought, with little interest and certainly without any concern, he was back.

Tight lipped, Tom told her William had returned nursing the effects of a hangover after spending the night at a tavern in Reading. Without bothering to seek him out, Christina took refuge in her rooms where she could hide and think about the pleasure Simon had given her. Nothing else mattered.

After leaving Christina, Simon rode directly to the magistrate's house. Not until he was dismounting did he look down and see traces of blood on his breeches.

In various stages of shock, his face was incredulous, before becoming a mask of tortured anguish. Something shattered inside him, splintering his emotions from all rational control.

The blood was Christina's. It had to be. Good Lord! She was a virgin. He had just ravished a virgin.

A savage curse exploded from his chest. Whatever thoughts of revenge and wounded pride had driven him to make her yield to him, they were forgotten in a moment. She was not the lying temptress he had thought she was. She had given him the most satisfying sexual experience of his life. Whatever she had felt had been real and uncontrived, without any experience at all.

A surge of sickening regret ripped through him when he remembered all the coarse, vulgar things he had said to her, each degrading word he had spoken, and how he had shown her no more tenderness and consideration than a drunken lout. He would never have subjected her to that had he known. How could he have done that to her? How vulnerable she must be feeling now—and how she must hate him—and how confused and lonely and frightened she must be. He had taken her in desire and lust because he could not help himself, and he had left so soon afterwards because he didn't want the complications that would plague him.

Contrary to everything he had believed, Bucklow had not touched her. She had been innocent of deviousness all along—as innocent of it as she had been sexually innocent before he had touched her. But then, innocent, respectable young women did not visit men of Bucklow's character in their bedchambers. When he had found her in Bucklow's bed, he had witnessed no struggle on her part—in fact, she had appeared most compliant to his advances, which had given him reason to think that, had he not interrupted them, she might well have been on the verge of yielding her virtue to him.

But looking back, when he had entered the room, knowing the man who had killed his niece was within his grasp, Simon's rage had blurred his vision and twisted his mind so that he had no room in his sight for anything else. He recalled how upset Christina had appeared as she had proclaimed her innocence, calling Bucklow a wretch who used people to serve his own interests, accusing him of treating her in a barbarous manner—and Simon hadn't given her a chance to explain further. Now he also recalled the emotions he had seen flitting across her face and how vulnerable she had looked—and very frightened. What was the real reason for her being at the Black Swan alone? Was she being threatened by Bucklow? Was that it—and if so, why?

Handing the reins of his horse to a groom, as he strode towards the house he considered how much of his findings into Bucklow's activities he should reveal to Sir John. The magistrate, along with everyone else in the surrounding district, knew nothing of how William Atherton had foolishly allowed himself to become involved with Bucklow. As far as he was concerned, there was no need for Sir John to know. In the event of Bucklow being captured and Lord Atherton exposed, then that was a complication he would deal with when it happened.

Where William Atherton's sister was concerned, overwhelmed with an attack of conscience and duty—and more than a little guilt—he would do his utmost to keep her out of it.

The following days were nerve racking for William and Christina as they awaited news. They both expected someone to come and question or arrest them—and the worse scenario was that Mark would find them and exact his revenge. When nothing happened, they began to breathe more easily, but they were not deluded into believing they were off the hook.

As Christina knew it would, William was affected by melancholy, for the fear of being arrested or accosted by Mark made him bad tempered and sullen. He spent most of his time in his room or prowling around the house, refusing to go out or to receive callers. Expecting the full extent of his involvement to be uncovered at any time, he could not bear to feel the eyes of his friends, his neighbours, speculative, curious, even grimly amused, as if his woes served only to mark another tragedy that one could relate to the next gossip avid for another's misery.

Christina forced herself to smother all thoughts and feelings for Simon. What had happened between them had been a sudden and overwhelming irresistible passion. It had shown her something of the man beneath the worldly, rugged surface. It was not so much what had happened between them, but his attitude afterwards that had affected her more deeply than she knew. He had walked away. He had left her, rejected her in some irreparable way, and in doing so he had hurt her deeply.

She wished he had never touched her—at least she was wishing she could wish he had never touched her and that she could stop thinking about the things he had whispered to her as his hands had moved over her flesh, expertly evoking a willing response from her traitorous body. Try as she might not to think of him, in her quiet moments her thoughts often turned to him, and even when sleep embraced her, she had no respite, for he filled her dreams. She knew every detail of his powerful presence—the unforgettable moulding of his face, his body, his eyes, the beautiful mouth—the look and feel of him, the clean fresh smell of him when he was close, things she should not know and would be better off forgetting.

Three weeks passed in this way, and the days began to blend into one long unvarying stream until it was finally broken by the arrival of the magistrate. After expressing his concern on finding William indisposed, looking well pleased with himself, over tea Sir John informed Christina that he had received stringent orders from Lord Rockley that it would be absurd to associate her in any way with Mark Bucklow, and that her name was in no circumstances to be mentioned in connection with the affair.

Everything the magistrate said was true, for beneath a remarkably forbidding exterior, Lord Rockley concealed a considerable degree of subtlety. Bucklow's capture, quickly followed by his escape from the Black Swan Inn, caused none of the stir that might have been expected. The only witnesses had been a handful of locals attracted by the commotion at the Black Swan, who had shrugged and gone about their business when it was all over.

'So you see, as far as you are concerned, my dear Miss Atherton, and the curiosity your presence at the inn aroused, Lord Rockley's speed to affirm your innocence in this matter was immediate and categorical.'

'I am grateful to Lord Rockley for his thoughtfulness and concern,' Christina murmured, carefully avoiding

Sir John's eyes. Though innocent of any wrongdoing, she felt as if she were guilty of the most diabolical subterfuge known to man, and had to wonder if her conscience would ever recover.

'That is exactly what he is—concerned about you. When you learned where Bucklow was hiding out, it was indeed a relief to Lord Rockley when you informed him and led him there yourself so as not to alert Bucklow to Lord Rockley's imminent arrival with the constables.'

'He—he told you that?' Christina hated falsehoods, but knew it was needful to cast suspicion away from herself as well as from William.

'Indeed he did, and he was quick to comment on your bravery in the matter.'

Christina listened to Sir John's words with an attentive frown. She thought she could not be more surprised, but Simon Rockley was an enigma. She didn't understand his sudden determination to exonerate both herself and William from the affair, but she was immensely relieved that he had done so.

But then came a feeling of hope and her spirits began to rise for the first time in months. She had been wretched for so long, but she was young and it was against her whole nature to remain miserable for long. Suddenly she felt that in some miraculous way things might not be as black as they appeared.

It was with difficulty that she said, 'I am indeed grateful to Lord Rockley. Please convey to him my thanks when next you meet.'

'I shall indeed. Lord Rockley's investigations have blown the whole sorry business wide open. Bucklow's organisation is in ruins. He is an outlaw and will be caught. And who would have thought it—to use your own chambers here at Oakbridge as his base—and right under your brother's nose. Why, the audacity of the man.'

'Indeed,' Christina murmured drily.

'But then, I understand the chambers have not been used in a long time and although they are connected to the house, they are some distance away. I would not think your brother would have known what was going on. To suspect him of doing so when he has always behaved as a sincere friend to me would be a monstrous thing to do.'

'Have you visited the chambers yourself, Sir John?'

'I have—and they are so concealed as to have been ideal for Bucklow's purpose. All manner of stolen goods—from jewels, paintings and silver to other costly treasures—were found there. All would fetch a tidy sum. If the horde is anything to go by, I imagine Bucklow has enriched the Jacobites by almost unbelievable wealth. The goods have now been removed and will be returned to their rightful owners. There is a tunnel connecting the chambers to the house, is there not, Miss Atherton?'

'Yes—which William has recently had sealed up to deter any unwelcome visitors.'

'Very sensible. Some of Bucklow's cohorts have been rounded up—others have scattered to continue their foul deeds in another county, no doubt. Lord Rockley continues to search for Bucklow and at present is following a lead given to him by one of the criminals—hoping for leniency—that he has gone to London to wind up some unfinished business, before fleeing to France to join his fellow Jacobites. If that is the case, then good riddance is what I say. We have news that the young James Stuart has sailed from Dunkirk with a large contingent of French troops in nearly thirty ships, and that he is heading for Scotland.'

'And what will that mean?'

'Well, I can tell you that the British fleet and its intelligence service are not asleep. Already a strong British squadron has taken up its station. In London there is a certain panic, but everyone has rallied to the Queen. Knowing this, perhaps Bucklow will hide out somewhere and wait and see what happens next.'

As Christina showed Sir John out of the house, she felt as if an enormous weight had just been lifted from her mind. Indeed, she likened the magistrate's visit to a reprieve from a death sentence.

When Christina told William of Sir John's visit and Lord Rockley's attempt to absolve him from involvement in Mark Bucklow's crimes, his melancholy vanished and his temper was restored, but his fear of Mark returning was never far away.

The magistrate's visit was immediately followed by the arrival of Squire Kershaw and his daughter, Miranda, who was dressed as always in the very height of fashion. With dark hair and deep brown eyes, Miranda Kershaw was a very pretty, happy and lively young woman. She was the precious only child of her widowed father, Squire Kershaw, a wealthy wool merchant in

Cirencester supplying the clothing trade. Miranda had been granted as much access to life as she could have wished for. With perfect manners, excellent conversation, being much travelled and with highly developed powers of social observation, her talents made her therefore uniquely positioned to become William's wife and mistress of Oakbridge.

On entering the house, she stood for a moment in the doorway, looking around her, and before Christina could voice her welcome, a joyful William stepped forward to greet his betrothed.

'Miranda! By all that's wonderful!'

There was a little scream from the delightful vision, then impetuous and rapturous, she ran forwards leaving a whiff of expensive perfume on the air as she passed Christina to fling herself at William, pressing her cheek to his.

'Oh, William—my own dear, darling William,' she enthused, pressing butterfly kisses all over his face. 'I have missed you terribly. You have no idea how much.'

For a moment both their voices merged together incoherently, both talking so quickly that it was impossible to differentiate what they said. Until, finally, straightening her bonnet, which had become disarranged in the excitement, Miranda stepped back and held out her hand to greet Christina, who stood beside Squire Kershaw, looking on with amazement.

'Christina—how good it is to see you. I am so happy to be at Oakbridge at last—which I hope to make my home very soon. Indeed, Papa and I would like you to come with us to Cirencester for the wedding.'

'Wedding?' William repeated, unable to believe Miranda's haste to bring about their union.

'Yes, William, my love,' Miranda cooed, stroking his face as if it were the most precious thing in the world to her. 'I have counted every hour and every minute of our long separation, and I cannot bear to be apart from you any longer. All I want in life is you. When we were apart I thought I would die, I was so unhappy. And yet there was nothing I could do.' She gave a deep sigh, as if the memory of her unhappiness still had the power to hurt her. 'Do say you want what I want—for us to be married as soon as possible.'

'But—of course—you know I do,' William answered, the glow in his eyes almost dazzling. 'Indeed, there is nothing in the world I want more, but—what of your father?' he said, looking directly at his future father-in-law.

'Papa is in agreement, is that not so, Papa?' Miranda said, looking at her sire with her big, eloquent eyes.

Squire Kershaw laughed lightly, holding up his hands in surrender, as he had done many times in the past. He would do almost anything to indulge this precious daughter of his. 'I have no objections—none at all. I trust you have no objections, Miss Atherton?'

'None whatsoever. I am so glad William will have Miranda to look after him—and keep him out of mischief.' Her words, though spoken lightly, had more meaning than either Squire Kershaw or his daughter realised. A slight indignant flush swept over William's face, but when he realised his sister wasn't going to enlarge on her statement, he relaxed once more. 'I am sure they will be very happy together.'

Miranda laughed, a light tinkling sound. 'I will let you into a little secret, Christina. I shall keep William very busy. A man who is busy has no time for mischief.'

'Are you quite sure you don't mind having a man for your husband whose wealth has taken a bit of a battering of late? If you are, it is what I want also,' William said with a humility that Christina would not have expected of him. He looked at the portly gentlemanly looking on. 'I'm sorry, sir, but the Oakbridge estate has seen better times and will do so again—only lately...'

Squire Kershaw held up his hand. 'Think nothing of it—we all suffer setbacks from time to time. Perhaps I can proffer some assistance in that direction, which we will discuss another time. All I know is that if you do not marry my daughter, then she will remain a spinster for the rest of her life.'

'And what a tragedy that would be, my love,' Miranda purred, placing her hand affectionately in William's. 'You would not wish that on me, would you, my love?'

'Absolutely not, so I suppose there is nothing for it but for us to marry very soon,' William murmured, kissing her hand once more.

They all travelled to the Kershaw residence in Cirencester for the wedding, which was a very happy, though quiet affair. It was attended by just close family and a handful of friends. On returning to Oakbridge, Christina found a letter waiting for her from her Aunt Celia. Knowing how Christina loved Oakbridge and the country, her aunt wrote that she did not imagine she could provide the variety of changes she sought, but on showing her niece the town and introducing her to new friends, she might not miss Oakbridge quite so much.

As Miranda settled into her duties as mistress of Oakbridge, Christina found herself looking forward to her departure much more eagerly. In his new-found happiness, William seemed completely oblivious to the fact that Mark Bucklow was still at large, and, until he was captured, posed a threat. Christina, however, was of a different mind. Mark believed they had betrayed him, and it would be a mistake to assume he would forget.

The testing time came when Mark rode boldly up to the front door at Oakbridge. Having seen him approaching from an upstairs window, Christina hurried downstairs and opened the door before he could dismount. He looked tired and unkempt, making Christina wonder where he had been hiding out—a thought she dismissed immediately. She really didn't care.

'What's the matter, Mark? Have you run out of places to hide? Then again, if you have thieving on your mind, I suggest you leave right now. Thieves who break into other people's houses hold no terror for me. We're fresh out of valuables at this house, so you'll be wasting your time.'

'Feisty, unafraid and as spirited as ever, I see,' he growled.

'I haven't changed, if that's what you mean. What do you want?'

He advanced his horse closer. His eyes narrowed and began to glitter dangerously. His smile was unpleasant. 'I need somewhere to lay low for a while. Oakbridge is big enough to put me up for a few days.'

His high-handed manner had an unexpected effect on Christina. She did not flinch before the barely concealed menace. Her shock on seeing him again gave way to anger rather than fear. How dare he come here? She had no intention of complying with his demands and she told him so. But with anger came prudence and she stepped back as he continued to nudge his horse forwards.

'I told you. I need somewhere to hide. No one will think to look for me here.' When he made a move to dismount, a voice rang out behind Christina.

'Remain on your horse and leave.' William appeared to stand beside his sister, a pistol in his hand. 'You are not welcome here.'

Mark shrugged unconcernedly. 'And you think I care about that, do you, William? You know me.'

'Aye, I know you. You're a wanted man.'

'Only because you betrayed me, damn you.'

'William didn't betray you,' Christina told him coldly. 'No one did.'

Mark's eyes shifted from William to Christina. 'I know you went running to Rockley. How else could he have known where to find me?'

'I didn't tell him. He must have followed me to the Black Swan Inn that day. But I told William that if you did not comply with my wishes and leave us alone, I would go to Lord Rockley and tell him everything.'

'What else did you tell William?' he sneered, shifting his gaze to her brother. 'Did she tell you how I nearly had my way with her? She looks real fetching when she's all worked up. There's no one I ever saw that has her beauty. And she's more resourceful than most. It's only thanks to Rockley's timing that she got away from me—slippery as an eel, she is.'

William's lips twisted with contempt. 'You'd be dead now if you had taken her. If you know what's good for you, you'll stay away from her in the future. It wrenches my gut to think I unwittingly had any part in your Jacobite affairs. To steal from people and instil fear into them is one thing, but your plot to kill the Queen and install the Catholic James on the throne was insane. You are not welcome at Oakbridge. Leave to whatever ends you might find—although I would advise you to have a care. Lord Rockley is still looking for you. If you don't want him to find you, you'd be advised to find a deep, deep hole in which to hide in. Otherwise I shall send for the magistrate and let him deal with you.'

'Like hell you will,' Mark snarled beneath his breath. 'Damn you, Atherton. I'll kill you first, you clever young pup.'

So saying, Mark swiftly produced a pistol from beneath his coat, but before he could fire, William had raised his own and fired, sending Mark's pistol crashing to the ground. Mark looked from the pistol to William, completely startled. It was apparent from the surprise on his face that he hadn't thought William had it in him to shoot anyone. It came as a shock to him to find that he wasn't just pursuing a helpless woman, but a gutless boy transformed to a spirited man, as well.

It was only when Mark clutched his shoulder that Christina realised that he'd been hit and only remained in the saddle out of sheer determination. Glowering at them both, without another word he dragged his horse round and rode away.

'Let's hope we've seen the last of him,' William said, placing an arm about Christina's waist. 'With any luck, Rockley will catch up with him before he escapes to France.'

Christina looked at her brother, admiring the way he had just asserted himself. He had become more sure of himself of late. She noticed his own pride in his accomplishments and knew she had Miranda to thank for bringing him out of his shell. She had given him understanding and love, and the will to stand on his own two feet and stop blaming others for his state.

It was the feeling of nausea that first alarmed Christina, its continuation making her feel thoroughly wretched. It happened all the time now. At first she thought she was sickening for something, then, as the tenderness of her breasts became apparent, the idea that she was with child, that she was carrying Simon Rockley's child, hit her like some cold, unwelcome shock wave.

In her innocence, she had not thought of this. As she had lain under him, she had not considered the consequences of his act. She had thought the failure of her monthly cycle to be because she was upset with everything that had happened. But now she knew differently. Choking back a sob of great agitation, she knew she was going to have a baby—a baby, by the man who had accused her of terrible things, had called her a whore before ravishing her and discarding her so cruelly.

There was no doubt whatsoever in her mind. How stupid and naïve she had been. She should have expected this from a man like him. Strong and full blooded, he had impregnated her with an ease she found maddening.

Slowly the wretched tears began to flow. She wrung her hands together. What could she do? How could she tell William? Everyone would know in a few months of her pregnancy. What would they say? People would say that she was a wanton woman, a strumpet—unless she went to a retreat somewhere where she could hide away for the rest of her life. Or she could go to her aunt in London right away. Faced with a situation she did not know how to deal with, the mere thought of her sensible, level-headed Aunt Celia raised her spirits. She would tell her what to do.

Chapter Eight

Aunt Celia, Christina's mother's sister, was also her godmother. She had married wisely and well a man with a high position in the government, who had died young. With no children of her own and no desire to marry again, at the demise of her sister, Celia had taken Christina under her wing. Indeed, she had wanted Christina to live with her ever since her father had died. Being of slight build, with a face that had once been beautiful and an abundance of snow-white hair for ever escaping its pins, Celia had a cool head about her. She was also warm, open and affectionate. But no matter how open-minded her aunt was, Christina knew that when she made her confession it would have its painful moments.

She occupied a very pleasant town house overlooking Green Park. It was somewhat old fashioned in its furnishings, but Christina had spent some very pleasant times here as she had been growing up, so both these qualities endeared the house to her.

Leaving the servants to unload Christina's baggage, Celia conducted her into the house, gazing at her in delighted astonishment, her kindly blue eyes twinkling at her. 'It has been too long since I last saw you, Christina—too long—and now look at you. You are even more lovely that your mother, beauty that she was. I am so glad you are here and that you have taken me up on my offer to make this your home. We shall have so much fun together. But good heavens, lovely you are, but so pale. Let me kiss you.'

And she did, taking her niece in her arms and hugging her with an enthusiasm that left their mutual feelings in no doubt.

'Come and sit by the fire and let me look at you. My maid will bring us refreshment and you can tell me all about Oakbridge and William's marriage to Miss Kershaw. How exciting it must have been. I'm so glad he's settled down at last. I also want to know what you have been doing.'

Christina smiled a little nervously. The moment she dreaded had arrived. She was determined to face up to it at once, without any attempt at prevarication. Over the years her aunt had become someone very dear. She deserved to be told the truth. Besides, she, Christina, longed to confide in someone, and she had no one else.

'The story I have to tell may not be to your liking, Aunt Celia.'

Settling herself into her chair on the opposite side

of the hearth, Celia dismissed Christina's words with a wave of her hand. 'Nonsense. I am passionately fond of stories. Take as long as you like. We have plenty of time. I will hear you to the end.'

'You cannot imagine the things that have been going on at Oakbridge since we parted. Indeed, there are times when I wonder if it was really true or just a dreadful nightmare.'

Celia sat forwards in her chair. Her sharp eyes saw that all was not as it should be, that something serious troubled her lovely niece, and it had nothing to do with leaving her beloved Oakbridge. 'What do you mean? I am beginning to worry. What has happened to you, child?'

'I will tell you,' Christina said quietly. 'It will not be easy—and afterwards you might want to send me packing back to Oakbridge.'

'Then you do not know me. Come, now, Christina, I will not be put off.'

And so Christina told the whole sorry story, telling her aunt of William's gambling, his debts, and how he had fallen into the company of Mark Bucklow and its dire consequences. The words seemed to come of their own accord and in the telling of all she had been through, Christina felt as though some of the burden was lifted, but William's behaviour brought condemnation from her aunt.

'That foolish, foolish young man,' Celia retorted crossly. 'What a disappointment he has turned out to be. He had every opportunity to make something of himself, to make his father proud and look after his sister.

Instead, what does he do? He throws it all away for the amusements to be found here in London. It's a disgrace, an absolute disgrace. And this Bucklow fellow? Has he been apprehended?'

'No, unfortunately not.'

'Then let us hope he is caught before he decides to avenge himself on your weak-minded brother.'

Christina blanched at these harsh words. 'It's what we all hope for, Aunt.'

'Of course you do. But there is more, isn't there, Christina?'

Swallowing hard, she nodded. 'Yes, I'm afraid there is.'

Telling her aunt about her relationship with Lord Rockley was a different matter entirely, for Christina found it difficult discussing such intimate things. For a moment she hesitated, but her aunt's fading blue eyes regarded her with such a spontaneous sympathy that, lowering her gaze, she continued with her story, falling silent after she quietly announced that she was carrying Simon Rockley's child.

Christina feared her aunt's reaction to this, but the old lady was not without experience. Leaning forwards, she patted her goddaughter's hand as it lay on her lap and sighed deeply.

'And to think I thought I had led an exciting life. You, my dear, leave me standing.'

Christina raised her eyes and almost timidly asked, 'You are not shocked?'

'Indeed I am. I would be lying if I said I wasn't.'

'I'm sorry. I know how disappointed you must be,'

Christina said forlornly, looking down at her hands. 'I've brought disgrace to my family.'

Celia smiled at her gently. 'Nonsense, my dear. Sometimes a girl cannot help the things that happen to her. She's just a victim of circumstance.'

'Or Lord Rockley,' Christina murmured.

'Or Lord Rockley. Thank goodness you did not try to keep this from me—although it was not what I expected to hear. I do not blame you. You found yourself in a situation where you had no choice—you merely followed your heart.' She cocked her head on one side and eyed her niece quizzically. 'This Lord Rockley. What are your true feelings for him? Are you in love with him?'

Christina shook her head. What could her aunt be thinking of to ask such a preposterous question? Had she not understood anything she had told her? For a second Simon's tall figure seemed to invade the quiet room, but Christina thrust it back.

'In love with him? No—no, of course I'm not in love with him.'

'So why do I see shadows in your eyes when you speak of him?'

'I allowed myself to become—vulnerable,' Christina whispered.

'And the child? Lord Rockley will do the honourable thing and marry you, I trust?'

Christina grimaced. 'If he does, he will do so for the child alone.'

'Christina, you are a lovely young woman, inside and out, whom any man would be glad to marry for herself alone. Lord Rockley is lucky to have you, regardless of the manner of it.'

'I wish I could believe that,' Christina replied. 'But even if we were to marry, it is all so complicated.'

Celia's eyes narrowed as a thought occurred to her. 'Am I to understand that he knows nothing of the child?'

Christina shook her head. 'No. I have not told him—indeed, I have not laid eyes on him since…'

'Then he must be told. He has a right to be told. Then you and he will work it out.'

So torn about her emotions was Christina that tears stung her eyes. 'It is not that simple. If he rejects me, how will I bear it?'

'Christina, none of us can predict what others might do. You care for this man. I know it—no matter how you try to hide it. You just have to allow love into your heart.'

'I don't know if I can,' Christina whispered at last.

'You will, and in the meantime we must work out what's to be done.' She glanced at her niece, a sudden frown creasing her brow. 'You—do intend informing Lord Rockley that he's to be a father, don't you, Christina?'

'Yes. I think I must. As you said, he has a right to know.'

'And the sooner the better. Where is he now?'

'I believe him to be here in London. He has reason to think this is where Mark Bucklow can be found.'

'I see. Then I shall make enquiries as to where he is staying. It shouldn't be too difficult tracking him down.'

* * *

The following day began a period of social activity for Christina as her aunt escorted her to several minor social events. Attending concerts, plays, visiting museums and one exhibition after another was part of a cultural repertoire that shaped Celia's everyday life. For Christina these were occasions when she could become reacquainted with old friends. It was only after two weeks of being in London, at a party given in the Assembly Rooms close to Charing Cross, that her aunt finally ran Lord Rockley to ground.

It was a well-attended affair. The noise of the throng, the heat and the music hit them when they entered the ballroom, where an orchestra played on a raised platform at one end of the room. It was a kaleidoscope of colour, of dazzling ball gowns, men in brightly coloured waistcoats of silks and satin, and powdered wigs of every description. Celia was a popular figure and was at once surrounded by her friends.

When Christina was being led off the floor by her partner after dancing a minuet, a man appeared in the doorway. Christina recognised Simon instantly. Her heart gave a fearful leap and she swayed on her feet. She caught a glimpse of his aristocratic profile and tall and erect figure, whose every line was eloquent with haughty contempt. She watched as he greeted a friend and then turned to survey the scene, a bored expression on his darkly handsome face.

As if he knew she was there, he turned his head slowly. His sombre gaze met her own and stayed there without flinching. His mouth lifted in a slow, amused smile, and, raising a finely arched brow, he inclined his head to her in the merest mockery of a bow. Conscious of those searing eyes upon her, Christina trembled. With unsteady fingers she clutched her gown at her bosom, remembering that powerful gaze that seemed to strip the clothes from her body.

He disappeared as the party guests surged around in a rough swell of movement. Christina turned away, but his presence was like a long, drawn-out torture for her. Throughout the evening she talked, smiled and graciously accepted the attentions and compliments that her beauty attracted. But all the while her eyes sought out Simon Rockley.

Celia rarely left her side. When a friend told her that Lord Rockley had arrived at the assembly, she scanned the guests until her gaze fell on the man she was sure was responsible for her niece's wretched condition.

'Is that Lord Rockley?' she asked Christina.

'Yes, that's him,' Christina replied, trying hard not to look at him.

'I thought so. He's terribly handsome, isn't he?' Celia noted that the gentleman was surrounded by several young ladies. With heightened colour on their cheeks and eager gazes, they all vied for his attention. Lord Rockley, she noted, was treating them with a bored, amused tolerance. His attention was on the only woman in the room who was immune to his magnetism. Christina.

* * *

Across the room, Simon had to drag his gaze from Christina and force himself to converse with his friends, so that he wouldn't meet her gaze and wouldn't start wanting her. *Wanting her?* he thought with bitter disgust. He had started wanting her ever since he had seen her that day by the stream, and he wanted her no less badly now, within minutes of seeing her again.

Clad in a gown of sapphire-blue silk spangled with silver, her hair perfectly arranged in curls around her perfectly shaped head, she made his body harden with lust. He glanced at two of the ladies in his group—both beautiful women, beautifully gowned and coiffed, their manners impeccable. Neither one of them would have considered removing their stockings and dipping their bare feet into an ice-cold stream, or attempting to rescue a dog from a trap of thorns. But then, neither one of them would have looked so wonderful had they tried.

In the past he'd thought Christina was some kind of sorceress because she'd mesmerised him so completely. Now he tried not to look at her, but he could actually feel her gaze on him. The glances were soft and inviting. They infuriated him and made him want her more, for didn't he know what it was like to feel her writhing beneath him, to have his hands all over her body? Christina alone knew what she could make him want—and make him remember.

He knew about her brother's marriage and that Christina had come to London to live with her aunt soon afterwards. He had also known that she would be at the Assembly Rooms tonight. Knowing this, he had been driven by a ridiculous eagerness to see her again. He had been tormented by the manner of their parting. He had left her in anger and confusion, when he should have offered her firm but gentle moral support. By now that beautiful, spirited girl had probably worked herself into a fit of rebellion because he had made no contact with her since he had taken her virtue.

Simon's loins tightened as he recalled the way she yielded to him, having surrendered her maidenly inhibitions. The sweet desire she felt for him had been there. She had wanted him, and he had wanted her more than he had ever wanted anything in his life.

Observing the beautiful young woman swirling around the floor in the arms of a good-looking young swain, suddenly furious with his weakening resolve, he excused himself and moved away from his group. He would leave and go to his club, where he intended to drink himself into a private stupor if that's what it would take to keep him from going to her. Yet there she was, standing beside an elderly lady—her aunt, he thought—and, as if his feet moved of their own volition, he found himself heading in her direction.

Christina watched Simon approach, her mouth dry. A tall, slender-hipped, broad-shouldered man, Simon Rockley was as handsome of physique as he was of face. Attired in silver-grey silk and white shirt and stock, he looked the part of landed gentry. His chiselled profile was touched by the warm light of innumerable candles, and the growing ache in her chest attested to the degree of his handsomeness.

Now the moment had arrived, Christina turned her thoughts back to her present predicament and cringed inside at the thought of the outcome. Suddenly she was reluctant to speak to him. As he strode nearer, there was something about his measured stride that suggested the implacable approach of Fate itself. Her heart suddenly started thumping wildly. It was this that she had been dreading, as Lord Rockley no doubt felt obligated to dance with her.

When she thought of the manner of their parting, that he had left her to face what he had done to her completely alone—and the cruel things he had accused her of prior to this—she was tempted to turn her back on him and walk away. But to do that or to refuse to dance with him outright would publicly humiliate him and herself, yet her fierce pride ached to do precisely that. He was a man of such arrogance, she would love to deflate him. He might have saved her from Mark Bucklow's lust and covered up William's part in that Jacobite affair, but she refused to be the object of any man's pity and was frantically searching for a way to balance common sense with pride when he halted before her.

Simon bowed with a grand, sweeping gesture. 'May I have this dance, Miss Atherton?' His heart slammed into his ribs when she raised her eyes and met his gaze. Try as he might, he'd been unable to wipe her from his mind this past two months, and now, being in the same room as her only made his desire stronger. Why did he lose all restraint when he was near her?

Doing her best to avoid her aunt's curious gaze,

Christina lifted her chin, keeping her voice low so only he would hear. 'You honour me with your request, Lord Rockley, but surely you would enjoy the dance more with another choice of partner.' She gave the slightest of nods to other young ladies plainly eager to dance with him.

Simon gave no more than a flicker of a glance in their direction before settling his eyes on Christina once more. 'I am single-minded in my pursuits. It is you I wish to dance with, Miss Atherton. Had I wished to partner anyone else, I would have asked them.'

'Then what can I say except that I accept. But before you whisk me into the dance, Lord Rockley, I would like to introduce you to my aunt, Mrs Celia Slater. Aunt Celia, you remember I told you about Lord Rockley and his pursuit of a certain criminal who was terrorising the neighbourhood around Oakbridge.'

Celia's eyes locked on to those of the handsome Lord Rockley and she smiled assuredly. 'You did indeed, Christina. It's a pleasure to meet you, Lord Rockley. I wish you every success in bringing that particular criminal to justice.'

'Thank you, Mrs Slater. I have every confidence that I shall—and I would like to say that it's a pleasure to meet you, too.'

Purposefully Simon took Christina's arm and guided her on to the dance floor as the strains of the music filled the room. They began to dance, slowly at first, until the rhythm of the music eased their tensions and they began to unbend. The enchanting chords began to entrance them as each was filled with the other's presence. They moved with the music and swept and swirled around the floor. Christina knew only that Simon's arm was around her and his dark, handsome face above her. He was conscious only of her softness within his embrace, the delicate scent of her perfume, and the dark, mysterious blue of her eyes.

'I must thank you for—for not divulging William's part in that awful business at Oakbridge,' Christina said when they had to slow down because of the sheer crush of dancers all vying for the same space on the floor. 'I have been thinking what would have happened to him if—if he had been arrested. I can only say thank you.' It was an effort to force the words from between her teeth, although in fairness she knew they must be said.

For a moment she thought he was going to laugh, but instead he replied, 'I did not do it for your brother. I did it for you. Had he been arrested, you would have been forced to share the grim consequences that would be immediate and unavoidable, for it would have been nigh impossible to convince everyone he didn't know what was going on at Oakbridge. You did not deserve that.'

'Yes—thank you. Although there is always the danger that someone will talk. After all, Mark's men were convinced William knew what was going on.'

'The men you speak of—those who are still at liberty—are scattered far and wide and only interested in saving their own hides. Worry not, Christina. You can relax. I have quashed any rumours connecting you and your brother to the crime. To his credit, William's abhorrence for the Jacobites is well known. No one will believe he allowed them to use Oakbridge to further their cause. Since I don't want it spread about any more than you, it will be our deep, dark secret.' He raised a brow as he queried, 'Do we understand each other?'

She nodded. 'Yes. Both William and I are grateful for what you have done. And—and Mark?' she dared to ask, hesitantly, bravely. 'You—have no word of him?'

Simon's lips twisted in a semblance of a smile, the angry look that entered his eyes telling Christina that the moment of intimacy that had kept them entranced at the beginning of the dance had vanished. As soon as the words had passed her lips, she regretted having asked, for as things stood between her and Simon just then, she might have been wiser to keep quiet. But she had never learned to resist the impulse of her heart, especially where important matters close to her family were concerned.

'It matters to you, does it, Christina, what happens to him?'

'I ask only out of concern. I—I would like to know what has happened to him—yes.'

'Then be content when I tell you that I am on his trail. I have approached several of his associates here in London—all connected to the criminal underworld, I might add. He has unfinished business with them— they owe him money apparently. He is bound to turn up soon. After that I believe he will try to make his way to France and his fellow Jacobites.'

'And you are sure of that, are you—that he is in London, I mean?'

Simon looked down at her, his brow furrowed. 'I

am—unless you have proof that he is elsewhere?' His frown deepened when she quickly averted her gaze and bit nervously on her bottom lip. 'Christina,' he said, his voice hardening, 'tell me what you know. I demand the truth.'

'Well—yes, I—I have seen him. Once,' she confessed quietly.

'Where? Where, damn it?' he demanded angrily, keeping his voice low so as not to attract the attention of the other dancers.

'At—at Oakbridge—just before I left. He—he wanted somewhere to stay until it was safe for him to move on.'

'And?'

'William refused to let him into the house.'

His eyes hardened. 'And did it not occur to you to report the incident?'

'William was going to do that.'

'I see.' Simon was beside himself with fury. He was incensed that she had seen and talked with Bucklow since they had parted. Thirty-one years of strict adherence to certain rules of etiquette could not be completely disregarded, and Simon kept his expression guarded, giving no hint of the rage boiling inside him like a fiery acid as his feet continued to move in time to the music.

He was silent for a moment as he turned the information she had given him over in his mind, and then, his expression as sardonic as ever, and neither candid nor even remotely friendly, with a mocking smile he said, 'There's no need to distress yourself, Christina.

If Bucklow is not in London and you have seen him at Oakbridge, then perhaps I should switch my investigations back there. Rest assured that I shall find him. I am determined to see him hang. And since you appear so concerned, I shall be sure to inform you of the fact so you can say your farewells before the noose is finally placed around his neck.'

His taunting smile seared Christina and brought a rush of colour to her face. He was cruelly laughing at her and her stung pride would not allow that. He was treating her as if there had been nothing between them, as if they had never shared the intense passion between a man and a woman. It was incredible to her that those firm lips had kissed her, that those hands had caressed her and given her such delight. It was this incredulity rather than resentment over his attitude to Mark that brought her chin up defiantly. She glared up at him.

'Were I a man you would not smirk so easily.'

He cocked a brow and chuckled unmercifully at her. 'Were you a man, my dear Christina, I would surely have demanded satisfaction from you already for what you have put me through.'

Christina's blush deepened. Infuriated and seething with anger and humiliation, with a sudden burst of pride and energy, she wrenched herself free from his arms. Fortunately they were on the edge of the crowded dance floor and no one appeared to notice the heated altercation between them.

'Excuse me,' she hissed. 'This is one dance that goes on too long for my liking.'

Spinning on her heel, she strode away from him,

pushing her way past those who got in her way. Trembling with fury and feeling a need to calm down and compose herself before she faced her aunt, she stepped through a door on to a small balcony, gripping the stone balustrade with trembling hands. Suddenly she stiffened when she sensed someone behind her.

'You cannot escape me so easily, Christina,' Simon said calmly. 'I am not so easily got rid of—as you must have realised on our last encounter.'

Christina's face turned ashen under the careless remark, and she swayed on her feet, feeling faint. Simon steadied her by placing his hand under her elbow and turned her to face him. Placing a finger under her chin, he raised it so he could gaze down into her eyes.

'You do remember, don't you?'

Christina stared at him. She felt all the warm and passionate memories well up in her and at the same time sadness, for dearly as she wanted to tell him she would never forget, that it was the most wonderful thing that had happened to her in her life, that she was only his and ready to obey him, that he could take her, to subjugate her—indeed, to do anything he cared to do to her—she was so unsure of his feelings and what it had meant to him that her pride would not allow her to reveal how she felt.

'Remember?' she bit back, jerking her chin away from his finger, her anger giving virulence to her tongue. 'Yes I remember everything. I remember how I let you take advantage of me,' she said furiously, remembering how she had enjoyed the things he had done to her, revelled in it before she had known he did not feel anything for her. Now, more than ever, she needed her forceful personality to keep her sane in what was to come. 'You have made it impossible for me to forget.' She found his sudden smile infuriating.

'I do seem to have a lasting effect on the ladies I make love to.'

'Don't flatter yourself, Simon Rockley. Don't you think I would forget what you did to me if I could? What you did was the most terrible thing that a man could do to an unmarried woman. It took me far beyond the safe bounds of carnal knowledge that has so carefully sheltered my life.'

He shrugged casually and raised a brow enquiringly. 'What are you talking about? Such anger is quite unnecessary. You look pale. Are you unwell?'

'If I am,' she flared, 'it's your fault.'

His body tensed, his jaw tightened and his eyes grew cold. 'My fault? How is it my fault?'

'I am to bear your child.' Christina threw it at him. She had not intended telling him like this, but he had got her so worked up. 'Small wonder the ladies you associate with can't forget what you do to them if you impregnate them the first time you take them to bed.'

Simon's face became thoughtful, his eyes narrowed speculatively. 'How long have you known?' He stood straight, his hands behind him, his face impassive—the expression he normally used to shield his thoughts when troubled or angry. A muscle began to twitch in his cheek.

Christina found the dead calm of his demeanour to

be more threatening than any display of anger. 'A-about a month,' she stammered.

'I see.'

'And don't you dare try wriggling out of it,' she flared, her eyes blazing at him. 'Never doubt that you are the father. You accused me of being Mark's mistress, which was not the case. You mistook what you saw at the Black Swan—in fact, before you arrived I had been fighting for my very life. I was never his mistress and it was insulting of you to assume I was.'

'I know.'

She gave him a dubious stare. 'You do? How?'

'Men know these things. I have no doubt that you were a virgin when I made love to you, Christina. None whatsoever.'

Simon's mouth sat in a bitter line, his black brows drawn in a straight bar across his eyes as he turned from her and fell into a brooding silence. When he had made love to her, initially she had fought him like a tigress, but she had surrendered like an angel, kissing him with such sweet, desperate ardour that had twisted him into knots of desire. If she was indeed with child, then he must accept that it was his and do the honourable thing and make her his wife.

The possibility that she might refuse was beyond the bounds of feasibility in his estimation. Parading before his eyes were visions of a bewitching girl lying in his arms, kissing him. He was well aware that her feelings for him were deeper than even she knew. She could not have given herself to him so completely if that weren't so. She was too sweet and innocent to feign those emotions. And yet he remained uneasy about her association with Bucklow—enough to make him doubt her.

He turned and looked at her lovely, frightened face. From the very beginning he had taken her reluctance to speak of that murdering scoundrel as a deliberate attempt to obstruct him in carrying out his investigations, and he still didn't know the reason why she had been in his bedchamber at the Black Swan that day. He recalled how he had felt when he had seen her in Bucklow's arms, and how, when she had pleaded with him not to shoot him, his heart had slammed into his ribs so hard it hurt. Feeling as he did, could he make her his wife? Would it be foolish to trust her in case he was deceived? And yet, since she was carrying his child, he was duty bound to do the honourable thing by her.

'I take full responsibility for what happened, Christina,' he uttered brusquely. 'You need not fear for your future.'

As she had watched him, fleetingly he had dropped his mask. The doubt was there, etched plain in the lines of his face. She felt an uneasy disquiet setting in. 'What are you saying?'

'That we will be married immediately.'

Christina could not quite believe what she was hearing. He sounded so dispassionate, she was not quite sure if she had received a proposal of marriage or a comment about some inconsequential issue of the day. 'I see.' She took a deep breath. 'And you are quite sure that you *want* to marry me, are you, Simon?'

'These are not the most romantic circumstances

under which to propose, and I am more than likely wounding you by discussing the arrangements in such a blunt way, but we have no choice.'

A lump of nameless emotion constricted her throat. He was treating her as if there had been nothing between them, as if they had never shared the intense passion between a man and a woman. 'That was not what I asked you.'

'My feelings have no bearing on this.' For the first time in his life Simon was finding it difficult to tell a woman—this woman—that she was the most alluring and as desirable as any he had ever known. Even now, when the consequences of his actions were so grave, he wanted her. She had become a passion to him, a beautiful, vibrant woman, and he had hurt her very badly. 'You are to bear a child—my child, as it happens—so we must marry. There is nothing else to be done.'

'Yes, there is. I don't *have* to marry you, and it is arrogant of you to assume that I would accept you. You speak as if I have no control over any of this. Well, I have. I am not making you do anything—just like the last time we were together, when you forced yourself on me. I am still hurting from that, and I will not chain myself to a man for the rest of my life who does not love me. I agree that marriage is the accepted mode in situations such as this, but where I am concerned I do not consider it necessary for us to marry.'

Simon looked at her with that straight, disconcerting gaze of his. The line of his lips was grim and hard. 'Don't be ridiculous. You must be aware of the stigma attached to an illegitimate child, that it will be an object for censure and ridicule throughout its life. Think about it. A woman alone with an illegitimate child is prey to the pitilessness of society.'

'I know. A harsh society that believes the sin is all the woman's, that she is to blame for being in the condition she has brought on herself and that the child, as well as herself, must be shunned lest it contaminates them—while the man who is to blame walks away without a blemish on his name. That said, Simon, I will not allow my destiny or that of my child to be dictated by circumstance, society or you.'

Simon looked at her hard. The expression on his face was difficult to read, but some new darkness seemed to move at the back of his eyes. 'I appreciate the wrong I have done you, Christina, but that does not alter my obligation. We will be married as soon as arrangements can be made, for I will not compound my wrong by abandoning my honour and my duty. It takes two to make a child, and you and I made the one you are carrying together.'

Christina pulled herself erect with as much composure as her shaking limbs would allow, but the silver-grey eyes meeting hers gave her no reassurance. She could have faced the blows from his hands better than the furious intensity of his gaze. She raised her head high, refusing to let him see her wretchedness.

'I know, but you went away. After you left me like that—alone and confused—to deal with what had happened, I could never be sure how you are feeling. So you see, after this I am having second thoughts about wanting you to be the father of my child.'

His expression changed, becoming harder still, and his voice changed also. It was clearly full of fury, his tone deadly quiet. 'What you want, Christina, is irrelevant. I am the father of your child, so let that be an end to it. It might not have been conceived in the kind of circumstances I would have liked, but I will use every means at my disposal to keep its reputation untarnished."

There was a silence. She looked away from him, now afraid, so terribly afraid that they had reached that point at which everything between them would be finished. Brusquely, she turned and went to the door, where she turned and looked back at him. His dark hair gleamed in the soft light as he moved his head, and as he looked across at her, there was a film of quick emotion across his eyes. Suddenly she felt bereft and so very lonely, confused and painfully aware that what she said next would scar her life.

Taking her courage in both hands, her voice was shaking with emotion before the directness of his brilliant eyes. 'I am not so forgiving that I will forget the cruel things you said to me at Oakbridge after you found me at the Black Swan. As I recall, you accused me of being Mark's mistress—and you called me a whore. I thank you for your offer, Simon, but I will not marry a man who doubts me and does not trust me. That is my final resolve. I will not be forced. Consider your duty towards me discharged.'

She left him then, feeling that something deep inside her had turned to ice. She suddenly felt utterly exhausted and very tired. She had lost everything she had ever wanted. There was nothing left except his anger, her disillusionment and the child inside her, clinging to the grudging life that awaited it. That was the moment when she knew the real, desperate meaning of isolation and the icy coldness of its grip.

Simon watched her leave, knowing he should call her back—wanting to with every fibre of his being. He was a soldier, trained to keep even the most riotous emotions in check, a skill that could mean the difference between precious life or certain death. Could he stand in silence and watch the only woman who'd ever touched him to his very soul walk away?

At a time when he was totally immersed in marital bliss, William looked on Lord Rockley's sudden arrival at Oakbridge with a mixture of concern and trepidation. After introducing him to Miranda, who greeted him with a genuine smile of welcome on her lips before disappearing to discuss the menu for dinner with Cook and to feed a ravenous Henry, they retired to the study. Simon lost no time informing William of his reason for the visit. He apologised for his hasty departure for London, but he was here now to discuss what had happened before that eventful day at the Black Swan Inn.

William listened to what he had to say, expressing his own concern for his sister and proceeding to give his own account of what had driven her to seek out Mark Bucklow that day.

'What happened to the Seniors upset her deeply. As a consequence of that she went to the Black Swan to beg Mark to leave Oakbridge and to leave us alone. I am ashamed that I wasn't man enough to do it myself,' he confessed, somewhat shamefaced.

'And why would she think Bucklow would do as she asked?'

'It was a gamble. It wasn't the first time she'd approached him about the matter. He always refused, but this time she hoped to pay him off.'

'You had money to do that?'

'No. You must have seen for yourself that we have precious little—which is entirely down to me,' he confessed somewhat sadly. 'Gambling debts—you understand.'

Simon did, all too well, for gambling ruined more men than it made. He felt a surge of anger for this privileged young man, who had had it all, only to throw it all away on the toss of a dice or the turn of a card. Christina deserved better than this for a brother.

'We have paintings and other objects of value scattered about the house we could sell that we hoped would appease Mark,' William went on. 'We were desperate. Before Christina left, she told me that if Mark didn't agree to our terms, then she would turn him in, even though it meant incriminating ourselves. And the mood she was in that day, I have no doubt she would have done exactly that.'

'Why did you go along with Bucklow? Why didn't you tell Sir John what was going on?'

William looked straight into his visitor's eyes, his expression grim. 'Because Mark threatened to burn Oakbridge down about our ears and us along with it if we didn't abide by his orders. He threatened both our lives—and believe me, Lord Rockley, when I tell you that Mark Bucklow would have disposed of us without a moment's compunction.'

'I see.' And he did see. He saw it all now—that everything Christina had done she had done out of fear for her brother and herself—and most likely in that order. 'So when she went to the Black Swan to confront Bucklow, she went knowing full well her life was in danger—and yet you let her go alone?'

Unable to look at the cold accusing eyes that pierced him to his very soul, William swallowed nervously and nodded, deeply ashamed of his actions that day. 'Yes,' he said, his voice hoarse. 'Believe me when I tell you that I'm not proud of myself. I didn't want her to go. It was reckless, but when Christina sets her mind to doing something she is not easily put off.'

Simon digested this stony faced, but he did not comment on it. 'And she had no qualms about doing that— she was not romantically attached to Bucklow?'

William stared at him aghast. 'What? Christina and Mark? Good Lord! She hated the man. She would as soon make up to the Devil as him.'

Simon's face was expressionless as he digested this with surprise and a terrible sense of guilt. 'Is this the truth?'

'All of it.'

'Then I have much to apologise for where your sister is concerned. I had no idea she was prepared to inform on him—or that he had threatened your lives.'

'She didn't tell you?'

'Unfortunately, I didn't give her the chance,' he

replied quietly, having to swallow down his wretchedness. 'I believe you saw Bucklow after that?'

William nodded. 'He came here hoping to hide out until the whole sorry business had blown over. We turned him away, of course. He became angry and threatened us with his pistol. Before he could harm either of us, I shot him.'

Simon stared at him in disbelief. 'You killed him?'

'No—unfortunately.' He smiled lamely. 'My shooting skills leave much to be desired, I'm afraid. It was a shoulder wound. How serious it was I cannot say because he rode off. I haven't seen him since.'

'And Christina? How did she react to him being shot?'

'With relief. She was glad to see the back of him. She—told me what occurred at the Black Swan Inn when you came upon her with Mark. You were wrong to condemn her. What you saw was not what it seemed. Had you not arrived when you did, he would have raped her.'

'Yes, I had already worked that out for myself.' Guilt seared through Simon when he realised just how hasty he had been to judge Christina, how wrong he had been, but it was important that he was made aware of all the facts. 'And the only time she saw him after that was when he came here?'

'It was. She ordered him to leave Oakbridge without giving him time to get off his horse.' He sighed. 'I rue the day I ever got mixed up with Bucklow. I was young and gullible. When he approached me I saw a means of becoming rich without much effort. That was all I could think of. I had no idea what it would involve, what it would do to Christina. As a brother I've failed her miserably. I got myself into a situation I couldn't get out of. Unfortunately, when Mark began running his nefarious trade from here, Christina became involved by association. Obediently and dutifully, she did as she was bidden because she was terrified, but she hated it. We both knew what would happen if we didn't comply.'

'I must ask you—did you at any time receive payment from your involvement with Bucklow?'

A pair of cool grey eyes held William's captive, measuring his response, judging it for the truth. With a dismissive shake of his head, William said, 'No. He lent me some money in the beginning, to pay off some gambling debts, which I failed to pay back. Little did I know he would use my debt to wheedle his way into Oakbridge. I swear I received nothing from the people he stole from. You—do believe me?'

Simon nodded. 'Yes, I do.'

William hesitated, still vaguely intimidated by Lord Rockley's aura of command, and yet grateful that he trusted him enough to accept what he said as truth. 'Christina didn't want either of us to benefit from Mark's crimes. I still cannot believe he was sending his ill-gotten gains to France.' He looked at Lord Rockley steadily. 'I was not actively involved, but I did know Bucklow was using the chambers, for which I could be condemned. I can't thank you enough for keeping my name out of it, but I know that in doing so you have deceived your superiors. I am surprised, since it was your duty to report everything to do with your findings.'

'What I do has got nothing to do with duty,' Simon said curtly, his expression suddenly grim. 'When I was asked to track down Bucklow, I agreed to do so for no other reason than to right a wrong Bucklow did to my family. When he held up my brother's coach late one night, issuing the usual threats and waving his pistol about, my niece was shot and killed. My brother was also severely wounded. Today he is the shadow of the man he was. Everything my investigations uncovered I passed on to the magistrate—leaving out your part in it. The reason why I did so I will come to in a moment.'

'I have let Christina down very badly, but I shall make it up to her.'

'I think I can help you there.'

'How?'

'I wish to ask her to be my wife—but I shall need your help in persuading her to marry me.'

William's eyes opened wide in disbelief. 'What? You and Christina? But—I had no idea...'

'No. You were preoccupied,' Simon reminded him bluntly. 'There is something else you should know. It is something she would probably prefer to tell you herself, but she isn't here. She is to have a child.'

Clearly shocked, William paled. 'A child? But—I don't understand. How can she? But—whose child is it?'

'Mine,' Simon answered, no longer in any doubt that the child was his.

William placed a shaking hand to his forehead and turned away, clearly upset. 'I—forgive me—but I am shocked. This is all so—surprising. You—have seen her?'

'Yes.'

'And you will marry her?'

'Without a moment's hesitation,' he answered, saying nothing about the terrible things he had accused her of, of how he had wronged her most grievously. Why, the poor girl must have been living under a nightmare for months, and he had done nothing but make matters worse.

'Then—what can I say? Does Christina want to marry you? Is she in agreement? Although with a child to consider she is left with little choice in the matter.'

'She has—reservations. In fact, she is dead set against it, which is why I would like your help in persuading her to accept my suit. I hold your sister in very high regard—indeed, I shall be proud to have Christina as my wife.'

William was uneasy about what Lord Rockley had told him, and reproached himself most severely for being so wrapped up in his own troubles he had not seen what was going on between Christina and Lord Rockley. At any other time and with any other man he would have taken him to task for seducing his sister, but he had much to be grateful to him for and he was eager to remain in his favour.

'Then Miranda and I will leave for London in the morning. I shall have a letter dispatched immediately to Aunt Celia telling her to expect us.'

Simon left Oakbridge and headed back to London, knowing that the longer he stayed away from Christina, her hurt and anger would be hardening into hatred.

Chapter Nine

Waiting for William and Miranda to arrive and excited by the prospect, Christina gazed out of the window. It was mid-afternoon when she saw her brother's coach pull up in front of the house. With her aunt, she went into the foyer to greet them, and a few moments later, amid a great deal of chattering and laughing, and Miranda being introduced to Aunt Celia, they settled down to refreshments. It was as William was sipping his tea that he casually told Christina of Lord Rockley's visit to Oakbridge to inform him of how his investigations were progressing.

Christina's spine stiffened and she looked at her brother warily, suspecting there was more behind Simon's visit to Oakbridge, but if there was, William was certainly not letting on.

'And when you left, Lord Rockley remained behind?' Christina ventured to ask.

'No, he and his valet left for London directly after leaving Oakbridge. In fact, I have taken the liberty of inviting him to dine with us later.' The smile he gave his aunt was so youthfully charming that it never failed to win her over. 'You don't mind, do you, Aunt Celia? I know how much you enjoy entertaining, and I didn't think one more would make any difference.'

'Of course not, dear boy—the more the merrier. I am expecting four of my friends to dine with us—Mr and Mrs Webster and Sir John Bainbridge and his wife, Emily, all of whom you are acquainted with. Besides,' Celia replied, avoiding Christina's curious gaze, who was beginning to think there was some kind of conspiracy at work and feeling the first stirrings of alarm, 'I would so like to become better acquainted with Lord Rockley. He's such a handsome man, I thought, when Christina introduced me to him recently at a party at the Assembly Rooms. I'm only sorry I didn't get the chance to become better acquainted.'

'There you are then,' William said smugly, placing his cup and saucer on the table. 'I'm sure you will be charmed by him—and you, too, Christina. I know you and Lord Rockley will have much to discuss.'

Instead of being stricken, Christina was slowly standing up, propelled to her feet by a boiling wrath. '*If* I have anything to say to Lord Rockley, William, I shall do so in my own good time. His visit to Oakbridge was to discuss me, wasn't it? Based on what you have said, it is obvious that this entire situation has been deliberately organised in a way to bring us together. You know, don't you? That—that insufferable man has told you that—that…'

William stood up and went to her, hating to see her so angry and upset. 'That you are to have a child. Yes, Christina, he did tell me.'

'He had no right,' she cried, beside herself with fury. 'No right whatsoever.'

'Since he is the father, he had every right.'

Christina stared at him in utter disbelief. 'He—he told you that?'

'He did. Why did you not tell me how things were between the two of you? I felt such an idiot when he told me.'

'I didn't tell you because there was nothing to discuss,' she replied flatly in answer to William's question.

'Apparently there was. I cannot say that I wasn't shocked when he told me—and disappointed that my sister would…' He halted himself before he said something insensitive that would hurt her. 'But what is done is done. We must make the best of it and look to the future.' He looked at his aunt. 'I expect Christina has told you?' She nodded. 'Then let us hope this can be sorted out as amicably as possible and the wheels set in motion for a wedding.'

Christina's head snapped up in anger. How dare Simon assume that she would marry him after she had told him she wouldn't? She was not without some pride. 'A wedding? But—I have not agreed to marry Lord Rockley—in fact, quite the opposite.'

William looked at her accusingly. 'Now, Christina, be sensible. You know the situation.'

'Of course she does,' Miranda chirped up, smiling sweetly at her sister-in-law. 'William has so much common sense. That is what I have always admired about him.'

William threw his wife a look that told her to keep out of it. 'I would be grateful if you would leave this to me, Miranda.'

'But of course, my love. I am sure you will make Christina see sense. Lord Rockley is extremely charming and I am sure he is very rich. The offer is a good one.'

'But I have told you, I have not agreed to marry him,' Christina persisted, only to realise that no one was listening to her, and with a sense of utter despair she realised her own impotence. What could she do? What could she say against these three people who were planning her future with an utter disregard for her own feelings in the matter?

'Your reputation has been harmed, Christina,' William went on, 'though I wish it were not so. You must prepare yourself for the thought of marriage to Lord Rockley. I shudder to think what kind of life you will have if you do not—an unmarried woman with a child. It is unthinkable.'

With the words said aloud at last, Christina felt her heart shatter and her eyes sting with tears. She felt humiliated and hopeless. How had this happened to her? When she'd watched Mark Bucklow ride away from Oakbridge that day, she thought she'd been delivered safe from the clutches of one man, only to find herself trapped with another.

* * *

With so much time to prepare mentally for whatever unpleasantness William had planned for her later, except for her treacherous heartbeats, which insisted on accelerating every time she thought of Simon, Christina had almost convinced herself she was well fortified against her fate by the time of Simon's arrival.

But nothing had prepared her for the moment she first set eyes on him. He was the last to arrive. He was wearing light grey velvet breeches and a dark blue frock-coat. His white silk vest had narrow silver stripes, and delicate white lace spilled from his throat and over his wrists. His dark hair was pulled back and tied at the nape with a black velvet ribbon. This elegant attire accentuated his virile good looks, for handsome he was, making him look like a story-book hero. A smile played on his beautifully shaped lips, and his eyes immediately sought her out where she stood alone in the doorway leading into the drawing room.

Her gown was a stunning creation of golden layers of silk fabric. It was as if she were clothed in a cloud that flowed in shimmering waves around her slender body. There was a duel of glances as his eyes challenged hers, drawing her to him, and Christina felt again the sudden heat of suppressed passion.

After introductions had been made, excusing himself to the others, he advanced towards her. Despite the civilised elegance of his attire, Christina thought he had never looked more dangerous, more overpowering than he did as he came towards her with that deceptively lazy, stalking stride of his.

'Hello, Christina,' he said, his penetrating gaze probing hers.

'Hello, Simon.'

Simon was a little taken aback by the courteous, but impersonal smile she gave him, but he refused to be discouraged. 'It is a pleasure to see you again,' he said, reaching for her hand. After the briefest of hesitations, she placed it lightly atop his outstretched palm. He felt her tremble as he curled his fingers around hers and slowly drew her hand to his mouth. He stopped within a hair's breadth between his mouth and her silken flesh. Glancing up, he again held her gaze, his senses aware of the feel and scent of her, and the way she caught her breath even as he used his own warm breath to caress the back of her hand, delighting in the soft flush that mantled her cheeks. He prolonged the contact for another couple of seconds, and then he gently touched her hand with his lips and released her.

'I wouldn't blame you at all if you refused to see me,' he said. 'I feel quite wretched about the way I treated you. My conduct was inexcusable.'

'It was indeed,' she replied as her hand drifted bonelessly to her side and her body tingled all over from the brief contact. This was the man who had stolen her virginity, got her with child, and then casually told her they would marry. Calmly she reminded herself that she was completely innocent, and that goodness and righteousness were therefore on her side. To further insulate herself against heartbreak, she had firmly put an end to her ritual daydreams about him. She would have to call upon the sturdiest reserves of her self-discipline to keep smiling, for keep smiling she would as long as the night lasted, and after that she would die.

'Do you want me to go away?' he asked.

'Yes, I do. I told you I won't marry you. I meant it then and I mean it now.'

'Then why are you blushing?' he asked softly. The colour in her cheeks and whatever flickered into her lovely eyes provided some insight into her true feelings, allowing him to see that she wasn't at all indifferent to him, no matter what she tried to make him—and herself—believe.

'I am not,' she said. 'If I have more colour than usual it can only be put down to the heat of the room. It is thanks to you that I have nothing left to blush about,' she remarked pointedly. 'Besides, I've always harboured a quiet contempt for women who blush and swoon at the slightest provocation. However,' she said breezily, leading the way into the drawing room where everyone was settling down to drinks before dinner, 'you are here now, so it's too late to do anything about it. The last thing I want is to cause a scene, so we must both put on a happy face and grin and bear it until it's time for you to leave.'

One corner of his mouth lifted as he met her gaze. 'That shouldn't be too difficult.'

'Not for you, perhaps. Personally I shall find it excruciating. Come and have a drink—William is about to pour. Oh, and you must let me introduce you to Miranda,' she said. Miranda had just joined them, having agonised all day about what she should wear, finally selecting a divine saffron-and-yellow satin, but discarding it at the last minute for an emerald-green silk. Christina turned and looked at Simon, managing to feign a wide-eyed, innocent expression. 'Oh, but I forgot. You have already met—at Oakbridge. Is that not so, Simon?'

'I have been to Oakbridge, and, yes, I have been introduced to your brother's charming wife.'

'And you had much to discuss with William, apparently.' Her expression hardened. 'How dare you?' she uttered for his ears alone, all her resentment rushing to the surface at such male arrogance. 'Had I wanted him to know about a certain highly sensitive matter, I would have preferred to tell him myself. You had no right.'

Completely unfazed by her anger, Simon shook his head slightly. 'I disagree. I apologise if I have upset you in any way, Christina, but since I appear to be the father of the child you are carrying, I considered I had every right.'

They were prevented from further discussion when Miranda drew them into the conversation. In the true spirit of a matchmaker, Celia had contrived to place Simon at the table across from Christina. Simon ate little of his meal—he was too preoccupied with the elusive, lovely young woman who had stolen his heart, but who seemed either afraid, or unwilling, to meet his gaze. He watched her chatting playfully with the handsome Sir John Bainbridge on one side of her, winding him round her finger, and jealousy pulsed through him. To add to his mounting frustration, he was seated between Sir John's wife and Miranda, who, delightful though she was, bored him and irritated him with her constant trivia.

As the evening wore on and there was quiet conversation and music, Simon was annoyed at the way Christina continued to avoid being alone with him. When she rose to bid everyone goodnight, pleading a headache, he followed her into the hall, where he halted her.

'What is it, Simon?'

'Must you leave quite so soon?'

She shrugged and looked away. 'I must. I am tired and I have a headache.'

He moved closer. 'What's the matter, Christina? It has not gone unnoticed that you have avoided being in my company all evening. Does my presence unsettle you? Is that it?'

Her chin rose high, but not aggressively so, and her shoulders were straight, but then she had nothing to be ashamed of or to defend, whereas Simon had wilfully and wrongfully accused her of terrible things, therefore the responsibility and the guilt and the shame were his, not hers. From the moment Simon had walked into the house, her senses had been screamingly aware of his presence. She felt as if she were being tortured inside, slowly and painfully. Even so, it was all she could do not to humble herself at his feet. Only one thing kept her silent and upright—pride—outraged, stubborn, abused pride.

'Yes, it does, and since you show no sign of leaving, then I must. Excuse me.'

Simon protested instantly. Following her to the

bottom of the stairs, he halted her, standing behind her and leaning close. 'Don't go.'

His voice was soft, so soft that if made something primitive stir deep inside Christina. She wanted to immediately affirm her desire to leave, but found the words wouldn't leave her throat. She half-turned and looked at him bathed in the candles' glow, his dark hair shining, his silver-grey eyes full of invitation. Why was he doing this? Why did he torture her so?

'If I wronged you,' he went on, 'I ask only to acknowledge it freely. William has told me everything. I now know that Bucklow was threatening you both—that he made threats against your lives if you did not do as he ordered. Ever since I arrived at Oakbridge intent on capturing Bucklow, you have tried to throw me off the scent. At every opportunity your deception has got in my way. Many times I have asked myself why— and now I know. I am sorry if I appeared judgemental, Christina. Truly. It was never my intention to hurt you. William also told me that you were on the point of coming to me to divulge Bucklow's whereabouts.'

'Yes, I was, much good it would have done me.'

'I would have listened.'

Christina stared at him, disbelieving. 'And you are sure about that, are you, Simon—because I take some reassuring. I understand when you ravished me it was because you thought I was a woman of easy virtue, that you thought I was Mark's mistress, and I would welcome any man's advances. My virtue was intact—until I encountered you.'

'I know that. You should have told me.'

'You were in no mood to listen as I recall.'

'That's because when I saw you with Bucklow you seemed—close, and fiercely protective of him as I remember when I was about to shoot him. I now know my judgement was faulty that day.'

'It was. Absolutely. You were too quick to judge and to condemn.'

Simon sighed deeply. 'When we returned from visiting Mrs Senior, do you remember that I asked you to trust me?'

'Yes, I do, and I cannot pretend that I wasn't tempted. But how did I know that I could trust you? And after what followed when we…when you left me so abruptly in the chamber—which made me think you didn't care—I knew that I could not.'

'I'm sorry, Christina.' When she turned from him he touched her arm. 'Please don't go. I am asking you to stay.'

She forced herself to remember their last encounter and shook her head, although she saw what this admission of his guilt had cost his pride. 'No. I am tired. Stay if you like. I am sure William would like you to—and Aunt Celia seems to be quite taken with you. Excuse me. I would rather leave.'

It cost her something to tear herself away so soon from the man she had longed to see, but it was more than she could bear.

Not wishing to make a scene in front of Christina's family, Simon let her go without further argument, but he had no intention of letting this be the end of it. She had displayed a marked antagonism towards him all evening and he had let it pass, but he was not done with her yet. He turned when William came to stand beside him.

'I'm sorry, Simon,' he said, watching his sister disappear up the stairs. 'Clearly Christina is not herself tonight.'

'No. Do you mind if I go after her? I would very much like to speak to her alone before I leave.'

'Well, it's highly irregular—but as things stand between the two of you, and since I have granted your request of my sister's hand in marriage, I can see no harm in it. I can only hope you succeed in sorting things out and the outcome will be a happy one.'

Christina was dressed and ready for bed when she heard a sharp knock on her door. Surprised, she went towards it, wondering if it was her aunt, come to bid her goodnight.

'Who is it?' she called.

'Simon,' came the abrupt reply.

Momentarily stunned, Christina stopped and stared at the door. So much for keeping him at bay in order to keep her feelings in check, she thought. He had to seek her out in her bedchamber. Closing her eyes, she inhaled deeply, struggling against a wave of despair and longing.

'Please go away,' she said without opening the door.

'Christina, I have to speak to you,' he remonstrated.

'Not in my bedchamber. It's not proper.'

'Considering the circumstances, it's too late for us to worry about what's proper.'

Irately, she opened the door and glared at him. 'I agree—and it's all thanks to you.'

He nodded gravely and stepped past her into the room, the image of relaxed elegance. 'I admit that I am to blame. I could cut out my tongue for the things I said to you. You've every right to be angry.'

'That is putting it mildly,' she retorted, continuing to hold the door open, resenting his casual manner. Even his expression was casual. If he thought she would ease his course of action, he was as mistaken as he was devious. 'You should have trusted me. If you had given me the chance to tell you about Mark, you would have realised there was nothing between us, before your fertile imagination invented a false tale,' she reproached harshly. 'Your charge rested on some dreadful misunderstanding. One minute would have cleared it up, but you were so pig-headed you refused me the opportunity of doing so. I did not lie. I was brought up to tell the truth, and I was deeply offended when you insinuated that I was a liar and accused me of being a whore. Now, since you have no reason to be here, I think it would be best that you leave.'

'Surely you must be sensible enough to know why I can't leave. Ever since I went to Oakbridge to see your brother, I felt I must see you, speak to you. Arrangements have to be made.'

'Arrangements?'

'For the child,' he said, stepping towards her and closing the door. 'Of course, we will have to be married.'

Christina gasped, feeling hot and cold all at the same time. 'Haven't you listened to anything I've said?' she flared. She looked away, wishing she could stare him in the eyes, but knowing she would be unable to control her heated emotions. 'And the child is enough reason for us to marry?' she responded incredulously. 'Forgive me, Simon, but I have been under the distinct impression that your feelings for me were anything but fond.'

To her rising disgust his eyes swept her body.

'I could not allow myself to feel anything for you when I believed you to be Bucklow's mistress. I now realise I was mistaken and wish to make amends. What more do you want me to say? I spoke with your brother tonight. We have discussed your marriage to me.'

He paused when she folded her arms over her chest and glared at him belligerently. He knew her pride, her courage, and was a fair way to proposing to her formally when she tossed back the shimmering curtain of her hair and through gritted teeth said, 'When I marry, Simon Rockley, the man I take to be my husband will be of my choosing, not William's. I want a man who will be a true husband to me, with whom I can share a love everlasting—not a man who will marry me for no other reason than that I am to bear his child. I am in charge of my own destiny, not you.'

'Not when you are carrying my child,' he stated coldly.

'You can't force me to marry you.'

His eyes glittered like shards of ice. 'No? We'll see about that. I always get what I want in the end. It would serve you well to remember that.'

'Always is a long time.'

'Don't be difficult, Christina. There will be no choice,' he stated bluntly. 'What man would have you when you are carrying another man's child? How could you hope for him to respect you? One of the most important things to bring to a marriage is respect.'

Christina was incredulous. 'Respect?' She heard her voice rise. She knew she should temper her ire, but his audacity proved too much. 'And how can I respect a man who mistrusts me? Why would you think I would tie myself to any man who would do that?'

Simon's mouth tightened. 'For the sake of our child.'

'How dare you?' she seethed softly, feeling the pain of knowing that he had deemed her so unworthy he could not bear to remain with her when he had ravished her. Her disappointment should not shock her, but somehow it did, deeply, and she felt the pangs of a woman who did not know if he could ever love her just for herself. 'You were quick to judge and to condemn when you found me alone with Mark at the Black Swan. How do I know you will not do so again if a similar situation should arise? I am only surprised how quickly your conscience has dealt with this. For myself, at this moment in time, I can neither forget nor forgive your cruelty.' The full force of her emotions roiling within her now burst forth and she was full of pain and anger.

'Christina,' he countered, his mien softer now, 'I am sorry. What more can I say? You must see the sense in our marrying. You cannot bear the weight of this alone, and the child cannot go through life with the stigma of being born out of wedlock. You have no choice now. I took that away from both of us when I allowed my desire for you to run away from me.'

'Aye, after you'd ravished me and left me to fend for myself.' Christina felt anger and frustration rising within her like a tide. He was talking as if she had no say in the matter. 'You talk as if I had no control over any of this. As I recall when we made love, it was a mutual decision. My—feelings were comparable with yours, I admit that, but that is all. Without trust—without love—I cannot marry you.'

He looked at her hard, and in his expression there was no hint of affection for her, only a resolute determination to have his way, an expression she was coming to know very well. 'I said you have no choice in the matter and I meant it.'

'I disagree,' she argued coldly. 'Marriage may be the accepted mode in situations such as this, but there are alternatives. I do have a duty to the child, I know that, and I will always do what I consider is in its best interests.'

The muscles of his jaw clenched tightly, banishing any trace of softness from his too-handsome face, and when he spoke, the softness in his voice was far from soothing. 'It is my child, too, Christina.'

'Whatever conclusions I have reached, I know you are an honourable man. I know you would take care of us and see that we are provided for. I don't think illegitimate children of men such as yourself suffer any great setbacks in life.'

Simon's face went white and he stiffened with all

the hauteur and dignity that befitted his rank. 'Good God, Christina! Are you suggesting that I make you my mistress?'

'Certainly not. Although I imagine that a man of your position is quite familiar with the appropriate arrangements for mistresses.'

'Whether I am or not is beside the point. This is about us. You and me.'

'I still think marrying me is an extreme step for you to take. If you are against making me your mistress—which I would not even consider in any case—is it not the usual custom for men of your position not to marry women who find themselves with child, but to pay them off?'

'It is clear that you know nothing of my character as a man. You insult my honour, Christina, and your own, I might add,' he said, his voice low and furious.

'It is you who makes me feel like that. Accepting your support for our child is one thing, marrying you is quite another. Despite the mad attraction you seemed to have for me in the past, you do not love me nor care for me in any sense that would make for a happy marriage. I cannot forget the things you said to me.'

'For which I have apologised.'

'Yes, you have, and you need not do so again. It is not necessary. I remember telling you I would not forgive you. I told you then that should you go down on your knees before me and beg my forgiveness, you would get neither pardon nor mercy from me. You replied by saying those were words I would never hear from you, that when it was all over you would forget me as if I had never been. How soon you changed your opinion of me. And how soon before it changes again, I ask myself, and I become a bitch again.'

Simon paled. 'That is unfair.'

'Is it?' She smiled. 'Don't worry, Simon. My heart was not broken on hearing your opinion of me. I was wounded and insulted, that was all.'

'I appreciate the wrong I have done you—in more ways than you will ever know—but that does not alter my obligation. We will marry. I insist on it, for I will not compound what I did to you by abandoning my duty and my honour. William and I have gone through the formalities. The wedding will take place immediately and as my wife you will be entitled to my full support.'

'This is not all about you, Simon. All I hear is about your duty, your honour and your obligation. Are you saying that if we marry your honour will be satisfied? I don't think so. Everything you say sounds to me like you are trying to appease your sense of guilt.' She saw him flinch. Drawing a deep breath, she went on. 'What happened between us happened and I will not turn it into something of which I should be ashamed, and nor will I tie myself to any man in his need to expunge his guilt.'

Feeling ill-used and furious, Simon glared at her. 'What the hell do you expect of me, Christina? What more can I say? You have punished me with your words as I have punished you. I am wounded that you think me capable of such an action, but I will tell you this, Christina. You can fight me tooth and nail, but you will marry me in the end.'

His words were those of reason, but she was not prepared to listen to such persuasive talk just now. Going to the door, she opened it. 'Go, Simon. Just go. Leave me in peace.'

Towering over her, Simon looked at her for a long moment. Her cheeks were flushed, her chest rising and falling with ire. Somehow she had become a woman as alluring, vibrant and desirable as any he had ever known. Even now, when the consequences of what he had said to her were grave, when the future of his heir was in jeopardy, he wanted her.

Without warning or hesitation, he bent his head and brushed her parted lips with his own. At first Christina drew back to resist him, but then her mind went blank before exploding with sensation. His kiss was slow and hot, pulling her under to some place deep, new and exciting. He didn't use force, but when the tip of his tongue touched hers, her lips opened a little more without any direction from her or urging from him. Some part of her wanted more, but Simon simply let his mouth linger a moment longer and then pulled away.

'I have hurt you very badly, Christina, I know that. And you are right—these are not the most romantic circumstances under which to propose marriage. In fact, I have probably hurt you once more by discussing our union in such a blunt manner. I suppose it was conceited of me to assume you would marry me, that you would accept our marriage as a matter of course because of the child. But putting all that aside, Christina, I do want to marry you regardless of anything else.' His eyes softened. 'Do not fight me, for I've wanted you from the first moment I saw you—resulting in jealousy and fury when I thought you might be Bucklow's mistress. I consider marrying you as simply the right and honourable thing to do.'

He lowered his head and his mouth came back to hers, bending her head back even as his tongue slid within to find her own. Christina was as helpless to the rising desire consuming her as she had been when first they'd kissed in the woods that day at Oakbridge. He tasted of wine and it drugged her senses. 'Christina,' he murmured against her mouth, 'I will go now, but I'll see you tomorrow. Now, what do you say about our marriage? You're a difficult woman to win over. What would you like me to tell your brother?'

Christina's senses were still spinning. She wasn't sure what bothered her more—that he had dared to kiss her or that he seemed so unaffected by it—or that she was beginning to realise that she was no longer able to control her own fate.

'Damn you, Simon Rockley,' she flared, pushing him away and folding her arms over her chest. 'I had made up my mind that I would never marry you, but you are right—and I hate you for being right. With the world as it is, if I am to give our child the best possible chance in life, then it will need a father—so, yes, even though my heart and mind rebel against it, I will marry you.'

'Good. That's settled, then.'

Without another word or a backward glance, leaving her with her pride, he walked out. Descending the stairs, he met William, who asked hopefully,

'Is it arranged? Did Christina agree?'

'You will be glad to know she has agreed that we will marry.'

William seemed to deflate with a sigh of relief. 'Thank God. The ceremony will take place as soon as it can be arranged.'

'I will arrange for a special licence, forgoing the banns. The sooner the better.'

At breakfast the following morning, the announcement of the impending wedding was greeted by everyone without surprise and much happiness.

'Simon is to obtain a special licence this morning, Christina,' William informed her.

'I see,' she murmured tightly.

'He's also going to see the minister to make the necessary arrangements for the wedding.'

Christina stared at her brother, feeling her hackles rise. This was not what she had expected at all. Surely there should be a loving discussion between the two parties concerned.

'Simon might have consulted me first,' she said heatedly.

'He did say he would call on you later. He's suggested the ceremony should take place as soon as possible.'

'As soon as possible,' she retorted crossly, quite furious at the way everyone seemed to be taking charge of her life. 'So I am to be married within days, and apparently I am to have no say in the arrangements for my own wedding.'

'Oh, but you have,' Miranda piped up cheerfully. 'Lord Rockley might arrange the time and the place,

Christina, but he cannot arrange what you will wear. I think a trip to the shops at the Royal Exchange is in order, don't you? There are some lovely shops upstairs, but I do so love browsing among the little stalls downstairs in the arcade.' Placing her napkin on the table, she rose. 'Order the carriage for us, will you, William, there's a dear, while I go and get ready. Come along, Christina. We shall have a lovely time.' Excited at the impending trip, Miranda swept out of the room.

While Christina looked solemn and subdued, Celia spoke of her happiness at the union and that a bright future awaited Christina. Her niece, however, did not share her optimism. She dreaded this union with Simon, for when she was with him she didn't know how she was supposed to feel. There was no denying or escaping the fact that he could make her feel things she ought not to want to feel, that there was no barrier high enough or solid enough to protect her heart from him. Her utmost fear was for the night following the ceremony and all the nights to follow, for if she let her guard slip just a notch, Simon would creep in and steal her heart and soul and make her need him.

The quiet marriage ceremony in the small church was held before just a handful of guests. The candles burned bright on the altar, making the group who stood there dark shadows in the otherwise dimly lit church. Christina's wedding gown was superb in its simplicity. The rich cream-and-silver brocade fell to her ankles, the stiff bodice finely embroidered with gold thread. A lace cap covered her head, with the lappets hanging down her back. She wore a necklace of warm amber and matching pendant earrings.

On quaking limbs, she looked at her husband-to-be. The candlelight touched his face, and for a second she was halted by the cold, stark features. She had an overwhelming desire to flee. The silver-grey eyes before her roamed over her face, making her tremble more violently. Simon held out a strong hand and offered it to her. Reluctantly she laid her hand in his, much warmer than her own.

Glancing down at her, Simon thought how lovely her face was, how elegantly her hand rested in his. Suddenly he was the captive of those fathomless deep blue eyes, and while doubtless those around them went on breathing normally, Simon felt as if he and his bride were alone in the world.

Tall and powerful he stood beside her, and time stood still as they were swept into the marriage ceremony. Every nerve, every sense Christina possessed, screamed out against the presence beside her. At that moment he was Satan—handsome, ruthless, dangerous. If she were brave, she would turn and run out of the church now, before they spoke their vows, but it was as if her legs were full of lead. All over the world women gave birth to bastard children all the time. Why was she not so courageous? Was it because she was drawn to a man who would never love her?

But even as she argued with herself, she got down on her knees with the man beside her and prayed for the blessing of God. One by one they pledged their troths with subdued voices—if the bride's voice was trembling, nervous and strained, no one would remark on it. The lean, well-manicured hands held her gaze as he slipped the wedding band on her finger. His closeness was overwhelming, as was the tangy, masculine scent of his cologne.

And then the priest pronounced them married. Again they bowed their heads before him, and then as Christina rose on shaking limbs, feeling as if she were dragging herself out of quicksand, she heard him say,

'I believe it is customary for the groom to kiss the bride.'

'I believe it is,' Simon uttered softly, turning to his bride.

Her knees were weak and her insides shaky, but as he took her hand, Christina would rather die than give him an inkling of how she felt. His long, lean fingers gently cupped the delicate bones of her jaw, while his other arm slid behind her back under the loose-flowing train. Suddenly all the things she held against him rose up to taunt her. Just the thought of those things were enough to hurt, but as he lowered his head and his mouth hovered so close to her own that she could feel his warm breath on her flesh, suddenly she wanted him to kiss her. Heaven help her, she did. She was a fool. Damn him for doing this to her. Damn herself, for this time she could not even summon the will to turn her face away.

Her heart began to drum in her chest as he parted her lips with his own, a lush, full openness that tasted her and enabled her to taste him. Even with everyone looking on, she wondered how anything as simple as this could bring so much pleasure. But despite this feeling,

Simon felt no response from her. She did not move or kiss him back. Instead, she remained rigid and still.

In that first minute of their married life, the last thing Simon wanted from her was resistance, and he knew he would need to entice her if he were to savour this delight in their marital bed. Kissing could be the prelude to all the delicious imaginings in his mind. The implications of his imaginings and having known the reality of making love to her had tantalised him unmercifully ever since he had left her that day in the chamber at Oakbridge.

Now, much as he wanted to deepen his kiss and forget about those present, he reminded himself that he was a gentleman, something that had never been this difficult to remember, and when he felt her lips tremble and soften, the first response to the featherlight caress of his tongue against her mouth, he managed to let go of her.

Taking her hand, he turned her to face her relatives, and, bending close to her ear, he murmured, 'Come. Everyone is waiting to congratulate us. There will be time for kissing later.'

At last Christina felt that she could breathe. Her quivering mouth burned from his blistering kiss, and her heart still had not slowed its rhythm. But she managed to smile tremulously as William and Aunt Celia came to congratulate them.

Afterwards, at Celia's house where the wedding breakfast was held and where they were to stay before leaving for Oakbridge in a few days' time with William and Miranda, Christina accepted the good wishes of those present, feeling like she was being assaulted on all sides as everyone sang her husband's praises. There was a good deal of laughter. Glasses were raised to one another, toasting whatever took their fancy. Christina looked on with indignation. Married but a few hours and Simon was winning over everyone—but her. Always, thoughts of her wedding night were not far away, and she was tempted to retire early and feign sleep.

She looked on it with dread. But then why should she, for what woman would not want to take Simon Rockley to bed? From the very beginning she had thought him a handsome man and his practised charm and lovemaking, even when he'd taken her in anger, had seemed to melt her very bones.

But a wedding night meant a complete giving of herself, which was not what she wanted to offer at this time, even though he had already taken her virtue. How could she surrender to him, when he had compromised her into this marriage?

Simon watched Christina through the celebration, his mind very much on his young bride. She spoke little and held herself back, as if she hoped he wouldn't notice her. Didn't she know that he noticed everything about her? Never had he felt for any other woman what he felt for her, that he could not imagine his life without her. He wanted her to feel the same way towards him. But her fears and doubts and mistrusts were strong, and he knew it would take much to overcome them.

When the festivities were over and the guests had gone, the fires damped down and the lamps turned low, when Christina had left him to finish his brandy, it took all of his control to allow her time to get ready for bed. Then he set down his glass and rose to his feet.

Alone in her room to await her husband, Christina made up her mind that she would not grant him his manly pleasures this night. When he had spoken of respect within marriage, she decided he would have to earn her respect. Attired in a delicate white nightdress, she drew on a thick velvet robe as if donning armour for battle.

She didn't have long to wait for Simon to come to her. He entered without knocking, closing the door firmly behind him. He had not expected to find her in bed waiting for him, and she wasn't. She sat in a large armchair beside the fire, her eyes watching him steadily, her face expressionless.

Slowly he made his way to where she sat, the sight of her in the flickering radiance of the candles almost taking his breath. Her long fair hair that tumbled in soft, glorious disarray about her slender shoulders created a vision beyond compare. His eyes swept over her in a lingering caress, evoking a blush that left her cheeks almost as rosy as her velvet robe.

He stopped before her, looking down at her upturned face. 'I'm happy to see you have not got into bed and gone to sleep.'

'I confess to having considered it.'

His face hardened. 'Then what stopped you?'

She stood up and faced him, hands on her hips like some avenging angel, knowing she was goading him too much, that he was a man of immense pride, but caring nothing for it. 'I wanted to be fully awake when I told you that you are not welcome in my bed and that I would like you to find somewhere else to sleep.'

'I see. And how do you expect us to begin our married life together if we are sleeping apart?'

'You have not yet earned my respect,' she said firmly.

'I will, but until then,' he said, taking hold of her arms and pulling her towards him, 'you are still my wife. I will have no one suggesting we are not legally married.'

'No one would do that. I think that in view of all that has happened, I'd prefer our marriage to be in name only, until a better understanding is reached between us.' She glanced at him. He was looking at her, a strange, enigmatic expression in his eyes.

'Our child is already on its way, Christina. What better understanding than that can there be for us to begin married life. One point I will make. Had I been opposed to marrying you, no man on earth could have forced me entirely against my will. I would have rotted in prison first. When you told me about the child, I spoke in anger to you. I accused you of terrible things and denied myself what I desired most. Call it my damnable pride, for in truth I sought to hurt you and avenge myself for things you were not guilty of. As it turned out, the revenge was not mine, but yours. So now I am through playing games in which I am the loser. I will have my due, Christina.'

'And if I refuse?'

'It is not my intention to take you by force, for I do

not want that kind of relationship, but nor will I play the monk. I will not live under the same roof with you never finding pleasure in you. I hardly think you will find me lacking in a husband's duties, as it will be my pleasure—and yours—to discover.'

Duties, Christina thought miserably. Was that all it meant to him—all the passion, the glorious sensations he awoke in her that made her delirious with pleasure when he made love to her?

'I know if I allow you to escape our bed tonight, tomorrow you will be in full retreat. We will share the same bed tonight and every night, whether we will be intimate or not.'

He removed his coat and walked towards the dressing room. 'I'll go and make myself ready for bed. When I return, I want to find you in bed.'

Christina was stunned and as the door closed behind him, a fierce rage flared within her. How dare he think that he could command her to get into bed with him? She was no longer the naïve young girl he had taken on the floor without the comfort of a bed. But the idea of being with him again excited her traitorous mind.

Sitting in the chair she was still for several moments, deep in thought. She remembered how it had been between them, how it had felt to have his lips on hers, on her breasts, his hands upon her naked flesh. Why was she making it difficult for them both? she asked herself. Was this not what she yearned for? Was she going to let her pride tear them apart?

Before she had time to answer her own question, Simon came back in, wearing a dressing robe. Suddenly she was filled with apprehension and her heart beat faster as, without a word, he crossed to where she sat, his manner purposeful. Taking her hand he raised her up, and she found herself standing willingly, his hands loosening the robe at her neck. Christina saw his eyes flare with heat when they took in her delicate nightdress, its simplicity clinging to her body like a second skin, teasing him, and she felt as if she were offering him a gift. His eyes swept her body in one long, passionate caress. Her breath caught in her throat at the promise and the heat of his touch when his hand caressed her cheek, then moved slowly downwards, drifting down over her collarbone and settling between her breasts.

Conscious of nothing but their heavy breathing, she did not resist. With one hand he cupped her breast that was pressing against the fabric, luring him with its eagerness to be set free. Smiling slightly as he saw the passion in her eyes, he slipped the shoulders of her nightdress down over her arms, releasing the soft orbs from their confinement. Bending his head, he placed his lips against her skin, warm and silky smooth against his mouth. And then he lifted her and carried her to the bed.

Placing her on the bed, he removed his robe, and even as he dispensed with that and his body was exposed in all its power, its strength and thrilling perfection, the evidence of his desire for her made her realise how much he truly wanted her. Laughing softly in his throat, Simon stretched out alongside her, facing her.

His gaze swept over her unbridled charms from head to toe. He was dazzled by her youthful beauty, and the glorious mass of her hair spread out over her shoulders and covering the bed behind her. Her ivory skin glowed softly in the candlelight, and by the golden flames he saw her breasts were generously and temptingly swelling, rising and falling slowly with her breathing. Slipping his arm about her narrow waist, he covered her mouth with his, kissing her with passion, engulfing her in a heady scent of brandy and cologne.

At first Christina almost recoiled with surprise at the warmth and passion he displayed. Then his mouth left hers and his lips trailed down her neck. And his long, heated body moved over hers. He seemed to luxuriate in the moment, so intimate, so tender it was, his lips finding hers once more, his kiss full, inviting and without reserve. As if her traitorous body were no longer her own, she slid her arms about his neck, and he drew her night dress up and over her head. She found herself pressing her soft breasts into the mat of hair that covered his chest. And then the hot flame of heat that reached to her very core enveloped her, consuming her so that she no longer felt herself.

At first he did not rush, but savoured each passing moment of pleasure, and in that time, a strange new budding ecstasy began to bloom and grow within Christina. She moaned and cried out at the exquisite pleasure and was not even aware of the precise moment she began to move and undulate her hips against his as he took her lips in another overwhelming kiss.

Having hungered and desired her for so long, Simon's long-starved passions grew until he was beyond himself, beyond reason, and he could only give in to the need of the moment. The intensity of their passion consumed them both and they forgot themselves as it mounted, each thrust forceful and hard. Lips and bodies were merged in a heated fusion that touched to the depths of their souls. Christina's cries were of pleasure as her world tore itself free of restraint and soared on to almost unbearable joy. They were two beings blended together in a whirling storm of passion. And then there was trembling release, the climax sweeping over Christina with a power she had thought unimaginable.

The storm at its end, a long quiet moment slipped past as everything drifted back into place. Simon lifted himself up on his elbows and looked down at his wife. Her face was gently flushed, her brow wet with perspiration, her eyes large and dark and slumberous. When he withdrew and rolled off of her and tried to gather her in his arms, as her mind came back from the far-flung ends of the universe, she moved away from him.

Simon rose and for a moment stared at her back, bewildered by this turn of events. His eyes coursed slowly over her body, and he could not but admire the well-turned hips and graceful thighs that had, a moment before, been his. 'Christina?' Reaching out, he placed his hand on her shoulder, but she refused his comfort.

'Leave me be.' Pulling a cover over her nakedness, she turned her face into the pillow so that if he looked he would not see her. Tears filled her eyes. She felt betrayed by her own body, for the pleasure it had taken in their lovemaking. It had been just like that other time, when she had lost all control, when she couldn't help herself, when she was driven by her desire.

How could he have been so cruel as to condemn her to a life with a man who did not love her? Yet in her heart she bore him tender feelings, feelings that had steadily grown, even as they were damaged by disappointment and confusion. Ever since that day at the Black Swan Inn, she had tried to close her heart to falling in love with him, but now she realised that she no longer had a choice in the matter. The one small salve to her pride was that she had not told him that she loved him, for love him she did, deeply, completely, and she thanked God she hadn't told him, for that would be the final humiliation. Her slender shoulders quivered with her quiet sobs. After a while they finally ceased and sleep came in their stead. But it was not an untroubled sleep—more like an exhausted one.

Simon reached out and gently arranged the cover around her. On a sigh he lay on his back and stared up at the ceiling, wondering if he had made a terrible mistake in taking her to bed. It wasn't that his lust had overcome his good sense, he had to make this marriage work, and he would not give up on his bride.

Snuffing out the candles at the side of the bed, he stretched out beside her, and his last thoughts as he fell into a sleep of his own was of her sweet-scented perfume and the warmth of her body close to his own.

It was during the early hours that Simon snaked his arm beneath the covers and round her waist, wishing to fit his body into the curve of her.

'Kindly remove your hand,' she cried, fully awake. 'If you don't, I swear, I shall find somewhere else to sleep.' Then she threw back the covers and got out of bed, making a grab for her robe and wrapping it around her naked body.

Surprised, Simon rose up in bed and looked at her wearily. 'I have no intention of hurting you, Christina. But your sharp tongue does rouse my ire, so be warned. If you continue in this vein, I have other ways to make you miserable.'

Christina looked at him, her eyes sad and uncertain, and her mouth quivered. Seeing her fear and distress, Simon let loose a curse and adjusted his pillows.

'For God's sake, woman, come back to bed. Yesterday was a long day and tonight I intend to get my rest.'

Christina's eyes snapped to him as anger replaced her fear. How dare he suggest she lie beside him now? She was not without some pride. Though there were still tears in her eyes she held her chin defiantly high. Going to the bed, she dragged a pillow and a quilt from it and took them to the sofa close to the window. Simon, with a raised eyebrow, watched her stonily as she spread them over the upholstery.

'Do you intend to sleep there?' he enquired with disbelief.

'Yes,' she replied. She settled down against the pillow and pulled the quilt about her.

'It's hardly a fit place for a pregnant lady to spend the night,' he informed her. 'There is a cold draught from the window. You'll get no comfort there.'

'Don't worry about me. I'll manage,' she said.

Simon swore under his breath and settled back among

the pillows. He stared at her. She shuffled beneath the quilt to get comfortable, and for a moment he thought she would fall on to the floor. He chuckled, despite himself, and from across the room she glowered at him and snatched the quilt tighter about her. Eventually she achieved some security, but she was anything but comfortable.

Simon watched her for a long time before finally lying down. He was aware of the empty space where she had slept, and he suddenly realised that he was going to miss her and her body's heat beside him. Raising his head, his voice was angry when he spoke. 'Christina, there's precious little heat in bed, so I can only imagine how cold you must be over there. I suggest we combine ours in bed together.'

She covered her prim nose and settled down. 'I am quite comfortable where I am.'

Simon drew the covers up about his head. 'Well, then,' he retorted, 'I am sure you and the cold draught will find ample companionship on that hard couch. I will not beg you again to join me. When you have had enough of playing games, just let me know and I will make room for you.'

Christina seethed on her uncomfortable bed and huddled deeper into the quilt as the cold began to seep through and she shivered violently. Already she regretted her actions, but she would freeze to death before she'd crawl back into his bed and let him mock her.

Chapter Ten

The following morning when Christina opened her eyes, rays of sunlight fell across the bed. She lay for a moment, her head aching, and it took a moment for her to realise that beneath the covers she was naked. It was then, with a terrible clarity, that she remembered what had happened the night before. Half-expecting to find her husband lying beside her, she turned her head, letting out a sigh of relief to find the bed empty. Only the indentations of his body and the scent of him remained.

When her eyes lit on the couch with the rumpled quilt, she remembered what had happened in the early hours, but could not recall getting back into bed. It was then that she realised Simon must have waited until she slept and carried her.

Feeling tired and in no mood for a fight, on a sigh she got out of bed. Dragging on her robe, she crossed to the window, thinking of the events of the night before. How was she to face him? How was she to deal with him? During the day she could distance herself from him, even show her wrath, but at night, in the privacy of their bedchamber, her body would betray her every time. Even now all she could think about were the things he had done to her and the pleasure she hadn't wanted to feel. Her traitorous body grew warm at the memory.

After she had bathed and dressed, she went down to breakfast. Everyone was already seated—everyone, that is, except Simon. Aunt Celia greeted her with a hug before holding her at arm's length and looking at her closely.

'Are you well this morning, Christina?'

'I am very well, Aunt,' she replied, a little too brightly, her aunt thought.

'You look radiant, Christina,' Miranda commented, flashing her a smile.

Christina turned to gaze at her sister-in-law, sarcasm quirking the corner of her mouth as she took her seat. 'Thank you, Miranda. Although I'm sure I don't look all that different than I did yesterday.' It was as though a night in Simon's bed was supposed to change her for the better. Could no one see that she and Simon were at odds over the state of their marriage? They might have made love on their wedding night, but they were still separated by a chasm of misunderstandings and anger.

'You do not ask where your husband is, Christina,' William said.

She shrugged. 'Have I not? Perhaps that's because I've never had a husband before.' She winced as her bitterness peered through her masquerade. 'Forgive me, William. I suppose I'll become better at my new role in time.'

Miranda reached out and put a hand on her arm. 'Every woman must learn the role of wife. The adjustments are not easy even when you're deeply in love with your husband, as you obviously are.'

'Yes, I am sure you're right, Miranda,' Christina said softly, feeling once again the sting of silly tears. 'I assume Simon's about his business somewhere.'

'He's gone to meet up with Henry and some of the men who are assisting him in tracking down Mark Bucklow. He said to tell you he expects to be back mid-morning.'

'Good. That's all right, then,' she replied coolly, buttering her bread.

When Simon returned and took one look at his wife's frozen features, he decided there and then that it was not a situation he would allow to continue. At one and the same time he wanted to take hold of her and shake her, and he wanted to scoop her into his arms and take her back to bed, no matter that he'd decided not to do so until she came to him.

Gazing at her lovely face and hidden curves, he knew his patience would not hold out that long. He was a fool to let her behaviour get to him this way, but not enough of a fool to storm off as he was sorely tempted to do at that moment. He would not give his infuriating bride that satisfaction.

* * *

The letter addressed to William from Oakbridge was delivered shortly after Simon's return. It was from Tom, informing him that the man Lord Rockley was seeking was holed up in the chambers at Oakbridge. If William wanted to see for himself, then there was a need for haste. The gunshot wound to his shoulder had festered and he was in a bad way. There was nothing anyone could do, and there wasn't much time.

Simon wanted to set off for Oakbridge immediately. Within the hour of receiving the note, after saying their goodbyes to Celia, the four of them were on their way.

It was dark and draughty inside the chambers. Having left Miranda at the house, accompanied by Tom and Henry, the three of them went inside. A slender shaft of light that entered through the open door and crossed the floor illuminated dusty footprints and bits of rubbish. Mark Bucklow lay on a low pallet, covered to the waist by a black cloak. He seemed to move from time to time with a restless shudder. The air was cold. On a box beside the pallet were a candle, which cast a flickering light around the chamber, and a pistol.

Moving towards the man he had been beginning to believe had eluded him for good, Simon now bent over Mark's prostrate form. He was obviously in a lot of pain. He was not asleep, for his breathing was ragged, and his hair lay wet against his damp face. The lines around his mouth were deep and his face was pale. His wounded shoulder was bandaged, but it was soiled with dry blood. He was obviously unable to move one hand, but on recognising Lord Rockley, he lifted the other and groped around for his pistol, already loaded with powder and shot. His fingers closed round the barrel and he raised it.

'Leave it,' Simon said. 'You're in no condition to put up a fight.'

Bracing himself on one elbow until his world stopped reeling, Mark aimed it directly at his adversary. 'I've enough fight left in me to kill you,' he growled with difficulty. 'Damn you, Rockley. Who told you where to find me?'

'I did,' Tom said, stepping forwards. 'You were too sick to take care of yourself when I found you in the woods. You couldn't go on running in the condition you were.'

Mark's visage grew red with rage, and his eyes blazed as he once again looked at Simon. 'Death, Milord Rockley,' he promised. 'Death to you!'

'Put down your weapon, Bucklow. Your time has come. You have too long escaped your fate.'

Seeing Mark's finger close on the trigger, Christina pressed a hand tightly across her mouth as her heart throbbed in sudden dread. Fear rose within her, and she could not beat it back as she watched Mark point the barrel at her husband and fire. A bright flash of light erupted from the gun and the sound was deafening in the small chamber, drowning out Christina's cry of anguish. Fortunately, Simon had anticipated what Mark would do and successfully sidestepped the missile, relieved when he heard it ricochet off the wall of the chamber. Immediately he snatched the pistol from Mark's hand and threw it down.

'You fool, Bucklow. That's the last time you attack anyone.'

The effort having proved too much for him, Mark's head fell back and he gulped in air. After a moment he opened his eyes, his gaze shifting to two of the other two occupants in the chamber, recognising them when they stepped forwards into the light. He struggled to raise himself. 'Damn you, William,' he gasped, his head falling back as the effort proved too much. 'You've done for me. You've finally got what you wanted, eh? This was not how I planned things. And you, Christina Atherton. To think I let you deceive me with your tricks.'

'It is Christina Atherton no longer, Bucklow,' Simon informed him curtly, pulling her close against his side. It seemed a direct challenge. 'She is Lady Rockley now—my wife.'

'Wife?' Mark hissed. 'Then—I damn you—twice, Rockley.'

'Damn me, just as your cause is damned. Before you die know that the French fleet carrying the young James Edward Stuart, the popish pretender, has been thwarted by the British navy in the Firth of Forth. Even now as we speak, the French are retreating round the north of Scotland, losing ships and most of their men.'

'And James?'

'On his way back to Dunkirk to report utter failure.'

Bucklow closed his eyes so that no one would witness his pain at James's defeat. 'Don't be smug, Rockley,' he gasped at last. 'James Stuart is steadfast in his religion. He will not renounce the cause that ruined his father. He'll come back with his followers. They will rise again—mark my words well—but I shall not live to see it.' And then he laughed, a horrible grating sound, which made a cold shiver run down Christina's spine. 'At least I've cheated the hangman—as I always said...I would.'

The words came haltingly from between his lips, and when his head fell back they realised there was nothing they could do. There came a sudden death rattle in his throat, and his whole body heaved as if in a convulsion. Even as Christina gave a little cry of terror, he collapsed.

For a long moment there was silence in the chamber as everyone realised Mark was dead.

Simon surveyed the faces that surrounded him as he took his wife into the shelter of his arm. 'There is nothing we can do. It is done. Let's get out of here.' When they were outside he turned to Tom. 'Ride to the magistrate and tell him what's happened, Tom. He'll arrange for someone to remove the body.' When Tom and William moved away and Henry went to fetch their horses, Simon glanced down at Christina, amazed to see her eyes swimming with tears. Tilting her chin with his finger, he said, 'What's this, Christina?' he murmured, brushing a curl from her cheek. 'Tears—for Bucklow?'

'No,' she gulped. 'Not for him. He was a criminal and deserved to die, but I—I thought he would shoot you.'

A leisurely smile lifted the corner of his mouth. 'Did

you think I would allow our babe to grow up without a father?'

Her tears flowed faster as the stress of the last few days, intensified by the last few minutes and the thought that she might have been holding her husband's lifeless body in her arms, was released and her fears were put to rest. She clung to him, wetting his coat with her tears, and she felt the gentle stroking of his hand and the touch of his lips against her hair as he held her close against him.

'Does this mean that you're warming to me?' he murmured.

She nodded, looking up at him with tear-bright eyes. 'I think I must be. I can think of no other reason why I am crying.'

'Not so very long ago you loathed me.'

'I'm a very complicated woman.'

'I'm beginning to realise that.'

Her smile was tremulous. 'Do you mind?'

'Not at all. I'm beginning to warm to you, too.'

'You are?'

'Oh, yes. You see, I love you, my lady. Very much indeed.'

Christina's heart soared and what was left of her tears trembled on her lashes. 'You do?'

'Absolutely.'

'And I love you—so very much. I've been such a fool. You see, I thought you were only marrying me for the child.'

'I would have made you my wife, child or no child, Christina. Believe that. I have been so blind.'

'Yes, you have—blind, stubborn and arrogant in your belief that I was guilty. But now you know the truth. The most serious mistakes concerning each other are behind us now. Thank goodness it is over and we can move on with our lives, but I am sure there will be many disagreements between us, being as stubborn as each other. But always know that I love you, Simon. I know that now, and I also know that, after last night, I couldn't go on fighting you, for what is the sense in rejecting the very thing I want most in the world? To belong to you and to live with you for the rest of my life.'

Deeply moved, Simon kissed her gently, his arms folding round her as if he would never let her go. 'From that very first moment I saw you by the stream, there has been a deep, magnetic attraction between us. My desire for you struck me like a knife. I wanted you simply and strongly as I have never wanted anything in my whole life, and to prove it, when we are back at the house I am going to lose no time in taking you to bed.'

Simon was true to his word. On reaching the house, after reassuring a distraught Miranda that everything was fine, Simon escorted Christina to their bedchamber. Come morning they would leave for his brother's house, where he would introduce her to his family, before going on to Tapton Park in Hertfordshire, which was to be their home.

When they were alone, to Christina's delight he immediately began removing his clothes. She came to stand before him, his glorious nudity a threat to her self-control.

'Now it's your turn—wife,' he said, his voice holding a note of playfulness as he began to undress her. 'I'm starved for you, my love,' he murmured between kisses.

'And I for you,' she whispered shyly, 'husband.'

He placed his hands on both sides of her face, almost mesmerised by the deep pools of blue. 'You cannot know how good it feels to hear you freely admit it at last.'

She smiled. 'You cannot know how good it feels to say it and to know that it's true. In fact, it's nearly as good as—' She got no further, for his hands were wandering boldly over her body, his purpose clear and arousing. He kissed every part of her as if learning all there was to learn about her, making her skin flush and setting her limbs a-tremble. Together they fell down upon the bed.

Gathering her against him, Simon began to make love to her until the passion that had always existed between them erupted in her mind and body, and in her heart.

Charles Antony Rockley did not enter the world quietly. His angry squalls could be heard the length and breadth of Tapton Park. Feeling a fatherly interest and pride in his son, Simon drew closer to the bed where his wife was nursing her new offspring. He smiled broadly as the infant drew up his knees and wailed louder, turning red with his anger.

'He surely is an impatient little man,' he said, laughing softly as the young Rockley opened his mouth and smacked his lips, anticipating his feed as his mother's nipple brushed his cheek. Immediately he latched on to it and for a while the world was at peace.

In a room downstairs, both families were congratulating each other and were wont to toast the child. But Simon and Christina saw little of this, for when they were not staring lovingly at their son, they were looking into each other's eyes and seeing a wondrous future spread out before them.

* * * * *

"The arrogance! To think that they can come here with their town bronze and sweep some heiress or other to the altar."

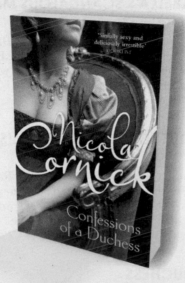

'Sinfully sexy and deliciously irresistible'
CHRISTINA DODD

Nicola Cornick

Confessions of a Duchess

When a feudal law requires all unmarried ladies to wed or surrender half their wealth, the quiet village of Fortune's Folly becomes England's greatest Marriage Market.

Laura, the dowager duchess, is determined to resist the flattery of fortune hunters. Young, handsome and scandalously tempting Dexter Anstruther suspects Laura has a hidden motive for resisting his charms...and he intends to discover it.

www.mirabooks.co.uk

HISTORICAL

Regency

LADY ARABELLA'S SCANDALOUS MARRIAGE
by Carole Mortimer

You are cordially invited to the marriage of Darius Wynter, Duke of Carlyne, to Lady Arabella St Claire... But sinister whispers surround the death of Darius' first wife—what is Lady Arabella letting herself in for?

Regency

DANGEROUS LORD, SEDUCTIVE MISS
by Mary Brendan

Heiress Deborah Cleveland jilted an earl for Randolph Chadwicke. But then he disappeared... Seven years later Randolph, now Lord Buckland, bursts back into Deborah's life! But this time he isn't offering marriage...

Regency

THE SHY DUCHESS
by Amanda McCabe

Lady Emily Carroll should have her pick of suitors. Instead, her shyness has earned her the nickname 'Ice Princess'. With her blushes hidden at a masked ball, Emily finds herself betrothed and her wedding night fast approaching...

On sale from 4th February 2011
Don't miss out!

Available at WHSmith, Tesco, ASDA, Eason and all good bookshops

www.millsandboon.co.uk

0111/04a

HISTORICAL

BOUND TO THE BARBARIAN
by Carol Townend

Sold into slavery, maidservant Katerina promised one day to repay the princess who rescued her. Now that time has come, and Katerina must convince commanding warrior Ashfirth Saxon that *she* is her royal mistress!

THE CATTLEMAN'S UNSUITABLE WIFE
by Pam Crooks

When cattleman Trey Wells's betrothed is kidnapped, blame falls on Zurina Vasco's brother—and a vengeful Trey demands she help him track them down. Trey soon realises Zurina is the only woman for him—but there is much to overcome before he can give her the love she deserves...

RECKLESS
by Anne Stuart

Adrian Rohan has only one pleasure: the seduction of beautiful women. Rich, charming and devastatingly skilled in the art of love, he never fails in his conquests...until Charlotte Spenser...

On sale from 4th February 2010
Don't miss out!

Available at WHSmith, Tesco, ASDA, Eason and all good bookshops

www.millsandboon.co.uk

REGENCY
Silk & Scandal

*A season of secrets, scandal and
seduction in high society!*

Volume 5 – 1st October 2010
The Viscount and the Virgin
by Annie Burrows

Volume 6 – 5th November 2010
Unlacing the Innocent Miss
by Margaret McPhee

Volume 7 – 3rd December 2010
The Officer and the Proper Lady
by Louise Allen

Volume 8 – 7th January 2011
Taken by the Wicked Rake
by Christine Merrill

8 VOLUMES IN ALL TO COLLECT!

England's Forgotten Queen

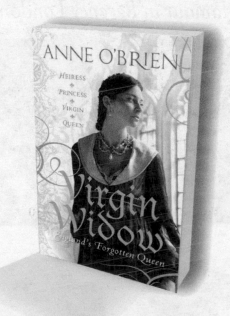

Anne Neville is the heiress and daughter of the greatest powerbroker in the land, Warwick the Kingmaker. She is a pawn, trapped in an uncertain political game.

When the Earl of Warwick commits treason, his family is forced into exile. Humiliated and powerless in a foreign land, Anne must find the courage and the wit to survive in a man's world.

www.mirabooks.co.uk

Sparkling ballrooms and wealthy glamour in Regency London

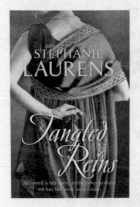

2 FREE BOOKS
AND A SURPRISE GIFT

We would like to take this opportunity to thank you for reading this Mills & Boon® book by offering you the chance to take TWO more specially selected books from the Historical series absolutely FREE! We're also making this offer to introduce you to the benefits of the Mills & Boon® Book Club™—

- **FREE home delivery**
- **FREE gifts and competitions**
- **FREE monthly Newsletter**
- **Exclusive Mills & Boon Book Club offers**
- **Books available before they're in the shops**

Accepting these FREE books and gift places you under no obligation to buy, you may cancel at any time, even after receiving your free books. Simply complete your details below and return the entire page to the address below. You don't even need a stamp!

YES Please send me 2 free Historical books and a surprise gift. I understand that unless you hear from me, I will receive 4 superb new books every month for just £3.99 each, postage and packing free. I am under no obligation to purchase any books and may cancel my subscription at any time. The free books and gift will be mine to keep in any case.

Ms/Mrs/Miss/Mr ———————— Initials ——————————

———————————————————————————————————————

Surname ————————————————————————————————

Address ————————————————————————————————

———————————————————————————————————————

——————————————————————— Postcode ——————————

E-mail ——————————————————————————————————

Send this whole page to: Mills & Boon Book Club, Free Book Offer, FREEPOST NAT 10298, Richmond, TW9 1BR